THE CANNONS OF LUCKNOW

Historical Fiction Published by McBooks Press

BY ALEXANDER KENT
Midshipman Bolitho
Stand into Danger
In Gallant Company
Sloop of War
To Glory We Steer
Command a King's Ship
Passage to Mutiny
With All Despatch
Form Line of Battle!
Enemy in Sight!
The Flag Captain
Signal–Close Action!
The Inshore Squadron
A Tradition of Victory
Success to the Brave
Colours Aloft!
Honour this Day
The Only Victor
Beyond the Reef
The Darkening Sea
For My Country's Freedom
Cross of St George
Sword of Honour
Second to None
Relentless Pursuit

BY DUDLEY POPE
Ramage
Ramage & The Drumbeat
Ramage & The Freebooters
Governor Ramage R.N.
Ramage's Prize
Ramage & The Guillotine
Ramage's Diamond
Ramage's Mutiny
Ramage & The Rebels
The Ramage Touch
Ramage's Signal
Ramage & The Renegades
Ramage's Devil
Ramage's Trial
Ramage's Challenge
Ramage at Trafalgar
Ramage & The Saracens
Ramage & The Dido

BY DAVID DONACHIE
The Devil's Own Luck
The Dying Trade
A Hanging Matter
An Element of Chance
The Scent of Betrayal
A Game of Bones

BY DEWEY LAMBDIN
The French Admiral
Jester's Fortune

BY DOUGLAS REEMAN
Badge of Glory
First to Land
The Horizon
Dust on the Sea

BY V.A. STUART
Victors and Lords
The Sepoy Mutiny
Massacre at Cawnpore
The Cannons of Lucknow
The Heroic Garrison

BY C. NORTHCOTE PARKINSON
The Guernseyman
Devil to Pay
The Fireship
Touch and Go

BY CAPTAIN FREDERICK MARRYAT
Frank Mildmay OR *The Naval Officer*
The King's Own
Mr Midshipman Easy
Newton Forster OR
The Merchant Service
Snarleyyow OR *The Dog Fiend*
The Privateersman
The Phantom Ship

BY JAN NEEDLE
A Fine Boy for Killing
The Wicked Trade

BY IRV C. ROGERS
Motoo Eetee

BY NICHOLAS NICASTRO
The Eighteenth Captain
Between Two Fires

BY W. CLARK RUSSELL
Wreck of the Grosvenor
Yarn of Old Harbour Town

BY RAFAEL SABATINI
Captain Blood

BY MICHAEL SCOTT
Tom Cringle's Log

BY A.D. HOWDEN SMITH
Porto Bello Gold

BY R.F. DELDERFIELD
Too Few for Drums
Seven Men of Gascony

The Cannons
of
Lucknow

V. A. STUART

The Alexander Sheridan Adventures, No. 4

MCBOOKS PRESS

ITHACA, NEW YORK

Published by McBooks Press 2003
Copyright © 1974 by V. A. Stuart
First published in Great Britain by Robert Hale Limited, London 1974

Cover painting: *Sir Henry Havelok at the Relief of Lucknow.*
Courtesy of Peter Newark Military Pictures

Library of Congress Cataloging-in-Publication Data

Stuart, V.A.
    The cannons of Lucknow / by V. A. Stuart.
        p.   cm. — (Alexander Sheridan adventures ; no. 4)
    ISBN 1-59013-029-4 (alk. paper)
    1. Sheridan, Alexander (Fictitious character)--Fiction.
    2. British--India--Fiction.   3. India--History--Sepoy Rebellion, 1857-
    1858--Fiction.   4. Great Britain--History, Military--19th century--
    Fiction.   5. Lucknow (India)--History--Siege, 1857--Fiction.   I. Title
    PR6063.A38 C36 2003
    823'.914—dc21   2002012358

Distributed to the trade by National Book Network, Inc.,
15200 NBN Way, Blue Ridge Summit, PA 17214
800-462-6420

Additional copies of this book may be ordered from any bookstore or
directly from McBooks Press, Inc., ID Booth Building,
520 North Meadow St., Ithaca, NY 14850. Please include $4.00 postage
and handling with mail orders. New York State residents must add sales
tax. All McBooks Press publications can also be ordered by calling toll-free
1-888-BOOKS11 (1-888-266-5711). Please call to request a free catalog.

Visit the McBooks Press website at www.mcbooks.com.

Printed in the United States of America
9   8   7   6   5   4   3   2   1

This book is for Dale L. Walker,
of the University of Texas at El Paso, in gratitude for his
kindness and encouragement and in the hope that he may find it
as factual as we both like our historical fiction to be.

➤➤➤ • ⬅⬅⬅

"One hundred years," the Moulvi said.
The Sadhu agreed with nodding head.
"And we have served an alien breed.
The hour is come—Hind shall be freed!"
The runners sped throughout the land—
The Sign was passed from hand to hand.
From every ghat and every khud
There came the call for British blood.
Night's horror gone, the peacock loud
Proclaims the waning star of Oudh.
The vulture, gruesomely replete
Sees blood-red dawn invade the street.
Here riven shako, bloodied sash,
Half-buried in the shrouding ash
Bear evidence that, once begun,
Treachery's cost is five to one.
Now day's reluctantly begun
As though, in shame, the very sun,
Seems in the mist to hide his head . . .
And over Oudh the dawn is red!

Delhi Rebels by W. B. Lindsay.
By permission of the author

AUTHOR'S NOTE

❯❯❯ • ❮❮❮

BASED ON published letters and accounts of the Indian Mutiny everything recounted in this book actually happened.

The only fictional characters are Alex Sheridan and his bearer, Mohamed Bux; all others are called by their correct names and their actions are on historical record although, of course, conversations with the fictitious characters are imagined. As far as possible, however, such conversations are based on their known views or actions. Sergeant Mahoney, of the famous "Blue Caps" serving with the Volunteer Cavalry, was awarded a V.C.; Timothy Cullmane of H.M.'s 64th was killed in action. No award of a Victoria Cross was made to any of the survivors of the heroic siege of Cawnpore, although repeated recommendations were made on behalf of Lts. Mowbray Thomson and Henry Delafosse. Both continued to serve in the Indian Army; Henry Delafosse retired as a major-general, after commanding the Blue Caps, Mowbray Thomas reached the honorary rank of general.

Gunner Sullivan died of wounds and cholera, after his escape: Private Murphy served with Havelock's Force and, on leaving the army, was made gardener in charge of the Cawnpore Memorial Well and garden, which post he held until his death. Lousada Barrow retired as a major-general, C.B., and General Havelock's son Harry was awarded a V.C. and he too, became a general.

I should like to thank the city librarian, Mr. O. S. Tomlinson and the staff of York City Library for their help in obtaining reference books for me, including out-of-print works which I could not otherwise have read.

I make no apology for appending a list of "Books Consulted" since I have tried to make this novel as factually accurate as lies within my power, for which reason I consulted them . . . and readers, whose interest in the Mutiny may have been stimulated, could well find the list of practical use as a guide to their future reading.

PROLOGUE

❯❯❯ • ❮❮❮

WITH THE SOUND of General Havelock's guns still ringing remorse-lessly in his ears, Dundoo Punth—Nana Sahib and self-styled Peishwa of the Mahrattas—stepped into the broad-beamed coun-try boat which had been tied up at the Bithur landing stage since early morning, awaiting his appearance.

His brother, Bala Bhat, sullenly nursing the wound he had received in the battle for Cawnpore, had preceded him, with the women of his household, and the women now crouched, fright-ened and shivering, in the forward part of the boat. Their dark faces were raised to his, seeking reassurance, but the Nana ignored them. He seated himself on the cushions placed beneath the oil lantern in the stern and gestured to the chief boatman to cast off.

"Maharajah . . ." The grizzled old *rissaldar*-major, whom he had promoted to the command of his cavalry, made a last effort to detain him. "How am I to pay my sowars if you leave us, *huzoor?* They grow insolent, they make demands which I cannot meet. They—"

"Their cowardice has cost us Cawnpore!" the Nana Sahib flung back wrathfully. "Let them plunder the British if they desire payment for their services, Teeka Singh—they shall have no reward from me. I go to my death on their account, fool that I was to

For *Historical Notes* on the Mutiny, see page 254, and for a *Glossary of Indian Terms,* see page 269.

listen to their false promises and trust in their courage." He turned away, his round, plump face suffused with resentful colour, and Azimullah Khan, his tall young Moslem *vakeel,* brushed the old cavalryman contemptuously aside as he, too, boarded the crowded boat.

"Cast off, dogs!" he shouted to the boatmen. "Pull into midstream!"

The men obeyed him, straining at their oars, and the mob of Brahmin holy men, beggars, and palace retainers, who had accompanied their Maharajah to the landing *ghat,* set up a chorus of mournful wails.

"Protector of the poor! Mighty Peishwa, do not leave us! How shall we fare without thee, when the British come seeking vengeance? Nana Sahib, take not thine own life, we beseech thee —stay with us!"

The Nana's full lips curved into a cynical smile as he listened, and Azimullah observed, smiling also, "The seed is sown, Highness. They will believe all when they see our lights extinguished."

"And tell the British that I am dead?"

Azimullah's smile widened. "Of a surety, Highness—and the accursed British will believe what they are told. Narayan Rao will see to it and buy us time. That is all we need—time to rally our forces."

"The dogs of sepoys are deserting our cause daily," the Nana objected. "They flee in the hundreds at the mere sight of a British bayonet. From whence can we obtain others?"

"Ahmad Ullah, the Moulvi, goes to Oudh to gather troops, and from Gwalior, Sindhia will send us more—Tantia Topi will see to that." Azimullah spoke confidently. "We shall retake Cawnpore, have no fear of that, Highness. This General Havelock has but a handful of white soldiers and he loses men daily from sickness. His gunners are old greybeards who must be carried in bullock carts and his much-vaunted steamer is worn out, with scarcely the power to make her way against the river current." The young Mohammedan snorted his contempt. "Let Havelock cross the river into Oudh—as he must, if he is to reach Lucknow—and we shall annihilate him."

"As we did at Panda Nadi?" Bala Bhat put in sourly. "And at Aong?" He gestured to his wounded arm, his eyes bright with anger. "The greybeard gunners, whom you affect to despise, shot the sponge-staffs from the hands of our *golandazes* and their aim was so true that Tantia Topi's elephant was killed under him with a single shot! I saw this, with my own eyes . . . and I saw also our mighty cavalry routed by a charge of less than a score of *feringhi* horse. What say you to that, Azimullah?"

"They were badly led, badly disciplined," Azimullah defended. "Teeka Singh is a weak commander. His sowars hold him in contempt, knowing that he cares nothing save to enrich himself."

"Teeka Singh will be given his just deserts now," the Nana said. His gaze went to the landing stage they had left and his smile returned, coldly malicious. "His own men will deal with him if he is unable to pay them. Perhaps he will buy his life by disgorging the gold and treasure he has robbed me of . . . although even that may not be enough."

But Bala Bhat was not to be placated. "Colonel Neill comes, they say, to serve our people in Cawnpore as he served them in Benares and Allahabad. He shows no mercy—he blows men from the cannon's mouth, hangs them with only a mockery of a trial, and has them buried in the foul earth, so that their eternal souls are damned! And those of *your* Faith, Azimullah, have their lips greased with pig fat before they are hanged and then their corpses are burnt!" His last few words were uttered with a satisfaction he made no attempt to conceal, and Azimullah bit back an angry retort.

Addressing the Nana, he said with dignity, "Your brother's information is not up to date, Highness—Neill has been made a general as a reward for his misdeeds. But do not despair, I beg of you—he, too, shall get his just deserts. This is a temporary set-back; the *feringhi* have been fortunate, but their luck cannot hold. And if *General* Neill does here as he has done in Allahabad, it will bring men of both your faith and mine flocking to your Highness's banner . . . even those who now doubt and waver. You will have the greatest army India has ever known, eager to restore you to the throne of your father the Peishwa! Wait but a little, until the Moulvi returns, and Tantia Topi, with the Gwalior legions. Lucknow will fall, now that Lawrence is dead."

"I am sorry for Lawrence's death," the Nana confessed, with genuine regret. "He was a good man—one I would have pardoned and enlisted in my service, for he had a true love for India . . . a love that transcended race and creed."

"He might have saved Lucknow," Bala Bhat reminded him. "Thou need'st have no regrets on Lawrence's account, brother."

The Nana's plump shoulders rose in a shrug. "I *have* regrets," he insisted obstinately. "On Lawrence's account and on that of the old general, Wheeler. He was my friend and his wife also. I ordered that they be spared, but those insolent dogs of sepoys disregarded my orders—seeking, no doubt, to implicate me so deeply in their murderous treachery that now I am compelled to flee from British vengeance with a price on my head. Even"—he waved a beringed hand distastefully to indicate the muddy waters of the Ganges— "to the extent that I must pretend to take my own life, in fulfillment of a vow I made under their coercion!"

In the flickering light of the lantern above their heads, Bala

Bhat and Azimullah exchanged uneasy glances, both aware that they, rather than the sepoys, had disregarded their master's orders concerning General Wheeler, giving ear, instead, to the Moulvi of Fyzabad, Ahmad Ullah, who had warned that none of the garrison must be spared. But the Nana offered no accusation and, emboldened by this, Azimullah said, passing his tongue nervously over his dry lips, "Highness, there are none left alive to tell of what happened at the Suttee Chowra Ghat, after Wheeler's surrender. The four who escaped by swimming and sought the protection of Drigbiji Singh will have had their throats cut by now. The Moulvi sent men to Moorar Mhow to attend to the matter before he left for Lucknow. Drigbiji's refusal to yield them up to your Highness's messengers was but a gesture on his part. He will not risk his neck to save theirs."

"You believe so? Drigbiji Singh is no coward."

"Neither is he a fool, *huzoor*. He will fear to incur the Peishwa's wrath."

"And the women are also dead," Bala Bhat added quickly.

His brother stared at him. "The women?"

"Those held prisoner in the Bibigarh. I myself made known thy wishes respecting them to Savur Khan, of thy bodyguard, and to the serving woman, Hosainee. As Azimullah says, my brother, there are none living to bear witness to the British against thee."

The Nana's shaven brows came together in a frown. "And no bodies? What of their bodies, Bala Bhat?"

"All have been disposed of, Nana Sahib," Bala Bhat assured him. "I entrusted Aitwurya and his *jullads* with the task and paid them well. As for those at the Suttee Chowra Ghat—why, they are long since picked clean by the vultures. Who can tell a man's race from his skeleton? In any case, the rising river has taken most of them away."

The Nana inclined his head, his anxiety partially allayed. He would be blamed for the massacre of the women, of course, and probably also for the slaughter of Wheeler's garrison. If the British were defeated, this would not matter and, indeed, might redound to his credit, but if they were *not,* if Havelock's contemptible little force of European and Sikh soldiers managed, by some miracle, to hold Cawnpore and relieve Lucknow, then it would be a different story. The British had vast resources in both men and money, but it would take time to transport reinforcements in any number to India and time was what he was about to gain for himself now. He raised his head, glancing astern to where the lights gleamed through the darkness from the palace he had been forced to vacate. The crowd was, he saw, still moving restlessly about the *ghat* and the riverbank—there would be witnesses in plenty to take the tale of his death back to General Havelock, but he ought, perhaps, to have left his womenfolk behind in the palace to give the story credence. Baji Rao's widows might with advantage have been abandoned—they were millstones round his neck, forever complaining and making demands on him, forever reproaching him because he had permitted European women to be put to death. Only this evening he had discovered, when the two were taken from their quarters, that they had hidden the wife of his lodge-keeper there in the hope of saving her life, and his own favourite wife, the lovely Kasi Bai, had been a party to their deception. She, too, had wept and made a scene when he had ordered the woman disposed of, and she was weeping now, her tears reproaching him. She . . .

"Highness—" Azimullah gestured to the distant *ghat*. "It is time."

"Very well," the Nana agreed. He rose, Azimullah's arm supporting him, his stout, richly robed figure visible to the watchers on the bank as the head boatman raised the stern lantern high above his head.

"Now!" Azimullah bade the boatman, and the two lanterns the craft carried were instantly extinguished. A wail went up from the waiting crowd, carrying quite clearly across the intervening water as the rowers, careful to make no noise, skilfully made use of the current to carry the boat to the opposite bank. It grounded, and two of them bore the Nana ashore on their backs to where the horsemen of his own bodyguard were drawn up to receive him, with curtained palanquins in readiness for the *begums.*

His nephew, Pandurang Rao Sadashiv, dismounted and made him a low obeisance; the erstwhile ruler of Cawnpore touched the young man's outstretched hands and, climbing into the nearest palanquin, drew the curtains and was carried swiftly away, his escort trotting after him.

The crowd on the Bithur *ghat* waited, still loud in their grief, but when half an hour had passed and there was no sign of the boat in which they had watched the Nana embark, the doleful wails abruptly ceased. Led by a Brahmin beggar in filthy, tattered robes, they made for the royal palace and proceeded systematically to pillage it, room by room.

CHAPTER ONE
❯❯❯ • ❮❮❮

ON THE afternoon of Sunday, 19th July, a detachment of the Madras European Fusiliers, Ferozepore Sikhs, and Volunteer Cavalry reached Bithur after a march of sixteen miles from Cawnpore.

The message from Narayan Rao, which had caused the British troops to be summoned from their Church Parade during the reading of the Lesson by General Havelock, had stated that Bithur was denuded of rebels, the palace abandoned and unguarded, and the Nana dead by his own hand. This—although, as the son of the late Peishwa's *dewan,* Narayan Rao's loyalty to the British cause was open to doubt—appeared at first sight to be the truth. The palace had been plundered of virtually everything of value save for sixteen serviceable brass guns and, after giving instructions for the guns to be hitched to bullock teams and sent back to Cawnpore, the officer commanding the detachment, Major Lionel Stephenson, ordered his Fusiliers to burn down the Nana's residence.

Returning from a tour of inspection with two other officers of the Volunteer Cavalry, Alexander Sheridan reined in his horse to watch, with oddly conflicting emotions, as the "Blue Caps" went about their business and smoke and flames began to rise from one after another of the pink- and white-washed stone buildings. He remembered the palace as it had been on one of his previous visits, before the sepoys had mutinied, when he— then a captain in the Bengal Light Cavalry—had been treated to dinner by the self-styled Maharajah of Bithur, together with other civil and military members of the Cawnpore garrison.

General Sir Hugh Wheeler and his gentle Indian wife had been amongst the party, Alex recalled with a sharp stab of pain. The old general, and Charles Hillersdon, the collector and chief magistrate, with Mrs. Hillersdon and, of course, his own beloved wife, Emmy . . . all of them now dead. The long table at which they had been seated—with its fine damask cloth and the incongruous mixture of priceless gold plate and cheap glass and silverware, set out for his British guests—had been smashed in an orgy of wanton destruction by the mob that had come here after witnessing the Nana's disappearance. And they, no doubt, had stolen the gold, for there had been no trace of it anywhere in the palace. The vast, echoing rooms were empty, stripped bare of their Persian carpets, their tapestry hangings, and their crystal chandeliers. Even the *zenana* had been ransacked by the mob; not only its rich furnishings but also the Nana's courtesans and dancing girls had vanished, together with the host of ayahs and other servants employed to wait on them.

The sole occupant of the once-luxurious women's quarters had been a pregnant Anglo-Indian girl, with her throat cut, left to die there—presumably on the Nana's instructions—and later identified as the wife of the lodge-keeper, an Englishman named Carter, whose fate was as yet unknown.

Alex's mouth tightened as he felt anger well up inside him. Leaving his companions, he walked his horse slowly in the direction of the river. Disappointed by the small amount of plunder left in the palace, the Sikhs, he saw, were now ranging further afield among the outbuildings and godowns on the riverbank, unrebuked by their formidable, white-bearded commander, Lieutenant Brasyer, who was watching them with an indulgent smile, like a father amused by the antics of his wayward children. Encouraged by this, a few of the older Fusiliers slipped away from their

fire-lighting in twos and threes to follow in the wake of their
Sikh comrades, keeping a wary eye on their own commanding
officer, lest they be ordered to return to their duties. But, like
Jeremiah Brasyer, Major Stephenson offered no rebuke, seemingly
blind to his men's temporary defection, as he superintended the
despatch of the bullock train and the guns started on their pon-
derous way along the dusty, rutted road to Cawnpore.

Alex silently applauded his forbearance, understanding the reasons which had prompted it. The spoils of victory were for the
victors and these men, both Sikh and European, had earned their
victory, although few spoils had come their way. Under the lash
of monsoon rain and in the remorseless heat of the Indian summer, they had marched 126 miles in nine days and nights, slept
tentless on the bare ground, and fought four actions against odds
which, in normal circumstances, any strategist would have deemed
impossible. Because they knew that some two hundred British
women and children were being held hostage in Cawnpore, they
had gone without food, charged, and taken enemy guns at the
point of the bayonet and risked their lives again and again in
order that there might be no delay in reaching their goal in time
to effect a rescue. In the last battle, after marching fifteen miles
under a blazing sun, a scant eight hundred men had faced as
many thousand mutineers, driving them from their entrenched
positions by the sheer fury and courage of their assault.

When they entered Cawnpore the following day, their triumph had dimmed when they learned that the hostages had been
brutally butchered in a final act of betrayal by the fleeing Nana.
Many of them had, like himself, seen the ghastly evidence of this
in a small, single-story building in the heart of the city, known
as the Bibigarh, and in the well adjoining that terrible house of
slaughter. To a man, they had been eager to exact retribution

from those who, if they had not committed, had quite certainly connived at the murders, but General Havelock had sternly forbidden reprisals against the civil population by his outraged soldiers. He had also issued orders that the city was not to be looted, which had angered them all—and the Sikhs in particular—although it had been a wise precaution, as Alex was aware. The bazaar contained large stocks of liquor, much of it champagne and bottled beer stolen during the siege, and liquor had always been the downfall of European troops, however well disciplined, when there was a lull in the fighting.

One or two officers had protested, Brasyer among them, but the dapper little general, who had asked so much of his troops in battle and driven them so relentlessly on the march, turned a deaf ear to their objections. A devout Christian and a lifelong teetotaller, he had made it abundantly clear that he would tolerate neither drunkenness nor the indiscriminate persecution of native civilians by the force under his command.

"Any soldier found guilty of looting is to be hanged in his uniform, gentlemen," he informed his assembled officers, adding crisply, before any of them could voice their dismay, "Mutineers, civilian traitors, and miscreants shall, I give you my word, be brought to swift and merciless justice—but barbarism must *not* be met by barbarism. Punishment is to be meted out to all deserving of it, but only in accordance with martial law and after a fair and properly constituted trial."

The savage vengeance taken by Colonel Neill in Benares and Allahabad—and, on his orders, by the advance force on the march to Fatepur, under Renaud—had shocked General Havelock profoundly. He made no secret of his disapproval of Neill's arbitrary method of quelling mutiny—and rightly so, Alex reflected grimly, although he himself thirsted for revenge as bitterly as any man, with more reason than most. Retribution must be reserved for proven traitors, and the Blue Caps' Colonel had not been too particular as to the guilt of those he hanged or blew from the mouths of cannon. On the admission of his own officers, many innocent villagers and harmless merchants had been victims of his wrath, a fact which, on sober consideration, might well have influenced the Nana's decision to put his British hostages to death.

It was perhaps unjust to question whether Neill's preoccupation with the punishment of mutineers at Allahabad had delayed the relief column he had been ordered to lead, at all costs, to Cawnpore but ... Alex sighed, in weary frustration. He *had* questioned it many times since his escape from Edward Vibart's leaking boat after the massacre at the Suttee Chowra Ghat in which his beloved Emmy had perished, with close on three hundred others. And ... he repeated his sigh. He had questioned it during the long, anxious days of waiting behind the crumbling walls of General Wheeler's entrenchment, when Neill's name had been on everyone's lips, including his own. Starving, desperate, dying under incessant attack, the garrison had clung to the hope that Neill was leading a relief column to their aid, but when day followed day and the telescopes sweeping the road from Allahabad revealed only reinforcements for the mutineers, even this hope had had to be abandoned ... and it had been the last hope any of them had had.

There were, of course, numerous sound military reasons for the delay—lack of transport and of supplies, the disruption of communications, the need to secure Allahabad and the road south to the railhead before the relief column could leave its base. James Neill had had only his regiment, a single steamer, and a few drafts which had struggled upcountry from Calcutta. Whatever might be said of his reign of terror in Allahabad, Neill was a good soldier and a brave man; no lack of courage could be imputed to him. It would therefore be the height of injustice to lay the blame solely at his door without full knowledge of the circumstances which had dictated his actions and caused him to wait for Havelock's reinforcements before attempting to reach Cawnpore. Havelock, God knew, with twice as many troops as Neill had had at his disposal, had been compelled to fight every mile of the way. Yet for all that . . .

"Sheridan, my dear fellow—see what I have looted!" Grateful for any distraction from his own thoughts, Alex turned, recognising the voice of Henry Willock, one of the displaced civil servants who had joined the ranks of the Volunteer Cavalry after their districts had mutinied. Cradled in his arms was a tiny Waneroo monkey with a jewelled collar about its neck. "Poor, pretty little creature," Willock said pityingly, stroking the monkey's wizened, half-human face with a gentle hand. "I found her in a cage in one of the godowns by the river, frightened out of her life. That foul swine of a Nana must have kept a good many pets when he was endeavouring to play the role of a British country gentleman. Two of our fellows have found a pair of pedigree bulldogs, if you please! And there are a number of zoo animals, locked in cages, as well as some very fine Arab horses."

"Arabs?" Alex exclaimed, with interest. "You mean—"

"They've all been taken, I'm afraid," Willock told him regretfully, forestalling his question. "If you were hoping to replace yours, you've left it a trifle late. Although I daresay you could purchase one—the Fusiliers are selling them to the highest bidder. Poor devils, they've no other chance to enrich themselves; everything else has gone. The Nana's own people have made a remarkably clean sweep of the place. *His* Brahmin priests and holy men, by all accounts, as well as the villagers and, I don't doubt, some of his murderous sepoys before they took to their heels. There's no liquor, of course, as Stephenson foresaw—even the Sikhs haven't found any." He laughed. "Poor old Brasyer's quite put out. He was hoping for great things here, when he realised that the general had omitted to include Bithur in his prohibition against looting."

He rode on, the gibbering little monkey perched on his shoulder and clinging to him, as if her very life depended on remaining close to her rescuer.

Alex smiled and trotted without haste back to the road, making no attempt to seek out the new owners of the Nana's Arabs. He had no money and, indeed, possessed only the clothes he stood up in—a makeshift uniform, consisting of a borrowed white cotton tunic, with regulation black pouch and cartouche belt, and the native-made boots and pantaloons in which he had escaped, worn with a pith helmet and puggree, also borrowed. If he wanted to buy himself a horse, he would have to seek out the paymaster and arrange for credit, but until now there had been no time to think of anything save practical necessities. In any event, the sowar's country-bred mare he was riding had served him well, despite her wound—Arab stallions, with long pedigrees, belonged to another life, another world. He patted the mare's scrawny neck and, seeing Captain Lousada Barrow—until the mutiny, commissioner of an Oudh district and now in command of the twenty-strong Volunteer Cavalry—crossed over the road to join him.

"Ah, Alex . . . just the man I was looking for. What do *you* think of all this, eh? Can you believe that the Nana would have abandoned his palace and all the treasure he's reported to have amassed, if he's not dead? Or"—he gestured to the guns, filing slowly past them behind their teams of plodding bullocks—"those cannon? Damn it, they're in first-rate condition! Maude will be delighted when he sees them, I'm quite sure . . . so why did they leave them for us, for God's sake? One thing these blasted Pandies never seem to suffer from is lack of ammunition. Why didn't they defend the palace? Surely it must prove that the Nana kept his vow and drowned himself, as he said he would if we defeated him and recaptured Cawnpore?"

"I don't know," Alex confessed. Lousada Barrow was an old friend and had been his mentor when he had first been seconded to the Political Service. He added, with feeling, "To be honest, I hope he isn't dead."

"You hope he's *not?*" Barrow stared at him in astonishment. "In heaven's name, why?"

"Because I had promised myself the satisfaction of being the one to bring him to justice, Lou. But if he has gone to meet his Maker, then I can only pray that the mills of God will grind exceeding small in his particular case." Conscious that his scarred face reflected more of his pent-up bitterness than he had intended to reveal, even to Lousada Barrow, Alex controlled himself and went on flatly, "I may be this garrison's only survivor—apart from Shepherd, who is a clerk—which leaves me with a debt to pay for all those who are no longer here to demand settlement. My wife and son among them."

"You are not alone, Alex," Lousada Barrow assured him. "By heaven you're not! After what was done to those poor innocents in the Bibigarh, none of us can rest until the debt is paid. And I don't imagine that any of us will forget what we saw here for as long as we live. But . . ." he broke off in sudden consternation. "Oh Lord, I'm sorry! I'm a thoughtless idiot, but there's been so damned little time to talk since you joined us. I . . . were your wife and son . . . that is, were they—"

"No." Alex shook his head. He had himself under stern control now, although it took a considerable effort of will to shut his mind to the memories his own words evoked. "They were spared that ultimate horror, for which I thank God with all my heart. The child, who was only an infant, died during the siege and Emmy . . . my wife was shot when they attacked us at the landing *ghat*. She died in my arms."

Barrow grunted his relief. He waved to the line of guns, as the last of the sixteen pieces lumbered past them and shouted out an order to his volunteer cavalrymen to form up as escort. "I told Lionel Stephenson that we would see our prizes safely delivered. Ride with me, Alex, if you would—I want to talk to you."

He set spurs to his big chestnut and Alex followed him through clouds of choking dust to the head of the column, where both reined in, slowing their pace to match that of the labouring bullocks. "Do you really suppose," Barrow went on, as if there had been no break in their conversation, "that you and the clerk—what's his name?—Shepherd are the only survivors of the garrison, Alex? Shepherd left the entrenchment before it was evacuated, did he not?"

"Yes," Alex confirmed. "General Wheeler sent him out, disguised as a servant, in the hope that he might be able to make contact with the Nunneh Nawab, Mohammed Ali Khan, who was said to have remained loyal to us. We sent out a number of others, servants and Eurasians mostly, and one loyal *jemadar*, but few of them managed to get back—apart from the pensioner, Ungud. Sir Henry Lawrence sent him from Lucknow originally and he contrived to take messages between us—I shall never know how. He's either a very brave man or an exceptionally lucky one—both, probably. And there was a Eurasian drummer named Blenman. Poor devil, he died in Eddie Vibart's boat." He felt his throat contract as be remembered the manner of the brave Blenman's death.

"What of the others who were with you in Vibart's boat?" Lousada Barrow pursued. "Did none of them get away?"

Alex frowned. "We made a final sally, thirteen of us, when our situation became hopeless. We didn't expect to get away. We just wanted to die like soldiers, taking as many of the Pandies with us as we could. When they surrounded us in a small temple and set it on fire, those who could swim decided to make a break for the river. The rest of us covered them. I saw four or five heads in the water. Mowbray Thomson's was one of them—he has . . . had red hair and it was unmistakable. I vaguely remember that an Irish lad named Murphy, of the 84th, was swimming beside him, helping him along, but they were under very heavy musket fire from both banks—I don't know how far any of them got. A couple of sowars rode at me and cut me down and I was unconscious for most of the day. When I came to it was dusk and I was pretty groggy, with great gaps in my memory. All I can recollect now is that I buried those of our men whose bodies I was able to find or dragged them to the river. The place was a shambles and there were clouds of vultures hovering about, so I couldn't leave them, I . . ." for all the effort he made to control it, his voice shook. "And the boat had gone, with the wounded in it."

Barrow laid a big hand on his knee. "Alex, old man, when you first joined us, you said you remembered almost nothing. But you're remembering now, are you not?"

"Yes," Alex admitted. "Unhappily I am."

"The general would like a report, you know, as soon as you're able to make one," the Volunteers' commander said gently. "Of the siege and your escape. And he needs the names of casualties, particularly civilian casualties, so that their relatives can be notified."

"Yes, I know. Harry Havelock asked me about it this morning. I promised I'd do the best I could, but there are still a great many gaps, I'm afraid." Involuntarily, Alex raised his hand, still grasping the reins, to touch the jagged scar which, although healing, puckered and disfigured his left temple and cheek. The sowar who had dealt him the blow had kept his sabre razor-sharp, he thought wryly, and probably thereby saved his life. He glanced at his companion apologetically. "Names and dates elude me, Lou. I remember some incidents vividly. When the Pandies launched attacks on our entrenchment and we held them off, every detail is clear, but—"

"I've seen your entrenchment," Lousada Barrow put in gravely. "And before heaven, I don't know how you held them off for a single day, much less for three weeks!" He swore under his breath. "Devil take it, what possessed old Sir Hugh Wheeler to attempt to defend such a place? The Magazine was intact, wasn't it, until the Nana had it blown up?"

"It was, yes. But—"

"You could have held out there for months. So why was it left to fall into the Pandies' hands?"

Alex sighed, reluctant even now to criticise his old commander. "Mainly, I suppose," he answered quietly, "because General Wheeler made the fatal mistake of trusting the Nana. He was promised Bithur troops to guard the Magazine and Treasury and the Nana assured him repeatedly that the sepoys, when they broke out, would march straight off to Delhi. The poor old man believed he would only have to defend himself against isolated raids by the city *budmashes,* but what really decided him was the promise he was given of reinforcements of British troops, which were said to be on their way from Allahabad at the beginning of June. A handful did reach us and General Wheeler sent them on to Lucknow, on receiving their assurance that Colonel Neill's column was behind them. Wheeler constructed the entrenchment within sight of the Allahabad road so as to enable Neill to get to us without having to fight his way through the city. When the Nana betrayed us and led the sepoys back here to attack us, it was too late to leave the entrenchment . . . and too late even to destroy the powder and ordnance stores in the Magazine. The Bithur troops seized them and handed the whole lot over to the mutineers who, of course, used them against us. But for all that, Lou, the old general's decision was a logical one, in the circumstances. The Magazine was six miles north of the Allahabad road and—"

"Did *you* consider it a sound decision?" the older man demanded.

"No," Alex was forced to concede. "A number of us didn't. But we thought we could hold out until Neill's column reached us. We were daily expecting its arrival."

"But Neill did not come." Lousada Barrow's expression was inscrutable. "Well, he had his problems, as you'll have realised by now—he had to deal with mutinies at both Benares and Allahabad."

"I *do* realise that, Lou. Indeed it was I who brought the message from Lucknow that Neill was held up in Benares—"

"You brought it?"

"Yes, by road—the electric telegraph wires had been cut between here and Lucknow. Sir Henry Lawrence sent me, and his warning was the first intimation poor old General Wheeler had that any delay was likely. We expected no prolonged delay—ten days, perhaps, or even a fortnight—because we knew that

Neill had been fully informed of our plight. I . . ." Alex hesitated, choosing, his words carefully before he went on. "No one has yet been able to explain the *length* of that delay, Lou, or to give me an entirely satisfactory reason for it. Lack of transport has, of course, been mentioned, as well as insufficient troops, and I'm aware that Neill had to ensure the safety of Allahabad, as well as that of Benares, before he could move to our aid."

"You mean," Barrow offered shrewdly, "it's been suggested that Neill spent more time than was strictly necessary hanging mutineers— and those suspected of being in sympathy with the mutineers—when he should have pushed on to Cawnpore at any hazard?"

Alex inclined his head. "Yes," he answered, tight-lipped. "Between ourselves, that has been suggested. He certainly appears to have behaved like the wrath of God in Allahabad. Estimates are at variance, but I've been told that he hanged over six hundred natives, some without trial. I don't know if that's true, of course, but I *do* know that he only despatched the advance force, under poor Renaud, on the thirtieth of June . . . three days *after* his failure to relieve us compelled our surrender. Spurgin's steamer left the same day, I believe."

Lousada Barrow settled himself more comfortably in his saddle. He took a cheroot from the case in his hip pocket and lit it, the lucifer cupped between his palms. Puffing smoke, he observed dryly, "James Neill has been promoted to brigadier-general in recognition of his services, Alex. Did you hear that?"

"No, I did not." Alex's tone was deliberately noncommittal. He offered no comment and Barrow frowned.

"Do not misunderstand me. I cannot approve of his drum-head courts martial or, indeed, of some of his other methods of stamping out rebellion—I've been a civil magistrate for too long.

"But,"—his broad shoulders rose in an elaborate shrug—"our new general *did* avert what could have been a very ugly situation in Allahabad and the surrounding district and he apparently did the same in Benares. His methods, if crude, are undoubtedly effective . . . and the Commander-in-Chief evidently thinks so, or he wouldn't have been promoted."

"I can't imagine that General Havelock will approve of them, judging by his remarks to us this morning," Alex said. "Barbarism must not be met by barbarism, he said."

"Quite so," Barrow affirmed. They were approaching a village, and he sent two of his cavalrymen to scout ahead of the column. Puffing once more at his cheroot, he went on, "Since this conversation is strictly between ourselves, my dear Alex, I can tell you that there's no love lost between Havelock and Neill. There hardly could be—they are such very different characters. Neill, understandably perhaps, resented having had command of the Movable Column taken from him, when he expected to be given it himself. And he said so, quite openly, as well as referring to his new commander as 'The Old Gentleman.' Before we even left Allahabad, Havelock had to pull rank on him more than once, and finally, when we did set off, he left Neill to follow on with whatever fresh drafts arrived from Dinapore or Calcutta. This, despite his long and distinguished service, is the first independent command our little general has ever had and he intends to make the most of it. He'll tolerate neither delay nor interference from Neill, I can assure you. He'll relieve Lucknow, if it's humanly possible to do so, without wasting a day."

"You really think he will?" Alex questioned doubtfully.

"I *know* he will. At this morning's staff conference, he instructed Fraser Tytler to begin preparations for crossing the river tomorrow morning. As soon as Neill gets here, Havelock will hand over the command of Cawnpore to him and press on."

"He's going to leave Neill in command here?" Alex echoed, unable to hide his dismay.

"A force of this size hardly requires two generals," Barrow returned. "And General Havelock doesn't—" he was interrupted by a shout from one of the two Volunteers scouting fifty yards ahead of the gun train, which was followed an instant later by a fusillade of shots coming from the village they were approaching. Ordering the train to halt and the rest of his small troop to close in and cover it against a possible attack, Barrow put his horse into a canter and rode toward the village, calling over his shoulder to Alex to accompany him. "Mutineers, I imagine," he added, when Alex drew level with him. "Holed up here with wounded, probably. We'd better take them alive, if we can."

The village was small, a mere cluster of reed-thatched huts running down to a stream and screened by trees. At first sight it appeared to be deserted, save for a little group of women engaged in washing their household linen at the river's edge who, with shrill cries of fright, flung themselves into the water at the sight of the approaching horsemen. Then a horrifying apparition emerged from one of the huts and came stumbling across the intervening space toward them, voice raised in an ear-splitting scream.

The fugitive was half-naked, a European or an Anglo-Indian, Alex decided, judging by the colour of his skin, but so hideously mutilated that his face bore little resemblance to that of a human being of any race. Nose, ears, and both hands had been hacked off and heavy iron fetters trailed from his ankles, as the unfortunate man dragged himself unsteadily through the dust and filth of the rutted cart track which served the village as a street. The crackle of musketry momentarily drowned his screams and three or four shots whined above his head or buried themselves in the dust at his feet. Intent only on escape, he ignored them, struggling manfully on, until a single, well-aimed shot stopped him in his tracks and he fell awkwardly forward onto his tortured face.

Barrow pulled up beside him and dismounted, jerking his horse round in front of him to serve as temporary protection for both himself and the wounded man. "I'll take care of this poor devil, Alex," he grunted breathlessly. "You go on and tell Birch and Stewart not to shoot those rebels if they can help it. I want the swine alive!"

Alex did his best to carry out these instructions, but by the time he reached the hut from which the shots had been fired, the two young Volunteers who had given the alarm were inside and he heard the roar of pistols being discharged at close range as he tethered his horse beside theirs and dashed in after them. Graham Birch turned, grinning, a smoking Colt in his hand, to point to the three bodies lying at his feet.

"Those devils won't fire on an unarmed Englishman again, sir," he announced triumphantly. "As for this cringing cur . . ." he spun the chamber of his Colt and levelled the weapon at the last remaining mutineer, who was crouching in a corner of the room, gibbering with fear, his empty musket held uselessly across his chest. "I have one round left that has *his* name on it!"

"No, hold your fire," Alex bade him. "Captain Barrow wanted them all taken alive, but since this man is the only one left, he'll have to do. Disarm and tie him up and then bring him outside, if you please."

Lieutenant Birch obediently lowered the Colt. He was a tall, good-looking boy, who had served for less than a year with his regiment, the 1st Bengal Light Cavalry. Like his comrade in arms, Ensign Stewart of the 17th Native Infantry, and a number of others—including Lousada Barrow himself—he had made a perilous journey through hostile country to Allahabad in order to serve with Havelock's Force and in the ranks of the Volunteer Cavalry. Death was no stranger to either of them now, but they exchanged wry glances as they pinioned the surviving sepoy's wrists and helped him, none too gently, to his feet.

Stewart ventured diffidently, "I'm sorry if we were a bit too impulsive, Colonel Sheridan, but they did open fire on us and . . . did you see that poor wretch they were holding prisoner? They'd inflicted the most ghastly injuries on him, sir, and I'm afraid it made me see red."

"I very much doubt whether the sepoys were responsible for the prisoner's injuries," Alex told him. "That kind of torture smacks rather of the Nana's executioners."

"You mean he was punished for some reason?" Birch suggested.

"Or silenced. It won't surprise me to find that his tongue has been cut out as well."

"His *tongue?*" Stewart passed his own tongue nervously over his lips. "I . . . see. The unfortunate fellow was making an odd sort of noise, as if he was trying to yell out and couldn't." His expression hardened. "The general says that we're not to match barbarism with barbarism, but after what I've seen here, I . . . damn it all, sir, I don't see what else we can do. They've betrayed us, they've murdered our women and children, they . . ." Birch silenced him with a sharp jab of the elbow. He jerked his head in Alex's direction with a warning scowl and the youngster reddened. "I'm very sorry, sir. I forgot that you—that is, I—"

"You forgot that I was in the Seige?" Alex finished for him. "And that most of the women and children who died in the Bibigarh were known to me? Well, continue to forget it, my young friend, because it's something that I'd give my immortal soul to forget. The general is absolutely right, you know. If we're to win back India, if we're to regain the trust of the ordinary people who have had no part in this mutiny, it will not be by meeting barbarism with barbarism."

"Yes, sir, of course," Stewart stammered. Still very red of face, he started to drag the pinioned sepoy from the hut. But, Alex thought, he would not forget; none of them would. What had happened here, what they had seen in the well outside the Bibigarh and in that other well, close to the entrenchment, was printed indelibly on their minds, as it was on his own. The fact that he had survived the massacre set him apart from these young officers with whom he now served; his scarred face and the empty sleeve at his right side set him apart too and erected an even more insuperable barrier than his brevet rank. Save in moments of stress or excitement, when they were in action, the young officers pitied him and fought shy of him, calling him "sir" and treating him with wary respect. In the Volunteer Cavalry he held no official rank; Barrow was commandant and the two officers who had escaped with him from Salone, Thompson and Swanson, acted as subalterns; he was entitled to no particular respect from even the youngest of them. Indeed, he supposed wryly, they had all—including Barrow, until their brief talk just now had made his feelings clear—expected him to be filled with a lust for blood, to seek vengeance as Neill had sought it. Whereas, in fact . . . he sighed, glancing at Birch.

"They *did* open fire on us, sir, as George Stewart told you," the young cavalry officer said defensively, careful to avoid his eye. "That was why we killed them."

"I'm sure that Captain Barrow will accept your explanation," Alex returned crisply. "Let's identify their regiments, shall we, in case a report is required, and then we'll get back to the train. It will be dark very soon."

Birch nodded. He turned over one of the bodies with his spurred boot, revealing a medal pinned to the dead sepoy's white undress coatee. "My God!" he exclaimed, sounding shocked. "This fellow fought at Chilianwala and Goojerat. He was in the 56th—one of the regiments that mutinied here. Don't tell me that you'd have spared *him,* sir?" He examined the buttons of the others. "They were all of the same regiment, all of the 56th." He dropped to one knee, removed the medal from the bloodstained jacket, and straightened up, the silver token of valour lying on the palm of his hand. "He won this and still betrayed his salt! Damn it, sir, I'm not sorry I killed him—after all, the punishment for mutiny is death, is it not?"

"It is," Alex agreed. "But now that we have retaken Cawnpore, our first and most essential task is to restore law and order. We have to substitute British justice, which *is* just, for the Nana's corrupt administration, don't you see? Mutineers and murderers will be punished—the general made no bones about that, did he? They'll be hanged or blown from cannon if their crimes warrant it, but each man is entitled to a fair trial, with his guilt proven against him."

"Yes, I understand that, sir, but I . . ." Birch hesitated, still not entirely convinced.

"Don't worry, the fellow you took alive won't escape, Birch." Alex laid a hand on his shoulder. "He was of the 17th and I have good reason for making certain that he does not. He'll be tried and his trial will serve as a warning to others, civilians as well as sepoys, who may now be wavering in their allegiance."

"You think it will influence them?"

Alex nodded. "Yes, I do. The ordinary people of Cawnpore

welcomed us back. You saw that for yourself when we marched in. But hundreds of them fled from the city, innocent and guilty, because they feared that we might follow our victory with looting and indiscriminate slaughter. They've suffered that already from the Nana's troops, who plundered them unmercifully. When they learn that we have taken no more than just reprisals, they will return—the innocent will, at all events. We need their help and loyalty if we're to hold on here and bring relief to Lucknow—theirs and that of the local rajahs and peasantry. We are far too small a force to do battle with the entire population between here and Lucknow. In any case, our quarrel is not with the *zamindars* and villagers; it's with the Nana and the sepoys he has subverted to his cause. We cannot allow what happened to the garrison here to be repeated in Lucknow . . . at all costs, it must be prevented."

"Well said, Alex!" Lousada Barrow's deep voice approved from the door of the hut. He came inside, mopping his face, which was damp with sweat. "All right, Graham, my boy," he said to Birch. "You did what you considered necessary and I'm not going to put you on the carpet for it. But remember, it's one thing to kill your enemy in battle and quite another to take away his life when he's ready to surrender. Besides, prisoners often provide useful information."

"Yes, sir," Lieutenant Birch acknowledged, crestfallen. "Will that be all, sir?"

"We're going to bivouac here and push on at first light," Barrow told him. "So cut along, like a good fellow, and see that my horse and Colonel Sheridan's are fed and watered with your own, would you? Captain Thompson is detailing a night guard—report to him."

"Very good, sir." Thankfully, the boy made his escape. When

he had gone, Lousada Barrow made a brief and impersonal inspection of the sepoys' bodies and said ruefully, as he led the way outside, "That poor devil's dead, Alex, the one who tried to escape from them. My boys are digging a grave for him now. He was an Englishman, but God knows who he was; perhaps you'd better see if you can identify him before we put him under. He might have been from the entrenchment, though I doubt it—he was too well fed. He's not a pretty sight . . . nose, hands, and tongue removed expertly and fairly recently. He tried to talk but I couldn't understand what he wanted to tell me. Something about a well, I think. That was the only word I could make out."

The burial party was at work under a clump of trees. Alex knelt beside the mutilated body, but was forced to shake his head. "To the best of my recollection I've never set eyes on him before, Lou." He rose, brushing the earth from his knees. "Have you tried the prisoner?"

"No, but we can do that now. Swanston offered to interrogate him. They're somewhere near—yes, over there, d'you see? We'll have a word with him." They walked across side by side. In the fading light, it was difficult to make out the prisoner's expression, but he seemed frightened and ill at ease and his interrogator, Lieutenant Oliver Swanston, greeted them with barely suppressed excitement. He had been Barrow's Assistant Commissioner in Salone and was a brilliant linguist.

"I believe we're on to something, Lou," he said. "This chap's a *subedar* of the 17th—Ramsay says he knows him well. His name is Bhandoo Singh and he was one of the ringleaders when the regiment mutinied at Azimgurh. I gather that he was the instigator of the theft of seven and a half *lacs* of treasure, which was being taken to Benares by a troop of Oudh irregular cavalry."

Barrow's bristling brows rose. "Was he now! Then he's quite

a prize, is he not? What happened to the treasure?"

Oliver Swanston laughed without amusement. "The *subedar* says they handed it over to the Nana Sahib."

"Is that the truth, Bhandoo Singh?" the cavalry commander demanded, addressing the man in his own language. "Did you yield up the treasure your regiment stole to the Nana?"

The prisoner inclined his head in sullen acquiescence.

"The Maharajah Bahadur insisted on it, Sahib, before he would permit the men of my *paltan* to serve under his command. One Azimullah Khan, the dog of a Moslem who stands at the Maharajah's right hand, took our treasure from us."

The three British officers exchanged glances and Swanston suggested cynically, "And did the Maharajah's *vakeel* use your treasure in order to pay his troops?"

"Nay, Sahib, he did not. His troops were not paid, save in promises." The man faced them indignantly, fear giving place to defiance. "Nevertheless, his soldiers fight for him, for the greater glory of Hind. They fight without pay, if need be, that they may rid this land of its oppressors; there are other leaders to whom promises are sacred. In Fyzabad there was such a one."

"In Fyzabad?" Alex's interest quickened, and he took up the questioning. "Went you to Fyzabad then?"

The *subedar's* dark eyes flashed. "*Ji-han.* From Azimgurh, we marched to Fyzabad, where the sowars of the Oudh cavalry told us that their leader, Ahmad Ullah, the Moulvi, had been seized and was held in prison, under sentence of death. The sowars of the Barlow *ki Paltan*, the Irregulars, together with our brothers of the 22nd, rose when we were yet a day's march from them, at Begumgunj, and broke into the jail. They released the Moulvi and other prisoners and sent word to us that their officers, with the Commissioner Sahib and some *mems,* would be seeking to make their escape by river. They besought us to intercept and stop them." He paused and all three officers, who were listening with growing dismay to his recital, again exchanged glances.

"The commissioner, Colonel Goldney, was at Fyzabad," Lousada Barrow supplied, his tone clipped. "He had left his wife and some of the other ladies at Sultanpore, believing that they would be safer there. They reached Allahabad with Grant, the assistant commissioner, before we left, having got away just before Colonel Fisher's troops rebelled. Fisher and several of his officers were killed, but Mrs. Goldney had had no news of her husband." He jerked the *subedar* round to face him and asked harshly, "What of the Commissioner Sahib and his party, Bhandoo Singh? Did you and your men molest them?"

Alex waited tensely for the reply to this question; old Colonel Goldney had been well known to him and he had been on terms of friendship with several of the Fyzabad officers, both civil and military. His heart sank when he saw Bhandoo Singh bow his head and he listened, barely able to restrain himself, as the man described, seemingly without contrition, how his regiment had met the four boatloads of fugitives with a hail of grape and musketry. One party had escaped, the *subedar* admitted; they had lain prone in the bottom of their boat and, unseen by the mutineers, had been rowed by their native boatmen downriver to Goruckpore. The rest had been murdered.

"The Commissioner Sahib stood trial before a court of our native officers. He was sentenced to death and shot. Others drowned, seeking to escape our attack."

"Poor old Goldney," Lousada Barrow said, his voice suddenly devoid of expression. No one else spoke and the prisoner continued his story, now boastfully, as if aware of the pain he had caused his captors.

After their ambush of the boats, the 17th Native Infantry had marched to Fyzabad. They had two guns with them, but their ammunition tumbrils contained only treasure, so they had been anxious to replace the powder and shot they had expended at the behest of the 22nd. Their fellow mutineers, however, had demanded a share of the treasure before complying with their request and, after considerable wrangling, the two regiments had parted company—the 17th with their spent ammunition replaced at the cost of Rs. 160,000. They had joined the Nana's forces at Cawnpore. The *subedar* was unable to give the exact date of their arrival but, pressed by Alex, finally admitted that it had been before the garrison had surrendered, on the Nana's promise of safe conduct to Allahabad by boat.

"I believe," Alex said, "That it was this regiment which pursued us along the Oudh bank. They had two light-calibre guns and it was they who prevented our escape. We could have held off the matchlock men and the sepoys with muskets; those two guns were our undoing. We weren't expecting them and we allowed ourselves to drift too close to the Oudh shore." He fired a spate of brusque questions at the prisoner, and the man lost his truculence as he attempted to evade them.

"I know nothing, Sahib. We obeyed only the commands of the *Sirkar,* the Maharajah Bahadur. True, we were on the Oudh shore, waiting to cross the river but—"

"But you knew of the British garrison's surrender?"

"We heard of it, but it was not our affair."

"You heard, no doubt, that your Maharajah Bahadur had sworn, on his most sacred oath, that if the soldiers of General Wheeler Sahib agreed to vacate their entrenchment, they should be permitted to march out under arms and be accorded safe passage to Allahabad?"

"There were many rumours, Sahib. We knew not which of many to believe." Bhandoo Singh was perspiring freely and Alex, feeling the familiar cold anger well up inside him when he remembered the Nana's betrayal, followed up his advantage.

"You lie, Bhandoo Singh! You and all the other rebel soldiers knew that the garrison was not defeated. They surrendered the entrenchment only on the Maharajah's promise that they should leave Cawnpore unmolested. You saw the boats being made ready at the Suttee Chowra Ghat, did you not?"

"True, Sahib. But we knew not for whom, we—"

"Did you not see them being roofed with straw, in order to accommodate *mem-sahibs* and *baba-log?* Four hundred coolies worked on them all through the night; were you then blind, that you saw them not?"

There were great beads of perspiration now on the *subedar's* dark brow. "We saw them but we did not understand their significance."

"Yet, next day, when the *sahib-log* embarked upon those boats you and the sepoys of your *paltan* opened fire on them with your guns—just as you had done on the boats from Fyzabad? That is so, is it not?"

"Steady, Alex," Lousada Barrow warned, a restraining hand on his shoulder. "The fellow will be tried. He—"

"Give me five minutes more," Alex pleaded. His savage anger faded. It was all past history, he told himself; the massacre, Emmy's death—nothing could undo it. This man's guilt was no greater than that of thousands of others like him. The Nana, Azimullah, the Moulvi of Fyzabad, and the infamous Bala Bhat, the Nana's brother . . . they were the guilty ones, they the betrayers. Bhandoo Singh had simply carried out the orders he had been given, but . . . damn it, he had been waiting, with his guns shotted and the port fires lit, in the concealment of a mango tope on the Oudh bank. Memory returned in all its hideous clarity and he saw again Emmy's face, the blood welling from her breast, and heard her voice, frightened and despairing, as she called his name before slipping from his grasp into the muddy waters of the Ganges.

"What orders had you from the Nana, Bhandoo Singh?" he asked, with icy calm. Although he had spoken quietly, something in his voice evidently struck terror into the prisoner. The last vestige of his earlier arrogance vanished. Wide-eyed and apprehensive, he stared at his interrogator, and then, the movement taking Alex by surprise, his pinioned hands fumbled with the cummerbund at his waist. From beneath it he drew out a rolled sheet of paper which he held out as if even to himself it was a noisome thing.

"These were the orders I received from the hand of Azimullah Khan," he confessed. "The paper bears the Nana's seal, as you will see, Sahib."

"Do you mind, Lou?" Alex took the small roll and, receiving Barrow's nodded assent, carried it over to one of the bivouac fires. Squatting on his heels beside it, he unrolled the paper and read the instructions it contained, the neatly penned Urdu script blurring before his eyes as smoke from the fire stung them.

The letter began with the customary Oriental greeting.* Health and prosperity to Bhandoo Singh, *subedar* of Barker *ki Paltan*. Your petition regarding your arrival with treasure, and your plan for the seizure of certain sepoys who have absconded, has been received and read . . .

---

*Among correspondence quoted by General Neill when he took command of the reoccupied city of Cawnpore.

Alex skimmed through the next few lines, and he drew in his breath sharply as he deciphered them.

> At this time there are no English troops remaining here; they sought protection from the *Sirkar* and said, 'Allow us to get into boats and go away.' Therefore the Sirkar has made arrangements for their going and, by ten o'clock tomorrow, these people will have entered boats and started on the river.
>
> The river at this side is shallow and on the other side deep. The boats will keep to the other side and go along for three or four *koss*. Arrangements for the destruction of these English may not be made here; but as these people will keep near the bank on the other side of the river, it is necessary that you should be prepared and make a place to kill them, and destroy them on that side of the river and, having obtained a victory, come here.

As Bhandoo Singh had claimed, the Nana had appended his hand and seal to the foot of the page. Alex stared down at it numbly as, one by one, the memories came flooding back.

Lousada Barrow joined him by the fire a few minutes later. "The man they were holding—that poor sod of an Englishman—was Carter, the lodge-keeper at Bithur, Alex. It was his wife we found in the *zenana*."

Alex scarcely heard him. Holding out the thin sheet of paper he had taken from their prisoner, his voice choked, he said, "Read this, Lou. Azimullah wrote it but it bears the Nana's seal and signature. It's proof that he betrayed us."

Barrow studied the damning document in silence. "Yes," he agreed heavily, when he had digested its contents. "It would certainly seem to be. The general will be interested to read this, I fancy."

CHAPTER TWO

➳➳➳ • ᴇᴇᴇ

THE COLUMN resumed its march at dawn next morning. As they rode toward Cawnpore, Lousada Barrow waved to Alex to join him at the head of the slow-moving train.

"I never managed to broach the subject I intended to discuss with you yesterday, Alex," he said. "And the interruption put it out of my head. You know, of course, that the general is anxious to increase our number for the advance on Lucknow? He's been hampered a great deal by lack of cavalry, since Palliser's Irregulars proved unreliable."

Alex nodded. The Volunteers had lost a man in the final battle for Cawnpore and now numbered, with Barrow and himself, a mere eighteen sabres. The loss of Palliser's fifty sowars, who had refused to charge the rebels at Fatepur, had been a serious one. Without cavalry, the victories so hardly won by Havelock's infantry and guns could not be followed up or the fleeing enemy harassed by pursuit. Mounted patrols, essential during the advance, were also hazardous for so small a number and the Volunteers ran the risk of being cut off or ambushed each time they scouted ahead of the main body.

"Are you proposing to enlist more recruits?" he asked, frowning. "From whence, pray, will you get them?"

"From the infantry," Barrow answered. "I've been offered fifty or so who say they can ride. Mostly from Her Majesty's Sixty-Fourth and Neill's Blue Caps."

"I admire their spirit, Lou. But they'll require horses, won't they, and at least some training?"

"We're to take over all Palliser's horses—and he, incidentally, is to join us, with his *Rissaldar*, who has remained staunchly loyal. In addition, we're to have all the horses which can be found or requisitioned in Cawnpore. Their mounts present less of a problem than the men themselves, Alex. They, as you rightly suggest, will need training, intensive and expert training, and we'll probably have less than a week in which to lick them into shape." Barrow paused, a faint smile playing about his bearded lips. "As I told you yesterday, the general intends to cross into Oudh as soon as Neill gets here, and he's expected today or tomorrow . . . which doesn't leave us much leeway, does it?"

Alex waited, voicing no opinion. He knew Lousada Barrow of old, knew that faint smile of his and what it portended. The Volunteers' commandant had made up his mind, decided what would have to be done and, like the general himself, to tell him that what he proposed was impossible served only to make him the more determined to prove that it was not. All the same, the prospect of welding some fifty raw recruits into an efficient and disciplined cavalry troop was a daunting one. The Volunteers, despite the fact that there were less than a score of them, *had* been welded into such a force, but they were all officers or officer material, good horsemen, and experienced campaigners, whose courage and discipline left little to be desired. During the advance to Cawnpore, they had proved their worth on countless occasions and more than once had charged and routed large bodies of rebel cavalry, who had shown a craven reluctance to stand up to resolute attack by even so small a force of Europeans.

"Alex," Barrow said, breaking the brief silence that had fallen between them. "How much cavalry drill do you suppose you could teach fifty infantrymen in a week?"

"Do you mean—" Alex stared at him. "You want me to undertake their training?"

"Yes, that's precisely what I want. You are the most experienced cavalry officer we have. You served in the Crimea, you handled Bashi Bazouk troops at Silestria, and you received your early training with the Eleventh Hussars. Not only that, but you served throughout the Punjab campaign and were in action at Chilianwala, were you not? For God's sake, old man"—he cut short Alex's attempted interruption—"no one else can do it. I certainly couldn't—I've spent the past four years in the Political Service and before that I was in staff jobs. I've never commanded troops in action and I've forgotten all I ever knew about cavalry training and tactics."

"You've done pretty well in command of the Volunteers Lousada. You—"

"And why do you imagine I was given the command?" Lousada Barrow threw back his head and laughed with genuine amusement. "Why, for the simple reason that, apart from young Cornet Fergusson, I was the only volunteer officer who had ever served with cavalry before! My grey hairs dictated the choice. I'd hand over my command to you were I at liberty to do so, believe me. Damn it all, my dear fellow, you outrank me with that brevet of yours! Even if the general keeps his promise and gives me promotion to major, you'll still outrank me and—"

"And what of my physical defects?" Alex put in wryly, indicating his empty sleeve. "They outweigh the brevet, I fancy."

"Did Sir Henry Lawrence—God rest his soul! Did *he* concern himself with the fact that you had lost an arm when he appointed you to the command of his Volunteer Cavalry?" his companion countered. He did not wait for an answer but went on briskly, "I confess that when you first joined us, Alex, I doubted whether you would recover sufficiently, after all you had endured in Wheeler's infernal entrenchment, to be capable of assuming any command or post of responsibility for a very long while . . . and I told General Havelock as much. You were lost in a world of your own and you spoke to no one—you just sat that broken-down country-bred of yours and waited for orders. Frankly, there were times when I wondered if you'd find the strength to do even that for much longer."

Alex sighed, making an abortive effort to remember. "Dear heaven, Lou, was I really that bad?"

"You were like a living corpse, old man," Barrow told him. "By rights you ought to have stayed in the field hospital, under the surgeons' care, but you wouldn't hear of it. Le Presle was worried about you. He predicted that you would drop from your saddle with exhaustion or that your head wound would kill you, if the sun did not. 'And then, Captain Barrow,' he informed me, with such severity that he clearly thought I was the one who insisted on keeping you with us, 'we shall have lost the only surviving officer of the Cawnpore garrison!'"

"Thank you for bearing with me. Good heavens, I—"

"You've made a miraculous recovery, for which we can both thank God. And now . . ." again a faint smile twitched Barrow's lips. "Now I'm asking you to do the impossible and make reasonably efficient cavalrymen out of fifty foot soldiers."

"In less than a week?" Alex demurred. "It's a hell of a tall order, Lou."

"I'm aware of that, but if you can't do it, then nobody can. I can let you have an officer to assist you—Palliser or young Fergusson, if you like, and Palliser's *Rissaldar.* Try, at least, Alex, if you will, because we need those fifty men very badly indeed. It's going to be harder to fight our way to Lucknow than it was to reach here, I'm very much afraid."

He was right, Alex knew. He bowed his head resignedly. "Very well, I'll try. I can't promise you that I shall succeed, but I'll do the best I can. Which," he added cynically, "would seem to prove— if proof is needed—that I'm still out of my mind! But it's a strange way to recruit cavalry, you must admit."

Lousada Barrow's smile widened. "Beggars can't be choosers, my friend, and this is a makeshift little army if ever there was one. We've too few men and too little of everything—except, perhaps, guts and determination. But they go a long way." He clapped a big hand on Alex's shoulder. "You can take over men and horses as soon as we get back to camp. I'll collect what weapons and equipment I can for you, but once Neill arrives, I imagine that the rest of us will be required on the Oudh side of the river." He shrugged. "At least you'll be better off in one respect than we are, Alex . . . we're in for a deluge by the look of that sky. And tents are, I understand, to be left behind—the general wishes us to travel light!"

The deluge he had predicted struck soon after the column reached Cawnpore. Heralded by a heavy thunderstorm which brought out every variety of insect pest, the monsoon rain hurtled down, soaking men, horses, and equipment, and turning the road into a quagmire. The patient bullocks, cursed by their drivers, strained and tugged at the heavy guns, and the Volunteer Cavalry men had to dismount and, reins looped over their arms, put their shoulders to the churning wheels. It was midday before the guns were delivered to Captain Francis Maude's newly established artillery park south of the city, and every man in the column was exhausted and filthy.

Alex changed into a clean shirt, snatched a hasty meal in the mess tent, and then went with Lieutenant Palliser and his *Rissaldar*, Nujeeb Khan, to take over the Oudh Irregulars' troop horses in the old Native Cavalry Lines. Each horse was furnished with saddlery and—their previous owners having been disarmed before being ordered back to Allahabad in disgrace—the weapons they had carried were in the custody of the 78th. Alex despatched Palliser with a small party and an ammunition tumbril to claim them and, aided by young Cornet Fergusson and the *Rissaldar*, led his new recruits to the old Cavalry Riding School to put them through their paces.

The Riding School, which had been used during the siege as the site of a twenty-four-pounder gun battery, was in a sorry state, its roof leaking and the once immaculately sanded floor covered with the filth and litter left behind by the mutineer gunners in their flight with the guns. The dripping men set to work to clear the place. There were curses and grumbles, but these were mostly good-humoured, for all the infantry men were enthusiastic and eager to assume the new role for which they had volunteered. Alex had to harden his heart when it came to selecting the best of them; there were only 53 horses, some of which, he knew, would have to be retained as remounts. *Rissaldar* Nujeeb Khan, a tall, fine-looking man with grey in his beard, was an expert judge of the potential skill of the would-be horsemen. He had been wounded in the head and legs when he had intervened to save his British commander from a threatened attack by the Irregulars, but he bore himself with stoic dignity and, seated astride a mettlesome grey stallion, trotted from group to group, offering advice and pointing out mistakes, his keen eyes missing little.

On his advice, eight of the volunteers were returned, crestfallen, to their regiment. The remaining forty-two mustered in two lines and, on Palliser's return with the tumbril, each was issued arms, and the three British officers, with Nujeeb Khan, took them in small groups for instruction in the rudiments of sabre drill.

It was a wearying business, with the heavy monsoon rain pounding relentlessly at the broken roof and the damp heat bringing men and horses out in what Palliser described inelegantly as "a muck sweat." But the foot soldiers managed well enough and finally, as reward for their efforts, Alex led them out onto the open plain to enable them to get the feel of their horses and of their unfamiliar weapons in a less confined space than the Riding School could provide. His new training ground was within sight of General Wheeler's now-crumbling entrenchment, but he scarcely spared it a glance, although the men, without exception, displayed a lively curiosity concerning its shell-pitted buildings and rode up to inspect, in the fading light, the battered ninepounders which still stood—as they had stood throughout the nightmare three weeks of the siege—as guardians of the place Azimullah had called "The Fort of Despair."

"I don't know," Palliser observed, after he too had ridden round the perimeter, "how this place withstood the attacks which were launched against it for as long as it did. To me it's inconceivable that close on a thousand men, women, and children found shelter inside it. With all due respect, Colonel Sheridan, poor old Wheeler must have been mad to select such a site for his defence. Damme, the walls could not have been proof against even musket balls . . . and a resolute cavalryman could have ridden his horse over it without much trouble."

"But only one ever did," Alex told him shortly.

"A sowar, you mean—a Pandy?"

"No, a British officer—young Bolton of the Seventh Light

Cavalry from Lucknow, halfway through the siege." Alex hesitated and then, his voice flat and without expression, he repeated the excuses he had made earlier to Lousada Barrow, feeling once more impelled to defend his brave old general's inexplicable choice of such a site. Turning away, he glimpsed, through the driving rain, a column of marching men moving slowly toward them along the Allahabad road and, thankful for a chance to change the subject, he drew Palliser's attention to them. "Look," he said, pointing. "Can those be our reinforcements from Allahabad?"

"Indeed they are!" the Irregulars' commander exclaimed eagerly. "And with General Neill riding at their head . . . *that's* a sight for sore eyes, is it not, sir? Shall I send word to General Havelock and form our men up to receive him?"

Alex gave his assent. Lieutenant Palliser trotted off to give the necessary orders, and Alex waited, sitting his horse in the rain and watching the approach of the column with a bitter sense of irony. Almost against his will, he returned in memory to the entrench- ment, and memory, sharp and poignant, peopled it with ghosts. He saw the sagging perimeter and the line of gaunt, unkempt riflemen crouching behind it, saw young St. George Ashe and Henry Delafosse, with their motley gun teams, working the worn- out nine-pounders, all of them in tattered remnants of clothing that had once been uniforms, their skins burned black by the sun. He glimpsed a dozen remembered faces—John Moore's, Francis Whiting's, Edward Vibart's, Mowbray Thomson's, Corpo- ral Henegan's, that of old General Wheeler himself—and heard the whine of shells overhead and the terrible, heart-breaking sound of a woman, screaming her agony aloud, as round shot thudded onto the rock-hard ground and bounced on its deadly way across the open compound.

The sweat broke out, streaming damply with the rain down

his cheeks and drenching his body. Then the vision faded and his gaze returned to the road. How often had those weary, half-starved defenders—himself included—looked out toward the Allahabad road and prayed for the sight of a relief column, with James Neill at its head, marching into Cawnpore? Alex shivered, remembering. That he was here to receive them was, he knew, little short of a miracle. He had never expected to live to shake Neill's hand or bid him welcome to Cawnpore . . . yet here he was, within sight of the entrenchment, whose stubborn, useless defence had cost the lives of almost a thousand others; here he was, waiting to greet the very man who might, had he come in time, have saved at least half of them. The man who might have spared Emmy and the rest—those poor ghosts he had just seen—from the horrors of the Suttee Chowra Ghat and the hideous slaughter which had taken place in the Bibigarh.

Dear heaven, he asked himself bitterly, how could he absolve Neill from blame, even in the clear, cold light of reason and with the excuse of military expediency? Neill had had a choice, but he had also had his orders.

Frowning, he studied the tall, upright figure in dun-coloured drill, riding a horse's length ahead of the trio of officers who accompanied him along the rain-soaked road. Like himself, James Neill had served with the Turkish Army in the Crimea, where he had won an enviable reputation as a cavalry commander. They had never met; Alex had been wounded at Balaclava and had returned to India after a brief convalescence, and Neill, who had arrived later, had remained with the Turkish Contingent until shortly before the war ended. He had commanded at Yenikale, with the rank of brigadier-general, in 1855, and had enhanced his reputation with the British High Command for the strict discipline he had managed to enforce among his unruly troops. He was said to have hanged a number of them for looting and similar crimes in order to achieve this end, Alex recalled, and the French troops, who had formed part of his garrison, had apparently regarded him with loathing.

But he had a presence, even at this distance, an air of almost arrogant authority which had evidently made itself felt among the men marching at his back. They formed a compact body, their rifles shouldered and every man in step to the beat of the drums and fifes playing them in. They were wet and obviously tired but they held their heads high and even the camp followers and the baggage train seemed to have kept pace with the rest of the column instead of straggling behind it, as most such cumbersome trains did.

Impressed in spite of his earlier critical thoughts, Alex rode over to join his own men. Lieutenant Palliser had formed them up in two lines by the road verge, intending to receive the new arrivals with the ceremony of a salute, but they looked a bedraggled little party in their sodden red cotton infantry tunics, and the horses were restive and hard to control. Four or five of the men failed entirely to control their mounts and, as they backed awkwardly out of line, they unsettled the horses nearest them, which had hitherto been giving their riders no trouble. One animal reared, depositing its rider in the mud; flustered and cursing, the others endeavoured to get back into line and Palliser, exasperated by their incompetence, roared at them to hold steady. They managed finally to obey him and reform ranks, but their salute, when General Neill drew level with them, was anything but ceremonious. He recognised Palliser and gave vent to a bellow of laughter.

"Devil take it, Charlie, what's this rabble you're with? They don't look much like cavalrymen to me. Surely these aren't the

Gentlemen Volunteers who've covered themselves with glory, according to the Old Gentleman's despatches?"

Palliser, scarlet with annoyance, shook his head. He was an admirer of Neill's and had served under him prior to General Havelock's arrival in Allahabad. During that period, his Irregulars had behaved in exemplary fashion, and their attempted defection at Fatepur still rankled. "Good Lord, no, sir!" he retorted indignantly. "The horses are mine—my fellows were made to hand them over with their arms. But the clowns who are now endeavouring to ride them are General Havelock's latest idea—recruits from the infantry, if you please."

"I see." General Neill permitted himself an amused and tolerant smile. "Well, perhaps you had better dismiss them, before they do any more damage either to themselves or their horses." His dark eyes rested for a moment, indifferently, on Alex's face, but he wore no badges of rank and made no attempt to introduce himself, and the older man was turning away when Charles Palliser, recovering his temper, made the introduction with a murmured apology.

"Lieutenant-Colonel Sheridan, sir. I beg you to forgive my bad manners, Colonel Sheridan, I—"

"Sheridan . . . *Colonel* Sheridan?" James Neill took in Alex's empty sleeve and the scar on his face and waited, lips above the recently grown black beard suddenly tightening. "Damme, I've heard of you but the connection eludes me for the moment. Aren't you a cavalryman?"

Alex bowed. He had his emotions under stern control and his expression was carefully blank. "Yes, sir, Third Light Cavalry," he supplied. "Brevet rank of lieutenant-cColonel, at present serving as a Volunteer in Captain Barrow's Horse."

"A lieutenant-colonel serving as a Volunteer . . . good Gad!

What times we live in." Neill was clearly puzzled but Alex did not enlighten him. Instead he answered quietly, "Indeed so, General. If you'll permit me, sir, I should like to take my recruits back to their lines. They've had rather a grueling first day on horseback and—"

"No, no, hold on, if you please." Neill's smile returned. "Let Charlie Palliser take 'em, for God's sake, and ride in with me. I've remembered who you are now—General Havelock mentioned you in one of his letters. Damme, you're the sole survivor of the Cawnpore garrison, are you not?"

"As far as can be ascertained, the survivors are myself and a Commissariat clerk, General," Alex admitted reluctantly. He hesitated, anxious to phrase his request so as not to give offence but determined, as much for Neill's sake as his own, to make his escape before he could be subjected to a barrage of questions. "If you would not consider it a discourtesy, sir, I'd like to remain with my men. I've been given a week in which to turn them into cavalrymen and I should be failing in my duty if I did not utilise every hour of daylight I have at my disposal for their instruction. They've a lot to learn, as I fear you will have observed."

"Yes, of course," Neill agreed, with unexpected readiness. His tone, as well as his smile, was friendly. "Congratulations on your escape, Sheridan. No doubt there will be another opportunity to talk to you about it when you're less pressed for time. But spare me Charlie Palliser, if you will—he can bring me up to date with the news before I present myself to General Havelock."

The column moved off with Palliser riding happily beside his old commander, and Alex led his crestfallen troopers back to the cavalry lines. He made a point of talking to them individually during the short ride across the flooded plain, offering advice and encouragement and, assisted by young Fergusson and Nujeeb

Khan, supervised them at evening stables. The men began to recover their spirits. Drenched and saddle sore though most of them were, they groomed and bedded down their horses with more enthusiasm than Alex had expected, and he made them a brief speech before dismissing them to their own quarters.

"It's not quite as easy as it looks, serving in the Cavalry, my lads," he warned them. "If you've only volunteered in the hope of saving your legs on the way to Lucknow, you may well wish you'd stayed with your own regiments before I've done with you. But you've all had to do with horses before—you know they must be fed, watered, and groomed before you can attend to your own needs, however bone tired you are at the end of a march." There was a murmur of assent from the assembled men. Alex outlined the training programme he hoped to arrange for them and ended with a few words of praise for their efforts during the afternoon, at which they brightened visibly. "I'll make cavalry-men of you," he promised, smiling. "But I shall have to make you work as you've never worked before. If any man is not prepared to give me all he's got during the next week, I would rather he said so now and I'll return him to his regiment without holding it against him. I want you to understand that a man who is unable, for any reason, to reach the standard I require will be a liability to his comrades—so think well, all of you."

He waited, but, after glancing from one to another of them, saw only one man step forward in response to his challenge, hesitate, and when no one else followed his example, step sheepishly back into the ranks again. He was a stocky, grey-haired private with a face the colour of teak, whose name, Alex learned from his list, was Cullmane. He was a good horseman, which made his change of mind the more puzzling, but he said no more and Alex let him go with the rest, making no attempt to question or single him out. As he himself was preparing to make his way to the mess tent, however, he found the stocky figure of his reluctant recruit barring his path.

"If I moight have a word wit ya, sorr," the man said, his voice betraying his Irish ancestry. "I'd take it as a favour."

"Certainly." Alex halted, eyeing him searchingly. "Before you do, though, I think I should tell you that you appear to be one of the best riders we have. And you did your horse well—you obviously know your way about a stable. What were you in civilian life, Cullmane, a groom?"

Private Cullmane's brown face split into a gap-toothed grin. "I was whipper-in to the 'Gallant Tips'—the Tipperary Hunt, sorr, in me younger days."

"Then there's not much I can teach you about horsemanship, is there, lad? You'll only have to master the drill, and you shouldn't find that beyond your capabilities."

"No, yer honour," the man admitted. "But 'twas what ye was sayin' about being a liability— 'twas that made me step forward. I wouldn't want to be lettin' yez down, sorr. But there's this . . ." He pulled back the sleeve of his mud-spattered red jacket to reveal an ugly wound which extended from forearm to elbow. It was partially healed and evidently of recent origin, and the elbow joint was so swollen that he had difficulty in bending it. "I got this at Aong, sorr, and 'tis me roight arm, ye see. I'll not be a great deal of use if I can't handle me sabre, will I, sorr?"

Alex inspected the arm. "Have you shown this to the surgeon?"

"Sure, sorr. He dressed it and sent me back to duty."

"I see. Well—can you handle a pistol?"

"I can, sorr."

"Then we'll use you as a galloper, Cullmane," Alex decided.

"Unless you want to go back to your regiment?" Receiving an emphatic headshake, he smiled. "Right, then. I don't imagine you'll be a liability after whipping-in for the Tips. But you'd better have that arm dressed again—you could lose it, you know, if it becomes badly infected."

"I'd be in powerful good company if I did, Colonel sorr," Cullmane said. "For haven't you lost your sword arm yourself now? Dammit, sorr, if ye'll pardon the liberty, if I could handle myself the way you do, sure I'd never miss it!"

"You would, my lad, you would," Alex told him quietly. Hardly a day had passed during the siege when he had not cursed the loss of his arm and found himself impeded by it. But at any rate, he thought, as he left the Cavalry Lines, if he could still give the impression of being able to handle himself well on horseback, then the years of patient practice with his left hand had not been wasted.

In the Volunteers' mess tent, he found Lousada Barrow at table and joined him there. After questioning him minutely concerning their new recruits, the cavalry Commander warned him that the time allocated to their training might be less, even, than he had anticipated.

"Neill's arrived, with 227 of the 84th, as no doubt you observed. The general received him with an eleven-gun salute and they're dining together now, but I gather from what Fraser Tytler let slip that the Highlanders are under orders to cross over to Oudh tonight."

"Tonight, in this deluge?" Alex frowned.

"So it would seem," Barrow assured him. "Tytler, who's something of an expert on engines, has spent the best part of the day putting the steamer's engines into working order. The Bridge of Boats was destroyed on the Nana's instructions, of course, but

Tytler says they've managed to collect twenty sizeable boats, with native boatmen to man them, and the steamer is to tow them across. They're to take a couple of field-guns with them but no tents, poor fellows."

"And Neill is to remain in command here, is he?" Alex was hungry, but he regarded the unsavoury-looking mess on the plate a servant placed before him with glum disfavour. "What *is* this? Is it edible?"

"It's curry," Barrow assured him. "And not as bad as it looks . . . try it. Yes, Neill's to command here as soon as all our men are across the river. The general has had hundreds of coolies working to build an entrenchment on the Baxi Ghat, where already he's had two guns mounted to cover the crossing. It's a well-chosen site, with the river on one side and the canal on the other, and it's high enough up to cover the approaches from the city as well. The coolies have worked well—the breastwork is considerably higher, even now, than poor General Wheeler's and I'm told that, when completed, the walls will be fifteen feet thick, turfed over, and fitted with sallyports and properly constructed gun platforms."

"Surely that will take time?" Alex ate his curry with unexpected relish.

Lousada Barrow shook his head. "The final touches will, but the general is satisfied that enough will have been done before he leaves with the main body to enable Neill to hold it with three hundred men." He laid a hand on Alex's shoulder. "It will be a different proposition altogether from Wheeler's, Alex, and the guns we brought in from Bithur will be used for its defence. Poor old Wheeler *did* make a grave error in siting his entrenchment so far from the river, you know, and mounting so few light guns."

Perhaps that was true, Alex thought unhappily. He pushed his plate away and shook his head to the mess *khitmatgar's* proffered basket of fresh mangoes. Barrow passed him a cheroot and they left the table together and went to sit in the tent which served as an anteroom. It was deserted save for two civilian Volunteers who were dozing over their coffee, and when Barrow had finished his, he took out his pocket-watch.

"The crossing is due to start about midnight," he said. "I suppose, in spite of the rain, we ought to watch it, don't you? But we can snatch a few hours' sleep before going down to the *ghat.*"

Alex agreed resignedly, stiffing a yawn. He was becoming accustomed to lack of sleep; it seemed a lifetime since he had been able to enjoy a full night's rest, but at least the few hours Lousada Barrow had promised him need no longer be spent on the bare ground with his horse tethered beside him, alternately drenched by rain and burned and blistered by the fierce June sun. Tents had arrived with the baggage train and were springing up like mushrooms within sight of the burned-out, looted ruins of the bungalows and barracks which had originally housed the garrison, so that some degree of comfort was now possible. For the next week, at any rate, all save the unfortunate Highlanders could count on being able to sleep under cover which, in view of the present ceaseless downpour, would make a welcome change.

"I think I'll turn in now, if you don't mind, Lou." Alex got stiffly to his feet, stifling another involuntary yawn. "I'm planning a fairly active day tomorrow. For a start I want to have the old Riding School cleared and the roof patched up—the Pandies had a twenty-four-pounder battery sited there and they've left it in a hell of a state. But I fancy the new boys will learn a good deal faster if they're under cover, and we'll knock up fewer horses if—"

"Good Lord, I nearly forgot!" Barrow interrupted apologetically. "My memory isn't what it was, I'm afraid. You won't be free tomorrow morning, Alex. The general has ordered the trial of that *subedar* of the 17th—the one we brought in from Bithur. The trial is to take place tomorrow morning at eight-thirty, at the Kotwalee, I think, under the presidency of one of the Queen's regiments' commanding officers . . . and you'll be required as a witness. You—"

"Oh, for heaven's sake!" Alex began in frustration. "If I'm to train those recruits, then surely—"

"The trial will not take up much of your time," Barrow assured him. "And I'll attend personally to the clearing of your riding school. But I understand that the general considers this trial of great importance, since it will be the first of its kind here. Justice must not only be done, it must be *seen* to be done. The death sentence is, of course, mandatory for all native officers and sepoys taken in mutiny, and the *subedar* will undoubtedly be sentenced to death. It's essential, however, that his guilt is proven, and you were there when we found the Nana's letter on him. You were also there when he carried out the Nana's orders and fired on the boats which managed to escape from the Suttee Chowra Ghat—which makes you a vital witness, Alex."

"I suppose it does," Alex conceded reluctantly. "And if the general wishes me to give evidence, I can scarcely refuse, can I?"

"Scarcely, old man. Well . . ." Lousada Barrow reached for his shabby cavalry cloak, which still smelled faintly of mothballs and bore the silver buttons and pale buff facings of his old regiment, the 5th Madras Light Cavalry. He drew it about him and led the way out into the rain-wet darkness. "They auctioned poor Stuart Beatson's effects this afternoon," he added, his voice muffled. "I bid for one or two items I'll be happy to share with you,

Alex. There's a splendid new cloak which I intend to hang on to, so you're welcome to this one, if you want it. The darned thing fitted me when I was a newly joined cornet—it doesn't now. And there are some shirts and cotton tunics and a very good pair of boots. If you come to my tent, I'll hand over anything you need."

Alex thanked him. The news of the death of the force's adjutant-general had not been unexpected—poor Beatson had been suffering from an attack of cholera since leaving Fatepur and had followed the advance in an ammunition tumbril—but nevertheless it came as a shock to him. And it would be a cruel blow to William Beatson, also, when he learned of his younger brother's sad end. Like so many brothers in the East India Company's service, the two had seen each other infrequently but they were the best of friends and had corresponded regularly. In the Crimea, Alex recalled, Stuart Beatson's letters had been read and read again by his onetime commander and closest friend. Disconsolately, he followed Lousada Barrow into his tent, where the garments he had purchased at the auction of the dead officer's effects had been laid out neatly on a folding camp bed.

"He was popular," Barrow observed. "The bids were high and the general bought a number of items, so there'll be something to send on to the poor fellow's wife and family. Not that it will console them for his loss." He sighed, slipping off his cloak. "Here's this thing. I'm sorry it's so wet but it will be an improvement on the horse blanket you've had to make do with, perhaps. Take anything else you require—your need is greater than mine."

"I shan't be able to pay you until the paymaster arranges a draft," Alex warned. "You see, I—" Lousada Barrow cut him short. "Oh, for heaven's sake, Alex! I don't want any payment and the cloak's a gift, in any case. Help yourself."

"I can't do that unless you'll allow me to repay you, Lou."

"All right, if you insist—pay me when you are in a position to do so. Try those boots; they're too small for me but I should imagine they're about your size."

Alex obediently measured the sole of one boot against his own. "They're fine," he said. "If you're sure you don't want them."

"I only wish I could get into them. Even these, which I've worn for years, seem to have shrunk." Barrow kicked off his own boots with a grunt of relief and, seating himself on the bed, gestured to the pile of shirts and native-made white uniform jackets. "Poor devil, he evidently expected a long campaign! He had rallied, you know, and Dr. Le Presle was hopeful that he'd pull through. He and Sydenham Renaud were both moved to a building known as the Savada Koti, which has been taken over as a temporary hospital. It was near the Nana's camp, I believe."

"Yes," Alex confirmed. "He kept some of his European captives there." He hesitated. "How is Renaud? Someone told me the surgeons were afraid they would have to take his leg off."

Barrow shrugged despondently. "They died within an hour of each other, I'm sorry to say. The funeral is tomorrow, with full military honours for them both. The Movable Column has suffered a great loss, Alex, in those two." He sighed. "They say no man is indispensable, don't they? All the same, they will be hard to replace, Stuart Beatson in particular. He was one of the best organisers I've ever met in my life."

"Has anyone been appointed in his place?"

"I heard that the general is to appoint his son, Harry, but I don't know if that's true."

Alex selected a shirt and two jackets. He waited, offering no comment, and Lousada Barrow went on, a thoughtful frown drawing his bristling dark brows together, "You haven't asked about Harry Havelock but I'll tell you anyway. He's young and he's a hothead but he's as brave as a lion and I think he'll go a long way. When he first came out, he ran himself into debt and, I'm told, caused his father a great deal of anxiety—he's not well off, you know, the general. He could never afford to buy his steps in rank; he won them all on merit, and it took him a long time. You can't blame him for giving his son a step up, in the circumstances . . . he's devoted to the boy, in spite of those earlier scandals."

"I did not say I blamed him, Lou," Alex pointed out mildly.

"No, you didn't. But I could see you wondering."

"Perhaps I was. It's an important job, adjutant-general to a force like this. I just hope young Havelock's up to it."

"Don't we all!" Barrow's tone was dry. "Well, I've brought you up to date with the news, good and bad, so perhaps we'd better call it a day. Those are the things you're taking? Good—then I'll have you wakened at midnight. Unless you're too tired and would rather sleep?"

"No." Alex denied it. "I want to watch the crossing."

The Nana would almost certainly have crossed into Oudh, he thought, as he made his way, wrapped in Lousada's cloak, to his own nearby tent. If, that was to say, the treacherous swine was still alive. His mouth twisted into a mirthless smile. The Nana, Azimullah, Tantia Topi, Jwala Pershad . . . all of them were still at large and all of them would have to be defeated and brought to justice. The Moulvi of Fyzabad also, for he, perhaps, was the evil genius on whom must rest responsibility for both the mutiny of the Oudh troops and the Nana's betrayal.

Alex groped his way over the recumbent forms of the two officers who shared the tent with him. They were sleeping deeply and neither stirred. Within a few minutes of casting himself down beside them, he was sleeping as deeply as they.

CHAPTER THREE
➽➽➽ • ⫷⫷⫷

IT WAS STILL raining heavily when Lousada Barrow led his small party of Volunteer Cavalry to the Baxi Ghat just before midnight, to find General Havelock and his Staff already there and the scene one of feverish activity.

The embarkation point was situated within sight of the wrecked pontoons of the old Bridge of Boats, which had once linked two small islands—both now under flood water—and carried traffic between Cawnpore and the Lucknow road. On a mound, sufficiently high above the landing stage to cover the approaches to it, the stark outline of the new entrenchment could just be discerned through the driving rain, the muzzles of two heavy-calibre guns protruding from the wall on the river side. General Havelock, Alex thought, eyeing these, had certainly wasted no time . . . and he was wasting none now.

The deluge had turned the riverbank into a quagmire, but in spite of it, the embarkation was proceeding with remarkable speed and efficiency. The small river steamer, the *Burrampootra,* in which Captain Spurgin, with a hundred Madras Fusiliers and two small guns manned by veterans of the Invalid Battalion, had battled his way from Allahabad, had already taken her complement of Highlanders on board. Under the expert hand of her commander, the gallant Indian marine lieutenant, Dickson, she was drawing away from the bank, smoke pouring from her single funnel and her ancient paddles noisily churning up the dark, muddy water of the swollen Ganges.

Colonel Fraser Tytler, the Force's A.Q.M.G., emerged from a native hut in which he had sought temporary shelter from the downpour and, a hurricane lamp held high above his head, watched her departure apprehensively. His normally immaculate white uniform was covered with oil stains, Alex observed, and his arms, bare to the elbow, were liberally coated with the same substance, but he beamed as he watched the little steamer swing round, holding her own against the current. General Havelock, recognising him, doffed his cap in salute and the Highlanders lining the upper deck gave vent to excited cheers.

Their comrades, waiting to embark in the small boats which the *Burrampootra* would take in tow, squatted down under the dripping neem trees in glumly contrasting silence as the native boatmen manoeuvred their craft closer to the *ghat*. Soaked as they were, they did not relish the prospect of wading out waist deep in order to board the *budgerows* provided for them, and several voices were raised in complaint when the order came for them to move. Havelock heard them and, dismounting from his horse, went across to speak to them. The swearing ceased the instant that the men saw the dapper little figure of their general picking his way through the squelching mud toward them, and they greeted him eagerly, clustering round him like a crowd of small boys unexpectedly vouchsafed a glimpse of their hero.

Alex was too far away to hear what he said to them, but the effect was heartwarmingly evident. The men lost their sullenness and cheered him spontaneously; Havelock, soon as wet and uncomfortable as any of his Highlanders, led them down to the *ghat* and stood, smiling encouragement, as they splashed into the water and, packs and rifles held above their heads, boarded the waiting boats.

"That, gentlemen," Colonel Tytler's voice said from the darkness, "is what I call leadership!" He was on horseback now, his stained uniform covered by a cape, but his handsome, patrician face still bore traces of his day of toil in the *Burrampootra*'s engine-room. He reined in between Alex and Lousada Barrow and went on quietly, "He's always had that quality, allied to a first-class brain and greater courage under fire than any man I've ever met. But until now, Henry Havelock has never been appreciated for the exceptional soldier he is . . . which is yet another argument against the buying and selling of commissions in Her Majesty's Army, I suppose."

"You've known him for a long time, have you not, Colonel?" Barrow suggested.

"For almost twenty years," the deputy assistant quartermaster-general admitted. "We were both in the Afghan campaign, although I, thank God, wasn't in Cabul in '41. We both started off as ADCs—Havelock to Sir Willoughby Cotton, with the Bengal Column, and I to Sir George Pollock, with the relief force. Havelock had just obtained his substantive captaincy in the 13th Light Infantry, without purchase . . . and with twenty-three years' service as a subaltern behind him!" He sighed reminiscently. "He was the moving force at Jellalabad, you know—not Sale, although Sale was subsequently given all the credit for it. A K.C.B., promotion to major-general . . . and eulogies from Lord Ellenborough fell to Sale's share, and Havelock, somewhat belatedly, was given a brevet-majority and a C.B. There's no justice, is there? But at least General Pollock had the good sense to appoint him adjutant-general to McCaskill's division—which he virtually commanded—and he had the satisfaction of helping to avenge the slaughter of the Cabul garrison. That was when I came to know him . . . and poor Henry Lawrence too. He was another who never got the rewards he richly deserved, and now, alas, it's too late for him. But at least it's not too late for General Havelock and—" the Colonel broke off, swearing under his breath.

Glancing round to ascertain the cause of his annoyance, Alex saw, by the light of the spluttering flares and torches on the *ghat,* that General Neill had also come to witness the Highlanders' crossing into Oudh. He had several officers with him, including Lionel Stephenson, his late second-in-command, and Palliser and Simpson, with whom he was apparently sharing some joke or anecdote which caused them uproarious amusement.

General Havelock heard their laughter, looked round, and nodded, but made no other acknowledgement of Neill's presence and Tytler grunted resentfully.

"Infernal fellow! I honestly believe he sets out to be offensive and really there's no reason why he should be. General Havelock is years his senior and has already proved that he's the right man in the right place. But Neill expected to be given this command and he won't let any of us forget it. Now he's furious because he's being left here while Havelock leads the advance to Lucknow, but damn it, a force of this size doesn't require two generals. Neill *has* to command the rear."

Normally a man of mild and even temper, Fraser Tytler bristled with rage when Neill, noticing the group of horsemen under the trees, came trotting over to join them, his smile expansive as he greeted several of them by name.

"I'd no idea your talents extended to mastery of the marine engine, Tytler," he said. "Congratulations. You have done a magnificent job on the old *Burrampootra.*"

Colonel Tytler muttered something, controlling himself with difficulty. He was about to move away, but Neill's next words brought him abruptly to a halt.

"I suppose the Old Gentleman made his accustomed oration

to his departing warriors?" he suggested, and before anyone could reply, he added, chuckling, "I've just heard about the speech he made to the unfortunate Veteran Artillery gunners Spurgin and Dickson brought up with them. Maude's had his eye on the poor fellows, it seems, and they were literally press-ganged into transferring to his field battery, in spite of pleading age and infirmity. The Old Gentleman had them paraded and, in true Napoleonic tradition, thanked them for 'so nobly volunteering to assist their country in her hour of need.' Whereupon, I'm told, one of their number stepped forward and interrupted him. 'Beg pardon, sir,' says he, with a regard for the truth that must do him credit. 'We ain't no volunteers, sir—no volunteers at all. We only come 'cos we was forced to come!' Damnably funny, don't you think, gentlemen?" He laughed, inviting his audience to share his mirth. "I gather the general was lost for words and dismissed the parade with almost indecent haste."

There was an embarrassed silence which, to Alex's relief, was broken by a burst of cheering as the last of the advance party boarded their boat and, with towlines attached, the *Burrampootra* started to chug toward the opposite shore. The slight figure of General Havelock could be seen standing, cap in hand, acknowledging the cheers of the departing 78th, and sensing that Colonel Tytler was about to explode into wrath, Alex attempted to stave off the threatened outburst.

"The Highlanders are in good heart, General Neill," he observed quietly. "Listen to those cheers! There can be no doubt that *they* volunteered willingly enough and that they appreciated General Havelock's presence here tonight."

Neill turned in his saddle, frowning when he identified Alex as the speaker. "Ah, Colonel Sheridan again, is it not?" His tone was restrained but his eyes held an odd, steely glint as he went on, "*Brevet* Lieutenant-Colonel Sheridan, late of the mutinied Third Light Cavalry and also, it seems, of General Wheeler's garrison. You're a mysterious fellow, Sheridan—damme, you are!"

"Mysterious, sir?" Alex echoed, more puzzled than alarmed. "I was not aware that there was any mystery attached to me."

"Ah, but there is," Neill asserted. "I have been making enquiries about you. I was astounded to learn that you had made no report on the siege and furnished no details of casualties to General Havelock, although you have been with the Movable Column under his command since it left Batinda. But no doubt there's a reason for your reticence?"

"Yes, sir. Unfortunately I was wounded in the head and—"

"We'll hear about that in due course. Let us first establish one or two pertinent facts. It would appear that you were appointed to command Sir Henry Lawrence's Volunteer Cavalry in Lucknow, for which reason, presumably, you received promotion to your present brevet rank? Rapid promotion—you were a captain, I believe?" Neill smiled.

Still not quite clear as to the purpose of his interrogation, Alex looked at him in surprise. "That is so, yes. But I—"

"But you turn up fifty miles from here, in the uniform of a native sowar, claiming to be one of only two survivors of the appalling massacre in which the rest of General Wheeler's garrison perished! That, in itself, has all the ingredients of a mystery, has it not? The more so, since your command is in Lucknow." James Neill's tone had been faintly jocular and he had not raised his voice, but he raised it now and the other officers, who had been conversing in a desultory way among themselves, looked round startled, as he demanded, "Well, hasn't it? It certainly has to me, Colonel Sheridan! Unless, of course, you had been sent to seek aid for the garrison?"

"No, sir, it was too late for that. General Wheeler had been compelled to surrender and—"

"Yes, so you told Palliser, I believe. But you've never explained why you were with General Wheeler's garrison, have you?" Neill's tone was deliberately provocative, his smile equally so.

"The explanation is simple, sir," Alex assured him, determined not to allow himself to be provoked.

Ignoring an attempt by Colonel Tytler to intervene, Neill exclaimed harshly, "The devil it is! Then pray let us hear it, sir."

None of the others spoke, but they were all, Alex could sense, listening intently to this strange and totally unexpected clash between James Neill and himself, as much at a loss to understand what had prompted it as he was . . . with the exception of Palliser. It had been Palliser's patrol with which he had first made contact at Batinda, and the Irregulars' commander had been at loggerheads with virtually everyone since his men—to whom he had been deeply attached—had been disgraced for their failure to charge the mutineers at Fatepur. He had resented their horses being turned over to the infantry recruits and, Alex decided wryly, he had probably also resented Lousada Barrow's choice of himself as training officer. Charles Palliser was a good soldier and an excellent cavalry leader; his resentment was, perhaps, understandable, but even so . . . he drew in his breath sharply as Neill prompted, "Well, Sheridan? Let us hear your simple explanation of how you came to be in General Wheeler's garrison and not in Sir Henry Lawrence's?"

Alex stiffened. He said, at pains to speak calmly and precisely, whilst racking his brain for the now only half-remembered details, "After the electric telegraph wires between here and Lucknow were found to have been cut, I volunteered to deliver a letter from Sir Henry Lawrence to General Wheeler. That was on the—

on the afternoon of Thursday the fifth . . . no, the *fourth* of June. The letter contained information which Sir Henry had received by telegraph from Calcutta and was—"

"You volunteered to leave your command in order to deliver a letter a *cossid* could have delivered?" Neill challenged scornfully. "Damme, Sheridan, why?"

"The message was urgent, sir, and of too much importance to be entrusted to a *cossid*. Had it fallen into the wrong hands, it—"

"But why *you*, Sheridan? For heaven's sake, surely a junior officer could have taken it?"

"My wife and child were here, sir," Alex admitted. "I was anxious to ensure their safety and Sir Henry Lawrence offered me the opportunity to come here, so that I might make arrangements for them to join me, if possible, in Lucknow."

"That was extremely considerate of Sir Henry!"

"Yes, it was, sir. He was considerate to all who served under him." Feeling Lousada Barrow stir uneasily beside him, Alex kept a tight rein on his temper. Of what use would it be to try to explain the reasons for Sir Henry's consideration, he asked himself, deciding against it. "As I said, sir," he went on evenly, "the message from Calcutta was urgent. It was, in fact, a warning that your relief column had been delayed by an outbreak of mutiny in Benares. General Wheeler was counting on the early arrival of your troops to reinforce his defence and to enable him, if it became necessary, to evacuate the women and children from what, he was fully aware, might become an untenable position . . . as, indeed, it proved to be."

"He chose it, did he not?"

"In the belief that he was to be reinforced by a European regiment, sir. General Wheeler was told repeatedly that troops were on their way to him. He had been assured that your column would reach him within a week or ten days. That was why he—"

"Yes, yes!" James Neill put in, an edge to his voice. "The devil take it, man, that's past history now—we all know why I was held up. I had to put down mutinies in both Benares and Allahabad, I had to restore order in the districts before I could move to Wheeler's assistance . . . and I had only one regiment to do it with. Damme, even with a regiment as good as my Blue Caps, I couldn't perform miracles!" There was a murmur of sympathetic agreement from several of the officers who had accompanied him to the *ghat* and Neill controlled himself with an almost visible effort. He added, less heatedly, "I sent poor Renaud, and Spurgin with the steamer, as soon as I could . . . it was Havelock who insisted on halting them at Batinda—not I, for God's sake! If he had allowed them to continue, they might at least have got through in time to save those tragic innocents who died in the Bibigarh. But . . ." his tone changed to the hectoring one he had used earlier. "It's your story I'm concerned with, Sheridan—*your* actions, not mine, that require explanation. Do you intend to explain them, damn it?"

"My actions, sir?" Alex echoed uncertainly.

"Yes, yours. You delivered Sir Henry Lawrence's letter and remained here, is that correct? You did not attempt to return to your command in Lucknow?"

Alex shook his head. "General Wheeler's troops mutinied within a few hours of my arrival. It was impossible for me to leave, I—"

"Impossible, Colonel Sheridan?" James Neill seized swiftly on his admission. His voice cut like a whiplash, and hearing it, Alex felt a sudden chilling apprehension. Of what, he wondered wretchedly, was he being accused? Neill leaned back in his saddle to glance at the officers grouped about him. The steady drumming of rain on the canopy of wet leaves above their heads had made it difficult for those on the edge of the group to catch every word that had been said, but it was evident from their expressions that they had all heard enough to realise that something out of the ordinary was going on, and now he had their full attention. Major Stephenson, meeting his gaze, shrugged uncomfortably; Palliser, who had been engaged in a whispered exchange with Simpson, whilst endeavouring to quieten a restive horse, wore a perplexed frown; Tytler and Barrow, who were closer than the others, were also frowning but both looked shocked and angry when Neill repeated his question, pitching his voice so that none of them could fail to hear it.

"Impossible, Sheridan, when your place was in Lucknow? Or did the fact that your wife was here influence your decision to remain with Wheeler's garrison?"

The question, with all its damning implications, hung in the air between them, striking at the very roots of Alex's disciplined control. He reddened furiously.

"Surely, General Neill, you cannot suppose that I remained here from choice? As heaven is my witness, I assure you, I—" Lousada Barrow laid a restraining hand on his shoulder, himself starting to voice an indignant protest, but Colonel Tytler cut him short.

"Leave this to me, Lousada." Turning to face Neill, he enquired icily, "General Neill, are you accusing this officer of some dereliction of duty? I am not at all clear . . . but if you are, may I suggest that this is neither the time nor the place to conduct an inquisition into Colonel Sheridan's conduct. In any case, accusations of so grave a nature as yours appear to be should, if they can be substantiated, be made the subject of an official enquiry."

Neill eyed him sombrely. "Official enquiry be damned! I am not *accusing* him of anything, my dear Tytler—I am merely endeavouring to throw some light on the strange circumstances of his survival."

"Strange circumstances, sir? I do not understand."

"Strange indeed, Colonel," James Neill asserted. "From all the reports I have heard, no one from General Wheeler's garrison escaped, unless—like the Commissariat clerk, Shepherd—they left the entrenchment *before* the Nana's terms for capitulation were accepted. A number of natives deserted, servants and the like, but Shepherd, I've been told, claims to have left in disguise several days before the surrender, on a mission for General Wheeler and with his consent. He was taken by the rebels and imprisoned, so therefore did not go to the boats with the rest of the garrison . . . which explains why he survived."

"Shepherd's story is not in dispute," Tytler pointed out. "General Havelock is quite satisfied with the account he has given. The rebels did not penetrate his disguise; he and a Eurasian drummer, who was imprisoned with him, were still wearing their fetters when our advance party found them on the outskirts of the city."

"Quite so," Neill acknowledged dryly. "But our friend Sheridan was found *fifty* miles from here, was he not, also in native guise but happily unfettered?"

"I confess that I cannot see the connection," Colonel Tytler said. He, too, gripped Alex's arm, warning him with a quick headshake, to say nothing, and Alex waited, very white of face now but aware of the need for caution.

"Can you not?" James Neill scoffed. "Oh, come now, my dear Tytler! I had hoped, for his own sake, that Sheridan would be able to tell us that he was at Batinda because—like Shepherd—

General Wheeler had sent him to seek aid for the garrison. That wasn't what he told Palliser, it's true, but he was wounded and confused; I was trying to give him the benefit of the doubt. But be still denies that Wheeler sent him—you heard him yourself, did you not?"

This was too much to stomach, and Alex could contain himself no longer. "General Wheeler was dead before I made my escape sir; to the best of my knowledge, he and all the others were massacred in the boats. I knew of no survivors, as I informed Lieutenant Palliser. Of what use to ask for aid when the whole garrison was destroyed? For God's sake, sir—" Neill silenced him with an imperiously raised hand.

"Wait—I'm not yet done. You've given your explanation and I have listened, although I, for one, find it far from satisfactory. Even the reason you gave for your presence in General Wheeler's garrison scarcely redounds to your credit. And as to your escape . . . not to put too fine a point on it, Sheridan, I don't believe that anyone *could* have escaped unless he had done so before Wheeler's surrender. When Palliser found you, he said that you remembered nothing of the siege or your own movements. You—"

"Sir—General Neill . . ." Palliser, flushed and clearly upset, broke his self-imposed silence. "I did not intend to imply . . . that is to say, sir, Colonel Sheridan had been severely wounded. What I told you was—"

"Hold your tongue, Charlie!" Neill bade him. "You told me the plain, unvarnished facts and I drew my own conclusions from them."

"I think you have said enough, General," Lousada Barrow put in angrily. "Colonel Sheridan is a most able and gallant officer, as I have every reason to know, since he's been serving with my

Volunteer Cavalry. He has a high sense of duty, sir, and a record second to none."

He would have said more but James Neill fixed him with an icy stare. "So General Havelock thinks," he said. "I dined with him this evening and he talked of the gallant Colonel Sheridan. He talked a great deal—damme, gentlemen, you'd have thought, to hear him, that no officer in the column had behaved with greater heroism! Or suffered more grievously at the enemy's hands . . . and this with poor brave old Renaud and Stuart Beatson barely cold. That stuck in my gullet, I'm bound to admit." His gaze went to Alex's scarred, unhappy face and rested there in morose appraisal. "The Old Gentleman heaped praises on you for your endurance and courage, Sheridan. He's even thinking of recommending you for a Victoria Cross, did you know that?"

Stunned, Alex shook his head. "No, sir, I did not. I assure you, it's the last thing I—"

It was as if he had not spoken. Neill went on scornfully, "He is not, perhaps, the best judge of what constitutes a deed worthy of the highest award for valour our country can bestow; he is also thinking of recommending his own son for the honour! And for what? Because the young puppy took advantage of the fact that their commanding officer had dismounted from an uncontrollable horse and led the Sixty-Fourth into the attack in his absence. The whole regiment will be up in arms if he makes *that* recommendation, I can tell you!"

"General Neill!" Tytler was outraged. "You are speaking of confidential matters. You have no right, sir, no possible right. You—"

"Have I not?" Neill blazed at him. "When my officers are ignored, their deaths not even mentioned or, it would seem, regretted?"

"That's not the case, sir. The general—"

"Ah, but it is, Tytler, it is, damn it all! I'm greeted with an eleven-gun salute and the news that I'm to remain in command here, whilst General Havelock has the honour and glory of relieving Lucknow. But until he goes"—Neill's voice shook—"I'm not to issue a single order. In God's name, what am I to make of that, sir? *You* tell me if you can!"

"These are confidential matters," Tytler again attempted to remind him. "They should not be discussed in public." He glanced round, as if hoping that the other officers might, without being ordered, vanish into the rain-wet darkness, but no one moved, although their faces, Alex saw, reflected varying degrees of shock and bewilderment and all, it was evident, wished themselves elsewhere. Sharing their feelings, he knew that he, at least, must remain; he had sparked off James Neill's outburst and—whatever the reason for it—he had to stand his ground until the matter was resolved. If it could be resolved . . . he expelled his breath in a long-drawn sigh.

That he had incurred Neill's bitter enmity he could no longer doubt—the attack on him had been personal and it had not been made without premeditation, but, try as he would, he could think of no reason to account for it. Nothing that Charles Palliser had said, surely, could have aroused such deep, vindictive feeling in a man to whom he was a stranger? Unless . . . there was a sick sensation in the pit of his stomach. He had expressed himself freely—too freely, perhaps—on the subject of James Neill to Barrow on Sunday evening, as they had ridden back from Bithur with the Nana's captured guns. Lousada Barrow would not have betrayed his confidence, of course, but there had been others riding fairly close behind them, who might have overheard more than he had realised. Dear heaven, if even part of that conversation had been repeated out of context to Neill, then his reaction was at least explicable. He was said to be sensitive to criticism, and criticism of his failure to relieve Cawnpore, particularly if it came from a survivor of the garrison, might well have struck him on the raw. As, evidently, General Havelock's reception had also struck him . . .

"Alex—" Lousada Barrow touched his arm. "The general's leaving."

Alex looked up. General Havelock, he saw, had mounted his horse and, shoulders hunched against the rain, was moving slowly past the second batch of Highlanders, to whom he addressed some words of encouragement as they waited for the boats to return. They did not cheer him; sodden and dispirited, even his favourite regiment failed to respond to his overtures, and Neill said, raising his voice again in unconcealed rancour, "What's Havelock done since he took command? Halted the advance column, disarmed Charlie Palliser's sowars—who behaved in exemplary fashion when *I* was commanding them—appointed his son D.A.A.G. in Beatson's place . . . my God, Tytler, there's no damned end to it!"

Observing General Havelock's departure, Fraser Tytler gave vent to an exasperated sigh. "Sir," he began, "If I may suggest—"

Neill ignored the interruption. "And now," he stated wrathfully, "he wants Victoria Crosses for his protégés, including one for the gallant Lieutenant-Colonel Sheridan, whose brevet rank, devil take it, was given him for a command in Lucknow which—because his wife was here—he's never actively held! I'm not satisfied with the account he's given of his actions. I want to know a hell of a lot more than he's seen fit to tell us. I want a full report and—"

Colonel Tytler managed at last to make himself heard. "As I

endeavoured to point out to you some time ago, General Neill," he said, with weary resignation, "this is neither the time nor the place to discuss such matters. Colonel Sheridan has been suffering from amnesia, as the surgeons will confirm, but I feel sure that he will submit a full report as soon as he able to. If you have any charges to bring against him, they can only properly be brought through official channels. Indeed, I think they will have to be the subject of an enquiry, in view of the fact that you have aired them publicly. I shall have to inform General Havelock of what has been said here, of course."

"Don't be such an infernal old woman, Tytler!" Neill snapped. "There's no need to make an official matter of this or to bring General Havelock into it. He has enough on his plate—damn it, he has to relieve Lucknow! I'm not proposing to bring any charges—certainly not until I've seen Sheridan's report, if and when he chooses to submit one. As to airing my opinions publicly, we're all entitled to our opinions, for God's sake, and Brevet-Lieutenant-Colonel Sheridan has seen fit to air his opinion of *me* equally publicly, or so I've been informed. Well, we're all officers and gentlemen here, are we not? The devil fly away with it, we can keep this matter between us, surely?"

There were eager nods and murmurs of acquiescence; for James Neill it was a climb down and they were all anxious, now, to escape from what had become an awkward and embarrassing situation. Several of them looked at Alex and Lousada Barrow said stiffly, "If Colonel Sheridan is satisfied—"

Unable to trust himself to speak, Alex inclined his head. The matter would not and could not end here, he thought wretchedly, but to attempt to prolong this bitter, humiliating scene would serve no useful purpose.

Neill's powerful shoulders rose in an elaborate shrug and he gathered up his reins. Addressing himself to Alex again, he said curtly, "I take it you intend to make a full report to General Havelock?"

"I do, General Neill," Alex managed, his voice devoid of expression.

"I shall read it with more than usual interest," James Neill told him. "And if I am wrong about you, Sheridan, I shall make you a public apology." He nodded and set spurs to his horse. Stephenson and the rest of his small staff rode after him; Palliser and Simpson, after a moment of indecision, followed in their wake.

"My God!" Tytler exclaimed, mopping at his streaming face. "My God!" He appeared otherwise bereft of words and Alex, miserably silent, was grateful that he asked no questions. Lousada Barrow swore, long and loudly.

"I think," he said at last, "that we'd all be better to sleep on this. You in particular, Alex."

"I have a report to write," Alex reminded him wryly. "And a court martial to attend at eight-thirty. If you'll forgive me—"

"Take all the time you need to write that report, old man," Barrow exhorted him. "I'll relieve you of your duties until it's done. Use my tent; you'll have no one to disturb you there. And you'll find writing materials in my valise. And now you really ought to get some sleep. Work on the report in daylight, when your mind's clear." In Tytler's presence, he said no more, but his sympathy, for all the gruff tone in which it was expressed, did much to raise Alex's flagging spirits. He followed his commander's sensible advice and slept until one of the mess servants wakened him, with *chota hazri* on a tray and the information that Captain Barrow wished to see him as soon as it was convenient.

When he reported to Barrow's tent, he found its owner already booted and spurred and a servant busy packing his valise and sleeping bag. Writing materials had been set out on a folding camp table and, waving an inviting hand to these, Lousada Barrow said, "All yours, my dear Alex . . . the tent, too. I shan't be needing it for some considerable time, alas!"

"You won't be needing it . . . but—" Alex looked round at the preparations for departure. "Are you following the Highlanders then?"

"Yes—I'm taking all our original Volunteers. Orders came first thing this morning. The Highlanders have formed a bridgehead on the Oudh bank, but they are being harassed by rebel cavalry, so we're to go across, together with a half-battery of guns." Barrow went into brief details. "As soon as sufficient troops have crossed, we're to move forward five or six miles to a walled village, Mungalwar, and establish our base there."

"I see. And what orders have you for our recruits?"

Lousada Barrow gave a mirthless laugh. "Your week is cut to a mere five days, Alex. They're to join us by Sunday evening at the latest, so you'll have to perform miracles, I'm afraid." He took his watch from his pocket. "Don't worry about this morning— Bob Thompson can take care of the preparations and, as we're not due to cross until three or four o'clock, I'll take your recruits and have the Riding School cleared out for you as promised. The court martial has been postponed, which is a blessing—the new provost-marshal, Bruce, who came in with Neill, wants to interrogate the prisoner before he's brought to trial. I suspect that's Neill's doing but"—he shrugged—"I may be wrong. Anyway, it's a break for you. It gives you this morning to write your report. Can you do it in one morning?"

Alex smiled. "I have a very powerful incentive, haven't I? My honour and possibly my future depend on it . . . yes, I damned well can do it, Lou."

"The sooner the better," Barrow advised him. "It must be in General Havelock's hands before he crosses into Oudh. I don't have to remind you that, when he leaves here, Neill will be in command."

"No, you don't have to remind me of that," Alex agreed, with feeling.

"I've ordered your meals to be sent over from the mess. I thought it would be ... that is, I—" the older man hesitated, reddening beneath his tan.

"You thought it would be better if I didn't meet Palliser and Simpson until this matter's cleared up," Alex finished for him. "Is that it, Lou?"

Barrow's flush deepened. "Something like that, Alex. It's obvious that they talked out of turn to Neill. Anyway, I'm taking them both with me, and I'm afraid I'll have to take young Fergusson as well. We're few enough, heaven knows. I can leave you the *Rissaldar,* if that's any help."

"Yes, he's good. So are some of the infantrymen, one in particular, a Tipperary man named Cullmane. Can I make any of them up to N.C.O.s?"

"They're in your hands, my dear fellow; after this morning I shan't set eyes on them. Just give me a troop of cavalry I can use." Lousada Barrow buckled on his sword belt and reached into his hip pocket for the cheroot case he carried there. He selected a cheroot, rolled its brittle leaves between his two big palms and, making something of a ritual of lighting it, went on, avoiding Alex's gaze, "What happened last night, Alex, I . . . oh, the hell with it! I was sickened, sickened and disgusted. And to have to sit there, not saying a word, when I knew what you'd been through—my God, I—"

"You don't have to tell me, Lousada," Alex assured him.

Barrow looked up, his expression relieved. "No, perhaps I don't. But I'd like you to know that it was I who suggested that you should be recommended for a Victoria Cross and by heaven, Alex, I'm going to see you get it if it's the last thing I ever do!"

Alex thanked him, his throat tight. When he had gone, a mess *khitmatgar* appeared with breakfast and he settled down at the camp table to collect his thoughts. Once he had started writing, he found the task less difficult than he had feared; describing incidents, he remembered names and faces, and his pen began to move across the paper with ever-increasing speed. Outside the tent the monsoon rain hurtled down, but he was oblivious to it; in memory he was back in the stifling heat of the entrenchment, his throat parched, his body tortured and dehydrated, his sight dimmed by the relentless glare, his nostrils filled with the terrible, unforgettable stench of human excreta and putrefying flesh.

But his must be a strictly factual report, he knew, giving details of each day's happenings and accounting for each day's toll of dead and wounded without emotion, expressed in stilted military terms. He shut his mind to the voices—and, in particular, to Emmy's voice—which rang in his ears and wrote prosaically under the date:

The rebels established twenty-four-pounder gun batteries in the Church compound, to the east, and in the Riding School, to the north-west, with which they kept up a heavy fire throughout the hours of daylight but did not launch any direct attacks on our position. Considerable damage was caused to both the hospital and the flat-roofed building by round-shot and several women and children, sheltering in the former, were injured by falling masonry.

Five other ranks of H.M.'s 32nd died this day of heat

apoplexy when serving the guns, and Lieutenant Dempster and a sergeant and two gunners of the 6th Battalion, Bengal Artillery, were killed by round shot. Colonel Williams, of the 56th Native Infantry, who had earlier suffered sunstroke, died of fever during the night . . .

It was odd how clearly he could remember those first few days of the siege. He had been fit then, alert and reasonably well fed, and the casualties, because they were the first and there had been comparatively few of them, stood out as individuals in his mind. He recalled the artillery sergeant's name—Murlow—and added it to the report.

Another date, more names . . . dear God, what a ghastly catalogue of misfortune it seemed, told thus, without any mention of those human touches and acts of kindness and self-sacrifice which had made the siege endurable! Alex sighed as the memories came flooding back and let his pen fall, momentarily distracted from his task.

There were the women, who had crawled so bravely across the shell-craters—Emmy among them—to bring water to exhausted gunners and riflemen, after they had stood all day at their posts . . . water, in pitiful pannikins, often stained with the blood of those who had risked their lives to draw it from the well. Water they had denied themselves. There had been other women, too, who had crouched behind the mud wall, in the full glare of the sun, loading and reloading the muskets and Enfields with which their husbands had driven off yet another of the mutineers' attacks, whilst their children lay, mute and apathetic, in holes scooped out of the bare ground beside them.

The women's courage, their resilience and resourcefulness, was something he could never forget. At first many of them had been afraid, but the example of a few, their cheerfulness in the face of danger and deprivation, which had grown as each day passed, had wrought a miracle. The initially fainthearted had lost their fear, the fastidious had learned to live with heat and filth and flies, the gently born to undertake menial tasks, dress hideous wounds and yet retain their dignity. . . . His own beloved Emmy had been of that brave company but, even so, he could not write of them now. Neill wanted facts, Havelock dates and names. . . . Alex wiped the sweat from his brow and, the pen held awkwardly in the damp palm of his left hand, went on writing.

A sortie was made, under the command of Captain John Moore of H.M.'s 32nd, consisting of eight officers and six other ranks of this regiment and H.M.'s 84th, to clear the uncompleted barrack blocks to the north-west of the entrenchment of rebel snipers, who had the drinking well under musket fire. This mission was successfully accomplished, with the aid of covering fire from Number Four Barrack, commanded by Lieutenant Mowbray Thomson, of the 53rd Native Infantry. Casualties were one officer, Lieutenant Wren of the 2nd Light Cavalry, and a private of H.M.'s 84th slightly wounded.

Those sorties had kept morale high; the Pandies had never stayed to contest the buildings they had occupied, however small the number of British soldiers who had left the entrenchment to attack and drive them out. John Moore had inspired, as well as led them; it had been his constantly reiterated wish, when the garrison's resistance was nearing its end, to lead the few able-bodied men in one final attack on the rebel gun batteries which had held the entrenchment within a ring of steel. But the women and children and the wounded could not be left; Moore's wish had not been fulfilled—instead, he had met his death at the Suttee Chowra Ghat, cut down, with the able-bodied men who had formed General Wheeler's guard of honour, as they sought vainly to push the overcrowded boats to safety in deep water. He had had his hour of glory before that, though, when the hospital had been destroyed . . . The pen nib spluttered on the damp paper. Neill should have his facts, blast his eyes! He should have chapter and verse, so that at least he would know what it had been like to wait and pray for the help that never came . . . Under the date 13th June, Alex wrote:

A well-directed shot from one of the batteries opposing us struck the thatched roof of the hospital building and set it on fire. We subsequently learned from a prisoner that the missile was a carcass, prepared for this purpose by an invalid *subedar* of artillery, Riaz Ali, who received a reward of Rs. 90 from the Nana for his action. Forty-two of the wounded perished in the flames, rescue having, of necessity, to be delayed whilst an attack on our perimeter was beaten off. The breeze being strong, the flames swiftly spread. The enemy poured their grape upon the burning building and, as the women and children fled from it, a heavy fire of musketry from the cantonment trenches killed and wounded many of them. Rebel infantry advanced to within sixty yards of our perimeter during the confusion caused by the fire, with the intention of taking by storm one of the nine-pounder guns commanded by Lieutenant St. George Ashe, of the Oudh Artillery. Lieutenant Ashe opened on them with grape and they were repulsed, with heavy losses.

The surgeons' store of instruments and medicines was destroyed, with the exception of one small box of drugs, and as a result, from this date, no amputations could be performed and many died from gangrenous infections of their wounds. Two hundred women and children were deprived of shelter, only a few of whom could be accommodated in other remaining buildings—the Quarter Guard, to which they were first directed, had subsequently to be taken over as a hospital for sick and wounded. The majority of the women, with their children, had to seek what protection they could behind the breastwork and in the trench behind it, over which canvas screens were erected. These were shot down or set on fire by enemy shells but, although left entirely without protection from the sun by day and the damp cold by night, the courage of the women never faltered. They handed round ammunition, encouraged the men to the uttermost, and attended to the wounded with tender solicitude.

Alex smiled as he read through what he had written. This small tribute, at least, he could pay, even in a factual military report, since the women had, after the burning down of their hospital, virtually joined the ranks of the defenders.

He started a fresh page.

The following died in the fire or subsequent to their removal from the burning building with their wounds imperfectly healed: Brigadier Alexander Jack; his brother, a civilian, after suffering amputation of one leg; Lieutenant R.O. Quin, 2nd Light Cavalry; Major W.R. Prout, 53rd Native Infantry, and his wife; Lieutenant N.J. Manderson and Sgt. Major Gladwin of the 2nd Light Cavalry; Mr. A. Miller, Railway Engineer . . .

He stopped, scowling at what he had written. The names eluded him. Emmy, he remembered, had spoken of them, had told him, her voice choked with tears, how many had died that night, and how many others, after lingering for a few tortured hours, had finally succumbed to shock and pain. She had named them—they had been among the patients she had helped to tend in the makeshift hospital in the Quarter Guard building—sick and desperately wounded men, who had been dragged from the blazing thatch-roofed hospital with a haste that, perforce, had taken scant heed of the agony even the smallest movement caused them. Women and children, babes in arms, like his own poor, sickly little son, whole families had been wiped out by the murderous fire of the mutineer gunners as they had fled from the flames, and then, next day, the charred bodies of those who had been unable to escape from the building had been brought out, to add to the butcher's bill. . . . Alex crumpled the page and selected another. It was no use submitting an incomplete list, he decided; he would leave the dead simply as a number in his report and later, when perhaps he would have more time, he would endeavour to compile a full list. . . . and then add to it the name of his infant son.

He picked up his pen once more and wrote on:

> At midnight on Sunday, 14th June, after Divine Service had been conducted in the new hospital and with small groups of defenders at their posts, it was decided to mount a sortie to surprise and spike the enemy's gun batteries to the north and north-east of our position. These guns had caused us much annoyance and it was felt by General Wheeler that a successful attack on them would raise

morale, which had suffered as a result of the burning of the hospital.

Fifty officers and men of the garrison, under the command of Captain Moore, left the entrenchment. The advance party was led by Lieutenant Henry Delafosse, 53rd Native Infantry, and Lieutenant Godfrey Wheeler, 1st Native Infantry and A.D.C., the main body by Captain Moore and Lieutenant Saunders, of H.M.'s 84th, and I myself, assisted by Captain Francis Whiting, Bengal Engineers, commanded the rearguard.

The enemy were taken completely by surprise and two 18-pounder and two 24-pounder guns were put out of action and a considerable quantity of ammunition blown up. On the alarm being sounded, we began our withdrawal, having first deterred pursuit by attacking a party of sepoys in a nearby mess house. Our party returned safely to the entrenchment, with three of our number slightly wounded, including Lieutenant Wheeler, and Corporal Henegan, of H.M.'s 84th killed in a gallant single-handed attack with the bayonet, as he was covering the rearguard's withdrawal.

Alex consulted his watch. It was ten-thirty; he had been working for over two hours. There was still a good deal to be added but . . . he rose and flexed his cramped limbs, then gathered the sheets of paper he had used and stacked them in a neat pile on the bed. He would have to go into very careful detail concerning the terms agreed upon by General Wheeler and the Nana's representatives for the evacuation of the garrison, he reminded himself—for all their sakes but especially for that of John Moore, who had negotiated them with Azimullah. Moore had gone to such pains to ensure that there could be no betrayal; the Nana had sworn, on his most sacred oath, that no harm should come to any member of the British force. Boats had been promised, fully supplied with provisions and properly manned; they had been inspected the night before the evacuation and found satisfactory; the *ghat* had also been inspected and no sign of treachery seen . . . yet they had been betrayed. He suppressed a weary sigh and went back to the table, reaching for his pen.

First he must report the final attack on the entrenchment, launched on the 23rd June—the anniversary of Plassey—when the mutineers had thrown overwhelming numbers of infantry against them, supported by cavalry and guns. Between seven and eight thousand, they had estimated, and to oppose them fewer than fifty unwounded but starving British soldiers and civilians, a handful of the less severely disabled men, who had come stumbling from the dark confines of the overcrowded Quarter Guard Hospital into the pitiless sunlight, a few brave women, and eight worn-out 9-pounder guns. Alex frowned, remembering, and then settled down once more to write.

> Our lookouts warned that large numbers of the enemy were massing for an attack, and a heavy cannonade was opened on our position from first light, which continued for two hours. The alarm was given and the breastwork manned, every available soldier and civilian, including a number who were wounded, answering the call to arms.
>
> Whilst the cannonade was still in progress, a message was received from Lieutenant Mowbray Thomson to say that his outpost in Number Four Barrack was in danger of being overrun. A party of 25 officers and men, led by Captain Moore, went to his assistance and aided him in driving off his assailants, at a cost of three wounded, including

Captain Moore, slightly. The rebels launched their attack soon afterwards, field guns, with a cavalry escort, advancing to within sixty yards of our perimeter. A large force of cavalry charged prematurely and was beaten off by our guns which, double-shotted, poured a hail of grape into their ranks. During this time a tumbril containing ammunition was set on fire by an enemy shell and Lieutenant Delafosse, commanding the two guns on the east side of the entrenchment, extinguished the flames, risking his life to do so.

Infantry skirmishers, under cover of bales of cotton, then came at us from all sides, followed by the main enemy force of at least four regiments, which advanced firing. The attack was led by the *Subedar* of the 1st Native Infantry, who displayed suicidal courage. It was pressed home with greater resolution than on any previous occasion and was eventually beaten off at midday, with heavy casualties on both sides, theirs being estimated at two hundred dead and probably at least this number wounded.

General Wheeler sustained a bullet wound in the leg when in the defensive post known as the Redan, commanded by Major Edward Vibart, 2nd Light Cavalry, which bore the brunt of the cavalry charge. We lost nineteen killed or mortally wounded, and one of Lieutenant Ashe's guns was blown up. This loss, in addition to damage to two other guns, lack of ammunition and food, and the number of men incapacitated by wounds and sickness, brought us to the realisation that we could offer no further effectual resistance.

After a truce called by the rebels to enable them to remove their dead, hostilities were resumed at long range by the enemy batteries next morning. The first of the monsoon rain fell during the night, causing our breastwork to disintegrate in places.

On the evening of 24th June, General Wheeler sent an appeal to Lucknow for aid, stating that we could no longer hold out without it.

The poor old general, Alex thought, lying helpless and well-nigh speechless from the pain of his shattered leg ... The admission of defeat had been wrung from him and he had wept as he wrote it, Surgeon Boyes had told him. "Surely," his despairing message had ended, "we are not to be left to die like rats in a trap, without any attempt being made to bring us succour?"

There had been no answer to that appeal, but General Wheeler had known, as they had all known by then, that Sir Henry Lawrence could send them no aid without grave risk to his defence of Lucknow. He had only one European regiment, the 32nd, two river crossings stood between Lucknow and Cawnpore, he possessed no boats, and already the mutineers, in their thousands, were preparing to besiege his Residency.

Only General James Neill could have sent succour to the Cawnpore garrison and he, too, had failed to send it. . . . Alex returned, grim-faced, to his report.

On the morning of the 24th, a Eurasian woman, Mrs. Jacobi—one of the Nana's captives—brought a letter, in the handwriting of Azimullah Khan, the Nana's *vakeel,* offering terms for our surrender. This was addressed to: 'The Subjects of Her Most Gracious Majesty, Queen Victoria,' and it invited 'All those who are in no way connected with the acts of Lord Dalhousie and are willing to lay down their arms' to surrender and receive safe passage to Allahabad. It was rejected by General Wheeler, on the grounds that we had not been defeated and therefore would not lay down our arms. The general insisted that the Nana must himself sign the letter before he would treat with him. A temporary cease-fire was proposed and agreed to and that evening Mrs. Jacobi returned with a letter signed by the Nana. Negotiations for our surrender commenced between Azimullah Khan and Jwala Pershad, on the Nana's behalf, and Captains Moore and Whiting on ours, with Mr. Roache, the Postmaster, on behalf of the civilians. This took place outside our entrenchment, in Number Four Barrack, and was conducted in the Hindustani language.

At no time, until these negotiations were concluded, were any of the Nana's representatives or the rebel troops permitted to enter the entrenchment, it being feared that the sight of our depleted defences and starving condition might cause harsher conditions to be imposed upon us. General Wheeler, although unable to be present, was kept fully informed. The conditions to which both he and the Nana finally agreed and each signed and sealed, were as follows:

Alex paused, searching his memory, and then wrote on:

In return for the honourable surrender of our entrenchment, with the guns, ammunition, and treasure held therein, we were to be permitted free exit under arms, with sixty rounds of ammunition per man. Carriage was to be provided for the wounded, the women and children, and the sick, and boats, furnished with provisions, were to be waiting at the *ghat,* in which our safe passage to Allahabad was to be guaranteed under the Nana's seal and signature and on his most solemn oath.

He paused again, reading through what he had written.

Now came the hardest, most heartrending part of his report and this, he knew, he could not write impersonally or without emotion. What he must say came from the depths of bitterness and despair and could not be expressed in military phraseology, with dates and a long list of the names and regiments of those who had been betrayed and slaughtered, without pity, by a ruthless foe. The boats, with their hastily thatched canopies of tinder-dry straw, had been ready at the Suttee Chowra Ghat, as the Nana had promised . . . but their boatmen had also been ready to set the canopies alight and then make their escape, wading through the shallows and leaving their craft to wallow, rudderless, in the muddy water, when the hidden guns opened up on them with grape and canister. Mounted sowars had been ready, too, to spur their horses into the water and, *tulwars* drawn, hack at any who attempted to follow the boatmen's example and return to the bank, whilst behind them, crouched behind rocks and bushes on the slope, sepoy snipers had unleashed a hail of musket balls into the drifting boats.

Emmy had been one of the first to die in the smoke and confusion . . . Alex felt the hot sting of tears behind his lids, as a vision of her small, sweet face swam before his closed eyes. For a moment, he had held her to him, seeking vainly to staunch the blood which flowed from the wound in her breast, and then two of the sowars had ridden at him and he had been compelled to let her lifeless body slip from his grasp in order to defend himself against their assault. He had killed the *rissaldar* by dragging the man from his horse, emptied a pistol into the chest of another of his attackers at point-blank range and then—he could not remember how—he had reached Edward Vibart's boat, someone had dragged him on board, and they had floated out into deeper water to begin the three-day bid to escape from a pursuit which never slackened.

He seized pen and paper again and started frantically to write, the words flowing so fast that they were beyond his power to control or to halt. He lost all consciousness of time and of his surroundings and when, nearly an hour later, Lousada Barrow came stumping into the tent, he looked up, dazed, as if into the face of a stranger.

"How's it going, Alex? Have you nearly done?"

"I . . . yes, very nearly, I . . ." The past receded; Barrow's familiar face came properly into focus and Alex leaned back on his stool, his whole body soaked in perspiration. "The report's done, thanks to you—I just have a page or two to add covering my escape. Although I could probably describe that in a single line, since I remember very little about it. The rest, the siege, the massacre at the *ghat,* all that is absolutely clear in my mind and I've set it down as it happened. The names of casualties will take longer; they'll have to be listed separately."

Barrow glanced at the pile of papers on the bed. He took off his cloak, letting it fall in a sodden heap at his feet, and crossed to the bed. "May I read it?"

"Of course you may," Alex agreed readily. "Indeed, I'd be grateful if you would, Lou, because I'm afraid I . . . that is, I may have put one or two points a bit too strongly."

"Too strongly for whom, pray? For Neill, perhaps?"

"For anyone who wasn't there."

"Good! I'll just dry myself off a bit and then read it. You carry on with whatever's left to be done." Lousada Barrow stripped off his jacket and shirt, towelled himself briskly, and, donning a dry shirt from his valise, picked up the pile of papers and went to lie full length on the bed.

"Those recruits are coming on quite well, Alex," he observed. "And they're keen, all of them. There's a hell of a lot to be done with them yet but . . . your ridingschool's ready for you. At least you'll be able to keep them dry during some of their training."

"Thanks, Lou. I'm grateful."

"Consider it my contribution to your impossible task." Lousada Barrow took out his cheroot case and offered it, smiling. "I've had to accede to a request from the *Rissaldar*, Nujeeb Khan, that he be permitted to accompany Charles Palliser. In the circumstances, I thought it politic to let him do so—Palliser's his sahib and he and the other native officers did remain true to their salt. Also, I don't want trouble with Palliser—he's a first-rate officer, with a temporary chip on his shoulder."

"Of course," Alex conceded. He struck a lucifer and held it to the tip of Barrow's cheroot. "What did you think of Cullmane?"

"A good man, handles horses well. Drink has been his trouble, I gather—he's been broken from corporal twice. Still, he'll get none here, if General Havelock can help it; all the liquor's been brought in from the city, I understand, and the Commissariat have it under heavy guard. The general has repeated his order that any British soldier caught plundering is to be hanged, in his uniform."

"*Has* he? Good God!" Alex was astonished. "Do you think he'll carry out such a threat?"

Barrow's broad shoulders rose in a shrug. "He's capable of it. In Havelock's eyes drunkenness is a crime, and there's been a lot of looting, you know, despite the initial order . . . shops and derelict bungalows broken into in search of liquor, even one attempt to steal from the Commissariat train on the march. That was before you joined us, and the men who did it were driven nearly mad with thirst. They'd have stolen water, if there had been any to steal. Havelock had them flogged, as an example . . . the British soldiers, I mean." He sighed. "The looters weren't all British but, as you know, by a strange anomaly, British soldiers can be flogged for breaches of discipline but Indian soldiers cannot. The Indians were sent back to Allahabad—they were some of Palliser's men and there was quite a bit of heartburning over the affair. Some heated words between our friend Charlie and one or two of the Queen's officers, which continued when the Irregulars were eventually found wanting and disarmed."

"Yes, I see." Alex returned to the table.

"That's all the news." Lousada Barrow settled himself more comfortably on the bed and, puffing at his cheroot, started to read the closely written pages of the report.

Alex completed the account of his escape and began to list the names of those who had died in the boats, aware that the list must, of necessity, be incomplete. The faces were there, enshrined in his memory—the gaunt, unshaven faces of scarecrow soldiers in filthy, tattered uniforms, of sick old men and boys who had lost all semblance of youth, of terrified, uncomprehending children, and of women whom Cawnpore had robbed of beauty and femininity—but the names eluded him, as they had done before. There had been so many . . . 437 had left the entrenchment, to walk or be carried in carts and palanquins to the Suttee Chowra Ghat on the morning of 27th June, almost half wounded or sick. Better, perhaps, if he were to list those who, like himself, might by some miracle have escaped.

Included among the thirteen who left Major Vibart's boat with me in an attempt to drive off our pursuers were the following," he wrote. "Lieutenants Mowbray Thomson and Henry Delafosse, 53rd Native Infantry; Sergeant John Grady and Privates Ryan, McNamee, and Murphy of H.M.'s 84th; Gunners Corkill and Sullivan of the Bengal Artillery; Privates Bannister, Wellington, Wooley, and Drummer Wood of H.M.'s 32nd. Sergeant Grady was shot down before we reached the temple in which we finally took refuge, at Sheorajpore. Six or seven men reached the river after we were driven from the temple, which the rebels had set on fire, but two or three of these were shot in the water. I believe that the others, if they were uninjured, may have found shelter with friendly villagers and would request that search be made for them or enquiries set in train."

Alex read through what he had written and smothered a sigh. Was there really any hope for those who had eluded the hail of musket balls from the shore or, he asked himself bitterly, had they found every man's hand against them in the riverside villages when, spent from their exertions, they had attempted to drag themselves from the water? He reached for a fresh sheet of paper and started to list those who had been left—to die at the hands of the Nana's executioners, it now seemed—in Edward Vibart's leaking boat.

For the next half hour the silence was unbroken save for the drumming of rain on the tent's tautly stretched canvas and the metallic scratching of his pen. Lousada Barrow read the report with complete absorption, his cheroot forgotten and burning to ash between his fingers. When at last he came to the final page, he jumped up from the bed in a sudden burst of energy and, crossing to Alex's side, clapped a hand on his shoulder.

"Merciful heaven, Alex, this . . . this is the most moving and the most appalling document I've ever read in my life!" He sounded shaken and his eyes, Alex saw, held the glint of tears. Recovering himself, he gestured to the sheets scattered about the table. "What are these—casualty lists?"

"The start of them, yes. They're not complete."

"Never mind, just give me what you have. I'm taking this report to the general at once."

"And Neill?" Alex questioned wryly, as he picked up the scattered sheets.

"Neill shall see it, have no fear on that score. And he shall read it, if I have to stand over him whilst he does. He owes you the public apology he promised you—dear God, if I had my way, he'd have to shout it from the housetops!" Barrow picked up his sodden cloak, wrapped it about him, and, with the report tucked carefully beneath it, drew back the tent flap.

"Just one more thing, Lou," Alex said. He held out a folded slip of paper. "I'd be obliged if you would also give the general this . . . but only if my name is on the list of those he is recommending for the award of a Victoria Cross."

"What the hell!" Barrow eyed the paper, frowning. "You're not asking for your name to be removed from the list, are you?"

Alex nodded, tight-lipped. "I've only Neill's word for it that my name is being put forward. But I feel, in the circumstances, that it would be best if it were not."

Lousada Barrow was silent for a long moment. Then he pocketed the paper, muttering something incomprehensible under his breath. "I'll see you on the other side of the river," he said aloud. "And I think you're a damned fool!" Head down, he went splashing out into the monsoon rain, yelling impatiently for his *syce*.

CHAPTER FOUR
➤➤➤ • ⋘⋘

ALEX WAS in the riding school soon after dawn next morning. He had been working with his recruits for nearly two hours and was about to lead a section out onto the open plain for more advanced training when, to his surprise, Major Stephenson made his appearance, accompanied by a tall, fair-haired sergeant. Both men were mounted, and the Fusiliers' Commanding Officer, after a courteous but somewhat tentative greeting, enquired whether another recruit would be acceptable.

"Not only acceptable but welcome, if he can ride," Alex assured him without hesitation. "Are you offering us your sergeant, by any chance?"

Stephenson nodded. "He's anxious to volunteer, Colonel Sheridan, and I think you'll find him a pretty good horseman. He was in charge of General Neill's horses when the general was with the regiment, and he's just been promoted for outstanding conduct during the advance from Allahabad. He's an excellent N.C.O. and—er—the horse comes with him. It's one of the general's."

Alex concealed his astonishment. James Neill, it seemed, was making a peace offering . . . and making it, surely, before he had had time to read the report on the siege which he had demanded in such offensive terms that night before last. Unless, of course, General Havelock had passed it on to him before himself perusing it.

"We'll be glad to accept both of them, major—thank you."
He turned to the new recruit. "Your name, Sergeant?"

"Mahoney, sir—Patrick Mahoney."

Another Irishman, although his accent was slight, and young
for his rank. Alex nodded approvingly, liking the man's alert, smiling blue eyes and general air of soldierly competence. He could
use a good N.C.O.; without Fergusson and *Rissaldar* Nujeeb
Khan, the entire burden of instruction and discipline fell on himself. He asked a few brisk questions and, receiving satisfactory
answers to them, sent his new sergeant off with Cullmane to
draw his arms and equipment. When he and Stephenson were
alone, he said, with well-simulated casualness, "I take it the general knows that you're gifting his horse to us?"

"Oh, yes, he knows. It was his suggestion, in fact, and he made
it spontaneously when I mentioned that Mahoney was keen to
volunteer. He—er—that is, Sheridan . . ." Major Stephenson hesitated. "General Neill wasn't himself the other night. I mean, it
wasn't like him to lose his temper with a brother officer. He *is* a
man of strong temper, of course, and he'd be the last to deny it,
but I've served with him in the Blue Caps for more years than I
care to count and he's one of the finest soldiers I've ever met.
I've never known him to be unjust or to behave as he—well, as
he did to you the other night. He had been very much provoked
and—"

"I did not, to the best of my knowledge, provoke him," Alex
defended. "If any remarks of mine—made confidentially and *not*
publicly—were overheard and repeated, I can only say that I regret
it exceedingly. But, as the general himself remarked, we're all
entitled to our opinions, and mine, as an officer of the Cawnpore garrison, may well have sounded critical. It may even be
biased, but I cannot, in all conscience, apologise for that, Major."

"No—er—in the circumstances, you had reason to feel strongly and I can sympathise, Colonel, I—" Lionel Stephenson avoided Alex's eye. "Some remarks of yours *were* repeated and unfortunately the general took exception to them. But as I said, he wasn't himself. Sydenham Renaud was one of his closest friends and the news of his death—the manner of it, too—distressed him greatly. When you add to that the reception General Havelock accorded him, his blunt demand that General Neill was to issue no orders here, and his refusal to permit him to accompany the advance to Lucknow . . . well, you can understand his feelings also, can you not?"

"Yes," Alex conceded, a trifle reluctantly. "I can. But surely, Stephenson, he—"

"And the strain of the outbreaks in Benares and Allahabad had told heavily on him," Stephenson persisted. "He performed miracles of organisation and improvisation to get the Regiment upcountry. The transport system was chaotic. Some of our men came by river, others by rail and *dak* and bullock train. Apart from two small detachments which arrived just before him, General Neill only had twenty-five men with him when he reached Benares. He found the native troops—three regiments of them—on the verge of mutiny and General Ponsonby incapable of taking decisive action. The Commissioner, Tucker, wanted the Thirty-Seventh disarmed—they were badly disaffected—but the old man flatly refused to listen to him. Neill was compelled to assume command in the middle of the disarming, which was deplorably mishandled by Ponsonby, when he did eventually agree that it was necessary. You never saw such an incompetent shambles, but"—he shrugged—"I won't take up your time by going into all that now. Suffice it to say that it was touch and go and, without any doubt, James Neill saved the day. I don't believe anyone else could have done what he did with the slender force of Europeans he had under his command. If he hadn't acted so firmly, the slaughter of our people in Benares would have matched that of Cawnpore, believe me . . . and the whole surrounding area would have risen up in arms against us."

"He acted very firmly in the districts, by all accounts," Alex said, with restraint. "I've even heard it said that he acted like the wrath of God, although, of course, not having been there, I can only go by what I've been told."

Stephenson bristled. "It was no time for fainthearted measures or kid-glove diplomacy," he asserted. "I *was* there and I know what I'm talking about. Whatever General Havelock may say about not meeting barbarism with barbarism, it's the only thing these people understand. We've got to show that we are the rulers; at the first sign of weakness, they'd be at our throats. They've proved it, time and again. I tell you, Sheridan, General Neill saved both Benares and Allahabad and, though he's as devout a Christian as General Havelock, he didn't do it by turning the other cheek!"

Conscious of growing impatience, Alex made a noncommittal rejoinder. The last thing he wanted was that his recruits' training programme should be disrupted by his absence, and, seeing that Mahoney and Cullmane had returned, he called them over and instructed them to carry on with indoor exercises. They obeyed him with alacrity and, watching them, he was pleased by the workmanlike way in which both men—and particularly his new sergeant—set about their task.

Major Stephenson, it was evident, held his late commanding officer in high esteem and, it was equally evident, had no intention of leaving until he had explained the circumstances which had caused Neill's outburst, however pressed for time his listener might be. After describing the measures taken to bring the Benares mutiny under control, he went on, "News that a similar situation threatened in Allahabad reached us by telegraph, but it was impossible for General Neill to leave immediately. He despatched two small parties by road on the sixth of June and he himself followed, on the evening of the ninth, with forty of our Fusiliers. He covered seventy miles in two night marches and had to fight his way across the river—the mutineers were holding the bridge of boats in strength. The general arrived exhausted and with half his force prostrate from sunstroke, to find that—thanks largely to Jeremiah Brasyer, who managed to keep his Sikhs loyal—the fort had been preserved. But the rest of the city was in a state of sedition. The jail had been broken into and the convicts released, a large portion of the Hindu quarter had been looted and set on fire, and every European who hadn't sought safety in the fort had been murdered. Some crazy Moslem fanatic had set himself up as ruler and the green flags of Islam were flying from the *Kotwalee.* Even inside the fort, there was trouble—the Sikhs had looted the stocks of liquor held there and poor Brasyer was uncertain whether he could control them."

Alex had heard Brasyer's account of this unhappy incident and he nodded, frowning. Yet these same Sikhs, whose love of drinking had made them such a problem in the Fort at Allahabad, had fought like tigers beside their British comrades during the advance to Cawnpore and now, Brasyer had told him with pride, asked leave from their commander to get drunk . . .

"General Neill restored order, both inside the fort and then in the city. He was so ill that be could not stand," Stephenson told him. "Indeed, he was barely able to sustain consciousness by taking repeated draughts of champagne and water, but he had himself carried into the batteries and there, lying on his back, he directed every operation. When I arrived, with two hundred of our men from Benares, Brasyer's Sikhs were given quarters outside the Fort and we took over the defence of the place from them and drove the mutineers from the city, together with their *moulvis* and their infernal Islamic flags." Again he went into details and supplied the names of officers who had been shot down by their own rebellious regiments who, he added regretfully, had included seven newly joined ensigns of the 6th Native Infantry. "Mere boys of seventeen and eighteen, Sheridan! Poor little devils—they heard the alarm and ran out of their mess house to find out what was happening and the Pandies cut them down. And"—Stephenson's tone was angry—"that was the famous Sixth, the *Gowan-ki-paltan,* who volunteered, to a man, to march against Delhi in May, for which expression of loyalty they had received the official thanks of the governor-general only the previous day! Their C.O., Colonel Simpson, protested their loyalty to the last and wouldn't hear of their being disarmed . . . yet they were in the forefront of the mutiny! It's been the same story throughout the province; officers of native regiments simply would *not* believe their men capable of betrayal until it was too late."

That, Alex reflected grimly, was the truth. In Meerut, where the smouldering embers of revolt had first been fanned into flame, Colonel Finnis of the 11th had not believed that his sepoys would betray their salt until they had shot him down on his own parade ground . . . and he had been only the first of many to die for his misplaced faith.

"You in Cawnpore," Stephenson was saying earnestly, "probably thought of our relief column *as* a column, of regimental strength, Sheridan, but I assure you, it was not. Two hundred and forty of our men didn't reach Allahabad until the 22nd of June. They had to come by river and their progress was delayed by lack of water, so that they had to make long detours. And cholera broke out soon after my arrival—we lost eighty men in three days, with twice that number disabled from various causes—sunstroke, fever, dysentery, and wounds. Men reported for duty and collapsed in the ranks; fresh drafts marched in and collapsed when they arrived. It's doubtful whether we could have held out against a sustained attack, but fortunately the mutineers didn't try it—we drove them off and they made no attempt to wrest Allahabad from us. To make certain that they did not, General Neill executed all the prisoners who fell into our hands, in public and in their uniforms. The ringleaders and native officers, when we caught them, were blown from guns . . . and it had the desired effect, the effect the general set out to achieve. Sedition among the civilian population in the city and in the villages was swiftly quelled, our base was secure, we were able to obtain transport animals and camp followers, and the general was able to despatch Renaud's column to Cawnpore with a reasonable hope that it would get through. Before heaven, Sheridan, General Neill did all that was humanly possible to save your garrison! Cawnpore was never for a moment out of his thoughts and all his efforts were directed to relieving you. If anyone is to blame for the failure to relieve Cawnpore, it is not General Neill. Lay it rather on our government's total unpreparedness for this mutiny—or at the door of those who were deaf and blind to the warning that it was coming and did nothing to prevent it."

He was right, Alex had, in all honesty, to admit. James Neill had done all and more than he could have been expected to do with one depleted regiment, a single gun battery of Europeans, and a handful of native troops of doubtful loyalty. He had saved two cities and kept open the road to Calcutta. Even the wholesale executions he had ordered and the reign of terror he had initiated had, according to Stephenson, been only the means to a wholly desirable end. Indeed, if his assessment of the situation was correct, it had been a question not of choice, but of expediency, so far as Neill was concerned. And there could be no denying that it had been successful—in Benares and Allahabad barbarism had been met by barbarism and the revolt suppressed, at a comparatively small cost in British lives. Whereas in Cawnpore, where over a thousand British soldiers and civilians and their families had been done to death by the most barbarous of all their enemies, General Havelock had issued stern orders that there were to be no indiscriminate reprisals . . . Alex sighed.

Would Havelock's Christian turning of the other cheek achieve more than Neill's covenanting campaign of vengeance, or would it, he wondered unhappily, be taken as a sign of weakness by a people to whom, in the past, might had always been right and the conqueror's power to govern had been vested in the fear he could inspire? Would Neill abide by Havelock's orders, when command of Cawnpore passed into his hands? It remained to be seen, but he, thank God, would not be there to find out.

"Well, I had better be on my way, I suppose." Stephenson's voice broke into his thoughts and he saw that the Blue Caps' commanding officer, his self-imposed mission completed, was preparing at last to take his leave. "I hope that what I've told you may have helped to—er—clear the air, Sheridan. General Neill wasn't happy about what happened on Monday night, you know, and it's worried him ever since."

"It has also worried me," Alex admitted, conscious that this was an understatement. They rode together to the doorless entrance to the riding school and he asked, reining in there, "Has General Neill read my report yet, do you know?"

"On the siege? No"—Stephenson shook his head—"but

General Havelock told him that he had received a report and he will, I feel sure, pass it on before he leaves here. I understand he hopes to cross on Saturday evening or Sunday at the latest. We're to begin our crossing on Saturday—the whole regiment. General Neill is to keep only the draft he brought in with him, young soldiers for the most part, and the Invalid Artillery men, stiffened by a few of Maude's walking wounded. A small enough force with which to hold Cawnpore in all conscience! However, the new entrenchment is coming on apace and the engineers have started work on gun emplacements. It's well situated and, unless an attack in overwhelming numbers is launched against him, the general is confident that he can hold his own. Have you seen the place?"

"Only in passing," Alex answered. He listened, hiding his impatience, to a description of the new entrenchment and Neill's plans for its improvement and, when Major Stephenson finally took leave of him, returned thankfully to his recruits.

For the next two days, he devoted every hour of daylight to his training programme, abandoning the shelter of the Riding School to exercise his troop on the open plain. The monsoon rain continued unabated, but the men were keen and, despite being constantly soaked to the skin, they worked well and he was pleased with their progress. Their crossing into Oudh was to take place on the afternoon of Saturday, 25th July, and this, which would involve embarking their horses on pontoons and standing to their heads throughout the two- to three-hour crossing of the flooded river, would, he was aware, test their abilities as cavalrymen to the full. But there was neither time nor opportunity for any form of rehearsal; all the available pontoons were in daily use, transporting guns and bullock teams to the Oudh shore, and the overworked little steamer, which towed them, was constantly breaking down. The most Alex could do was to set up an edifice of planks in the riding school and demonstrate with this the way in which the horses would have to be handled.

For the rest, he concentrated on drill, aimed at familiarising the men with their weapons and on welding them into a disciplined body, with each man part of his horse and both instantly obedient to any order they might receive. If they fell some way short of perfection, it was not due to any lack of effort on their part, he thought wearily, as he pulled up after leading them in a charge across the rain-soaked morass to which their training ground had been reduced. In the limited time available, they had done better by far than he had dared to hope and he told them so before dismissing them, in Mahoney's charge, for evening Stables. To his surprise, wet and tired though they were and with two hours' grooming and tack-cleaning still before them, the men cheered him, and Cullmane observed with wry humour, "You've beaten the hides off us, sorr, that I won't deny but b'Jaysus I t'ink Sheridan's Troop will hold their own wid the rest o' Barrow's Horse now . . . and wid the Pandies, given the chance!"

"If you don't drown too many horses tomorrow afternoon, Corporal Cullmane," Alex retorted, smiling, "I believe your forecast may be right. We'll parade at the usual time tomorrow morning, but I'll let you off at noon to prepare for the crossing. Thank you for your hard work, lads. Sergeant Mahoney!"

"Sir . . ." Mahoney was beside him. For the first time since he had joined the troop, the tall young sergeant looked flustered. He gestured behind him. "The general, sir—it's General Neill with some of his officers and they're coming this way."

Recalling the last occasion when General Neill had seen his embryo cavalrymen, Alex smiled to himself. He called them to attention and formed them up in two impeccable lines, wheeled them round to face the approaching horsemen, and, when the new arrivals drew rein, brought them to the salute with drawn sabres.

Neill acknowledged the compliment, his face expressionless but a fugitive gleam of approval in his eyes.

"Something of a change, I perceive, Colonel Sheridan," he said. "A rabble transformed into a very passable troop of cavalry in less than a week! That's a remarkable achievement and I congratulate you."

"Thank you, sir," Alex answered, with wary formality.

Neill eyed him speculatively for a moment, as if to gauge his reaction, before requesting, his tone clipped, "Dismiss them, if you please. I have something I must say to you in confidence. Ride back to camp with me. My staff can precede us."

Alex obeyed, and when his troop trotted off under Mahoney's command, he returned to find the general waiting for him alone.

"I've read your report," Neill told him. "And I owe you an apology, Colonel Sheridan. I offer it in all humility. I hope you'll feel able to accept it?"

"Sir, I . . ." Alex hesitated, stony-faced. But it would be useless to bear a grudge, he decided, and he had no desire to make an enemy of General James Neill who had, in any case, honoured his promise and made a handsome apology. "Of course, sir, gladly."

"I've written to the other officers who were present with us at the *ghat* on Monday night," the general went on. "Those, that's to say, who have already crossed with their regiments into Oudh, and I shall see Colonel Tytler at the first opportunity, in order to explain the position to him. He spends most of his time patching up the engines of that infernal steamer, which is why I haven't managed to contact him before this. But rest assured that I shall."

"Thank you, General."

"I trust you will consider that I have done my best to set the record straight?" Neill sounded genuinely concerned and the question was asked without a hint of arrogance.

"Yes, I'm satisfied that you have, sir," Alex said. It was not easy, he knew, for a man like James Neill to apologise. "Think no more about the matter. I shall not; I—"

"But *I* shall. I lost my temper. . . . A great many things had combined, that particular evening, to make me lose it, as I believe Major Stephenson explained to you. Even so, I had no right to vent my spleen on you, no right at all. Reading that report of yours, I . . . damme, Sheridan, I felt ashamed and that's the truth. It was a story of extraordinary heroism—heroism on the part of the entire garrison—that brought tears to my eyes; I . . ." Recovering himself, he went on with an abrupt change of tone, "I intend to act on your recommendation, of course."

"*My* recommendation, sir?"

"Yes, indeed. Your own escape was little short of miraculous—I'd have given odds of a thousand to one against it, my dear fellow, damme I would!" At his ease once more, General Neill appeared almost genial. "So we'll send out patrols to see if there's any trace of the officers and men you think may also have escaped. Those two subalterns—Mowbray Thomson and Henry Delafosse—before heaven, I'm not going to let *them* die of wounds or at the hands of hostile villagers if there's any chance of finding them! Do you think there is?"

Alex sighed. "I pray there may be, sir. All I can tell you is that six or seven men did reach the river and Thomson was one of them. Two were definitely hit and I saw them go under, but the others I'm not sure about. They were strong swimmers, although, of course, they weren't in good physical condition. There's perhaps an outside chance that some of them survived."

"Then we shall search for them and try to discover what fate befell them. One thing, though . . ." Neill paused, a thoughtful frown creasing his dark brows. "Captain Bruce, my Provost-Marshal, has been going through some of the documents in Bala Bhat's office—his brother, the Nana, appointed him Governor of Cawnpore, as you probably know, and his *babus* kept conscientious records of his administration. They make incredible reading! But, more to the point, Sheridan, amongst the papers was the draft of a letter sent to Rajah Drigbiji Singh, demanding the return of some European captives he was holding at Moorar Mhow. There's no record of Drigbiji Singh's reply and no indication that the Europeans were from Cawnpore, but the Rajah has always been loyal and the letter to him was dated a few days *after* General Wheeler's surrender. I think it's worth investigating, don't you?"

"I do indeed, sir," Alex agreed eagerly. Slight though the hope might be, at least it was hope. Moorar Mhow was in Oudh and some distance from the river, but Drigbiji Singh's territory included a number of river villages, all of which lay below the point where they had landed from Edward Vibart's boat to make their last stand in the small, white temple at the river's edge.

"That *jemadar* of the Seventeenth Native Infantry—what's his name?" Neill snapped his fingers, as if impatient at his own failure to remember. "The one you and Barrow brought in from Bithur, who admitted that he fired on your boats from the Oudh shore?"

"Bhandoo Singh, sir," Alex supplied.

"That's the fellow, yes. He said at his trial that he'd heard rumours that five or six sahibs had escaped from one of the boats but he couldn't tell us where they were."

"His trial, sir?" Alex questioned, surprised. "Has he been tried?"

"Tried and condemned," Neill returned, with a satisfaction he made no attempt to conceal. "I believe General Havelock suggested that you might be called to give evidence against him, did he not?"

"Yes, he did, sir. I understood that the trial had been postponed and I expected to be informed if—"

Neill brushed that aside. "My dear Sheridan, there was no need to call you. It would simply have been a waste of your time—time you've put to a much better use with those recruits of yours. The fellow admitted his guilt and there was the Nana's letter to prove it. The whole affair took less than half an hour. The death sentence was pronounced on him and on five others this afternoon. They included a *jullad,* whom witnesses identified as being one of the carrion who took the bodies of our women and children from the Bibigarh and cast them into that ghastly well. I won't revolt you with a full account of what they did. Suffice it to say that they first tortured and then brutally killed any of the pathetic creatures left alive by the Nana's executioners . . . and there were a number, according to the witnesses. Children, Sheridan, whose mothers had tried to protect them with their own poor bodies, even as they died! One or two, rather than endure the torture, flung themselves, still living, into the well. But they shall not go unavenged, I swear to God they—shall not!" Neill's eyes were blazing and his voice shook with the bitter intensity of his feelings. "I intend to make an example of that foul jackal and of the *jemadar.* Before heaven, it's got to be done— and in the only way these heathen understand!"

Alex turned in his saddle to study him uneasily, conscious of the first instinctive pricklings of alarm, but in the fading light was unable to see his face clearly. Only Neill's eyes blazed back at him, lit by some inner fire.

"Are the men not to be hanged, sir?" he asked. The old Mahratta custom of blowing men from guns had, he recalled, been resorted to in Allahabad—Stephenson had admitted as much —so that perhaps . . . he drew in his breath sharply.

"Yes, they're to be hanged," Neill returned harshly. As swiftly as it had arisen, his anger faded and his voice was coldly reasonable as he added, "I have ordered the gallows set up in the courtyard of the Bibigarh, and the executions will take place tomorrow, half an hour after noon. But these murderous traitors shall not go undefiled to their gods. They have innocent blood on their hands—blood that still lies, inches deep, on the floor of the Bibigarh. I intend to make them wipe it clean."

"You intend to make them . . ." Alex's mouth was suddenly dry. "To make them *what,* General?"

"Each man will be ordered, before going to his death, to cleanse one yard of that blood-smeared floor, Sheridan. And if he refuses, then by God, I'll have the swine flogged until he does what he's been ordered to do!"

"But Bhandoo Singh is a Brahmin—he'll be breaking caste if he carries out such an order. And that means—"

"Devil take it, I *know* what it means! It's easy for these men to die when they believe that their souls will be reincarnated into a higher sphere than the one they're leaving." James Neill's lips parted in a mirthless smile. "But if, instead, they are hurtled into eternity believing themselves condemned to return as some noisome reptile or lower form of animal life, I fancy it will be a different matter, don't you? They will be less stoical when they face the hangman. Damme, Sheridan, I saw the men we blew from guns in Allahabad go nonchalantly to their deaths, until we hit on the idea of having the faces of the Hindus first smeared with bullock's blood, and those of the Moslems with pig fat. That changed their tune, I can tell you. And now, after they've been dispatched, the Moslem corpses are burnt and the Hindus buried."

"But, sir . . ." Alex was profoundly shocked by this revelation and it took an effort of will not to reveal the revulsion he felt. "These men are soldiers. Their lives are forfeit as the penalty for mutiny, but haven't they the right to die like soldiers?"

"They are soldiers who betrayed their salt," Neill corrected. "In my view, they have merited such treatment. They have taken up arms against the lawful government, murdered their officers, as well as countless innocent women and defenceless children. What would you have me do—make heroes and martyrs of them, for God's sake? That will not deter others from following their example, will it?"

"No, sir." Alex had himself under rigid control now and his voice was flat and devoid of feeling. "But it won't encourage any of those who might regret their action to return to their allegiance. Or, indeed, sir—"

Neill cut him short. "Damme, there speaks a typical Company officer! I had not expected *you* to hold such views, Sheridan. Have you been to the Bibigarh—have you seen what they did there? An eye for an eye, that's the language they understand, and that's what I intend to exact from them. They shed the blood— let them clean it up. I see the hand of God in all this. Believe me, after much prayer and meditation, my Christian conscience is clear. We are fighting for our faith as much as they are, and it was they who called their revolt a holy war, was it not? Did they give Christian burial to their unhappy victims in the Bibigarh— damme, Sheridan, did you *look* inside that well?"

Alex shook his head. "No, I did not."

"Couldn't stomach it, eh? I don't blame you, many couldn't . . . and the poor victims were known to you. It was a truly terrible sight." Neill drew a deep breath and added, less harshly, "I've had both burial wells covered in now and I shall see to it personally that memorials are set up over them."

"I'm glad to hear that, sir," Alex managed. They were in sight of the camp now and lights flickered in the darkness ahead as oil lanterns were lit and men moved about the forest of tents, seeking food and shelter and the chance to change into dry clothing. He hesitated, feeling sickened and wishing that Neill would dismiss him.

"Well, here's where we part company," Neill said, as if reading his thoughts. "But I trust with no ill feeling?"

No ill feeling . . . Alex bit back a sigh. "No, General Neill, none on—on my part, sir."

"You're a strange fellow, Sheridan," the general observed thoughtfully. "Those poor dead creatures are crying out to be avenged and you worry about the Pandies' souls. But . . ." he shrugged. "When does your troop cross into Oudh?"

"Tomorrow afternoon, sir. We are to start embarking the horses at four o'clock."

"Then attend the executions and see for yourself how effective a deterrent they will prove. I shall count on your presence— half an hour after noon. That's understood? Right—then I give you good evening, Colonel Sheridan."

Phrased thus, the invitation was tantamount to an order, and, without waiting for a reply, Neill kicked his horse into a canter and went to join the members of his staff, riding thirty yards ahead of him.

Alex was depressed and anxious when he returned to his tent, but his depression lifted when he saw a familiar white-bearded figure awaiting him there. Flinging his reins to his *syce,* he ran the few yards which separated him from the entrance to the tent, and old Mohammed Bux salaamed, tears streaming down his lined brown cheeks.

"I had not thought to look upon your face again, *huzoor*," the bearer said.

"Nor I on yours, my friend," Alex told him, his own throat tight. "How came you here?"

The bearded lips curved into a smile. "Word reached my village that the sahibs were once more in Cawnpore and had driven the vile Mahratta into the jungle. So I returned, Sahib, without the hope that I might find you. All those who had defended the entrenchment had been slain, we were told, even the *mems* and the *baba-sahibs*. I had not waited—the sahib sent me, in the uniform of a sowar, to my village and I went, sahib, as you had commanded, casting off the uniform before I entered. But later I cursed myself because I had not waited."

"You have nothing for which to curse yourself, Mohammed Bux," Alex assured him. "When I sent you hence, it was in the belief that the Nana would honour the promise he had made to give us safe passage to Allahabad. He did not honour that promise."

"So we heard, *huzoor*. And we heard also that the Nana vowed to take his own life, should he lose Cawnpore. That vow he also failed to honour. He is alive, Sahib, in Oudh, gathering a new army about him." Graphically, the old man recounted the rumours that had reached his village concerning the Nana's treachery as, resuming his accustomed role, he assisted Alex to pull off his boots and divest himself of his sodden, mud-spattered clothing. "When I came into the camp this morning, I questioned the other servants and from them I learned that you were alive, Sahib. At first I feared that they were lying. I could not believe what they told me, but one of them brought me to this tent and now I see, *huzoor*, that he spoke truly, praise be to Allah!" He broke off and, fetching a towel, knelt with it in his thin, work-worn hands. Looking up into his master's face, he asked sadly, "Is it only you, Sahib, who is left? My *memsahiba* . . . the *chota baba-sahib* . . . have all gone from us?"

"Yes," Alex confirmed bleakly. "All are dead, Mohammed Bux." As he spoke of the manner of Emmy's death, the faithful old servant wept without restraint. Until the last day of the siege, Mohammed Bux had been in the entrenchment, refusing to leave even when opportunity was afforded him, performing the most menial of tasks and silently enduring all hardships, he had continued, until the end, to serve. Looking down, at him now, Alex was deeply moved by his devotion. He had, at long last, obtained a draft from the Paymaster and had cashed it that morning; he got to his feet and took half the money from his valise.

"This is for you, Mohammed Bux. It is not adequate reward for what you did, but I shall seek you out when this war is over and give you then what you deserve. Take it and go back to your village. You are free of my service."

"You are sending me away from you, Sahib?" The old man was bewildered. He frowned at the money in his hand and let it fall, uncounted, to the ground. "You are sending me, for the second time, to my village?"

"I go to war," Alex explained gently "We are to fight our way, if we can, to Lucknow. Conditions will be hard, we take no tents. It will be no place for an old man, Mohammed Bux. You have earned—you have more than earned an honourable retirement and I would give it to you, as a measure of my gratitude for the long years of your service."

"*Nahin,* Sahib, *nahin!* My parents are dead, my wives also, and my children grown to man and womanhood. In my village, I am as a stranger. I would stay with you."

Subjecting the wizened dark face to a searching scrutiny, Alex saw that the old man was in earnest. "If that is your considered wish . . . have you thought well, Mohammed Bux?"

"*Ji-han,* Sahib," the bearer assured him. "I have thought well and it is my wish to serve you." He rose, with dignity, from his knees and, taking Alex's hand, pressed it to his forehead in token of the bargain sealed between them. Then, bending down, he picked up the coins from the *dhurry*-covered floor of the tent, counted out ten of them, and laid the rest on the camp table. "I have taken the wage owed to me, Sahib," he said, smiling. "I go now to prepare tea."

The tent flap closed behind his retreating back and Alex, with a sigh of thankfulness, started to don the freshly laundered garments laid out for him on the bed.

Next day, after dismissing his recruits for their midday meal, he rode back across the canal and into the city, taking the road which skirted the Orderlies' Bazaar and the burnt-out ruins of the medical depot. The Bibigarh was a small, single-story building, painted with fading yellow-ochre wash, which stood enclosed in its own walled compound, a mere thirty yards from the Old Cawnpore Hotel, in which the Nana had taken up residence at the conclusion of the siege.

The hotel, Alex saw, a trifle to his surprise, was back to its normal business—indeed, to exceptional business, judging by the number of officers now emerging from its portals and heading—with considerably less reluctance than himself—for the house in which the massacre had taken place. Outside the wall of the compound and lining the road leading to it, a large crowd had already gathered, held back from both road and gateway by a guard of the Fusiliers and the 84th. Leaving his horse in the hotel stable, he joined a group of young Fusilier officers and walked with them to the gateway. They had lunched well—at their commanding officer's expense, it seemed—at the hotel and now, like schoolboys granted an unexpected holiday, they were in cheerfully festive mood, laughing and joking with each other. Their laughter faded, however, when they entered the precincts of the Bibigarh and Alex, who had been trying vainly to shut his ears to their ribaldry, was conscious of relief.

Inside, the scene differed from the normal solemn procedure laid down for military executions in that there was no hollow square drawn up in disciplined alignment and no band playing the Funeral March. The troops present, of whom a high proportion were officers, gathered in groups as spectators rather than witnesses and in place of the band, four drummers of the 84th stood with their provost-sergeant on the verandah of the building, their instruments piled in front of them.

It wanted fifteen minutes to the appointed time for the executions, but the six condemned men, under a strong guard, were lined up beneath the gallows which had been erected within the courtyard, their arms pinioned. The guards were natives, in the dun-coloured uniforms and red turbans of the newly recruited civil police—drawn, Alex had been told, from men of sweeper caste, under Eurasian N.C.O.'s—all armed with steel-tipped lathis. The prisoners, with a single exception, were sepoys, in uniform but stripped of their buttons and badges of rank, bareheaded and with their jacket collars open at the neck and significantly turned back.

The exception was the *jullad,* a hulking brute of a man with a pock-marked face and in soiled white robes, who was standing apart from the rest, an outcast, even from the sweeper police. He was showing visible signs of apprehension, sweating profusely in the steamy heat and looking this way and that, his gaze lingering on the small knot of native spectators gathered at the rear of the gallows, as if in the hope of rescue. By contrast, the sepoys maintained a dignified calm, outstaring the noisy, hostile crowd of British soldiers which surged about them, their own eyes full of hate. Two of them were wounded, Alex noticed, but in spite of this and their pinioned arms, they were careful to avoid physical contact with their guards—and the guards, for all their new and privileged status, treated them with the awed respect which Hindus of lower caste always accorded to Brahmins.

At twenty-five minutes past twelve, the provost-marshal, Captain Bruce, called the assembled troops to attention and General Neill and his escort rode in through the gateway. Dismounting, the general strode to the verandah of the Bibigarh and, acknowledging Bruce's salute, gave him permission to proceed. First in English and then in Hindustani, the provost-marshal read out the charges against each man and the sentences, the drums rolled, and Bruce, after a brief pause, continued to read from the papers in his hand.

"By order of the brigadier-general commanding in Cawnpore, the brigadier-general has determined that every stain of the innocent blood which was shed in this House of Massacre shall be cleared and wiped out, previous to their execution, by such of the miscreants as may be thereafter apprehended, who took an active part in the mutiny, to be selected according to their rank, caste, and degree of guilt. Each miscreant will be taken under guard to the house in question and will be forced to clear up a small portion of the bloodstains, and the provost-marshal will use the lash freely in forcing anyone who objects to complete his task. After having the portion properly cleared up, the culprit is to be immediately hanged and, for this purpose, a gallows has been erected close at hand."

There was a stunned silence. The British soldiers looked at one another, as the meaning of what they had just heard slowly sank in. They were standing to attention and, since no order had been received which would have permitted them to demonstrate their feelings, they remained silent. Some of the younger officers who were not officially on duty raised a cheer, but this was not taken up by the rest, and beside him Alex heard a subaltern of a mutinied native regiment say incredulously, "But this is meeting barbarism with barbarism! Surely General Havelock did not sanction such an order?"

"General Havelock crossed into Oudh at noon," a Fusilier captain reminded him. "General Neill commands here now."

The provost-marshal waited until the spasmodic cheers had died down and repeated the order in Hindustani. One of his staff, posted beside the group of prisoners, also translated it to them and, for the first time since their ordeal had begun, the condemned sepoys lost their stoical calm, as they waited tensely for the names of those who were to suffer this ultimate punishment to be read out.

The *jullad*'s name was called first. Already terrified, the man burst into a torrent of weeping, but he gave his guards little trouble and stumbled across to the verandah of the Bibigarh without having to be coerced. Two of the drummers, one carrying a cat o' nine tails slung over his shoulder, preceded him into the house; the provost-sergeant contemptuously propelled the abject prisoner into the inner room and General Neill stood, arms akimbo, in the open doorway to watch his sentence carried out. The whip, seemingly, was not applied, for no cries of pain reached those in the courtyard outside, but when the *jullad* emerged five or six minutes later, he came on his hands and knees and, flinging himself at the general's feet, pleaded with him for mercy.

"*Huzoor* . . . Protector of the Poor, I beg you to grant me my life! I have a wife and children, who will starve without me . . . and I did only what my masters bade me do. I am guilty of no crime, Great One—I did but take from here the bodies of those who were slain by others. I killed none—"

Neill gestured to the guards and, grasping the ropes with which he was bound, they dragged the man, screaming incoherently, to the gallows, where two of their number, acting as executioners under the supervision of a British sergeant, abruptly silenced his screams. The body was still jerking spasmodically at the end of its noose when the name of Bhandoo Singh was read out, and Alex, watching the *Subedar's* face, saw the expression on it change from indifference to horrified disbelief.

The native officer, it was evident, had not imagined that the hideous punishment meted out to the *jullad* could possibly be inflicted upon himself. He had waited bravely enough for death but not for *this* death, whose prelude would rob him of his immortal soul. True, he had heard the order read out, but in his interpretation of it had not supposed that his own crimes would merit his selection, and before he could stop himself, he shouted his protest aloud.

"I had no part in what was done here! I shed no blood in this house . . . hear me, I speak truly!"

The guards, in obedience to an order barked out by the sergeant to secure him, took a few paces in his direction and then hesitated, reluctant even now to lay hands on the person of a thrice-born Brahmin. A low-voiced argument ensued and then, without warning, the *Subedar* motioned to them to stand aside and they did so, unthinkingly. He made as if to walk of his own accord toward the Bibigarh and they prepared to fall in behind him, but instead he turned and flung himself on to the wooden ladder leading to the gallows. Hampered by his bound hands, he somehow reached the top and was attempting to thrust his head into the trailing noose when the sergeant kicked the ladder away. Bhandoo Singh fell with a sickening thud onto the platform, his right leg doubled up beneath him.

"Is he alive?" Neill's voice thundered, from the door of the Bibigarh.

The sergeant bent over the recumbent man and he called back breathlessly, "Yes, sir, he's alive. But I think he's broken his leg, sir. Shall I—"

"Bring him over here, man!" the general ordered irritably. "Carry him if you have to but get him here. The sentence will be carried out."

The sweeper police, smarting under the lash of the sergeant's tongue and anxious to make amends for their mistake, lifted the *Subedar* without regard for his injuries, and four of them carried him, moaning, into the shadowed interior of the Bibigarh. The two drummers with their cat and the Provost-Sergeant followed them, and a few moments later a high-pitched shriek and the unmistakable swish of an expertly wielded lash told those outside that Bhandoo Singh's fight against his defilement was not yet over. But it did not and could not last much longer; within ten minutes the limp body was carried out and on its return to the gallows, willing hands lifted it up to enable the noose to be put in place. A strange, almost animal murmur rose from the watchers as the dark body, with the telltale weals crisscrossing back and shoulders, swung twitching from the gallows like some grotesque marionette performing a macabre dance of death above their heads, as the air was slowly choked from his lungs. The sergeant, cursing his untutored executioners for a botched-up job, put a swift end to the victim's agony by hauling downward on his legs, and as the twitching ceased, the next name was read out.

"Naik Sita Ram, First Sepoys!"

Alex turned and made his way with slow deliberation through the closely packed crowd to the gateway, not caring whether Neill noticed his departure or not. He had stood enough, he thought, sickened. War was one thing but this . . . dear heaven, this was quite another, and as a soldier he deplored it. Reaching the gateway, he turned for a moment to look back and saw, a few paces behind him, the young Native Infantry officer who had earlier questioned General Havelock's sanction of his successor's order. The boy was white and tense but he managed a wan smile, and when he realised that Alex was waiting for him, caught up and walked with him through the gateway.

"I could not stick any more of that," he confessed. "But I was afraid I'd have to until I saw you leaving, sir. I kept thinking, you see, about those who died here . . . the women and children, I mean, who were massacred in that house. Would they have wanted to be avenged in such a manner? *Could* they have wanted it?"

"'That it may please Thee to forgive our enemies, persecutors, and slanderers, and to turn their hearts,'" Alex quoted softly. "I found that passage from the Litany heavily underscored in a prayer book which one of them dropped, so I think the answer to your question is—no, they would not. They kept their faith to the end and I feel sure that not one of them would have wanted to deprive even their murderers of the hope of life after death."

"Did you know any of them, sir, or have relatives among them?" the boy asked and, when Alex nodded, he went on, a catch in his voice, "My eldest brother was in General Wheeler's garrison, with his wife and two little girls. Edward Vibart . . . he was a major in the Light Cavalry. He—did you ever meet him, sir?"

"Yes, I did." Alex looked at his companion with quickened interest. Eddie Vibart had talked of a brother, he recalled, when he and Francis Whiting had consigned a brief, pencilled account of their ordeal to a bottle, which they had dropped into the river on the last day of their flight. "Didn't you go to Fategarh to visit friends?"

"No, that was John. I'm Tom—Thomas Meredith Vibart, sir, Thirty-Seventh N.I. Poor old Johnny is missing too. I'd hoped that *he* had managed to escape, but they tell me that none of the Fategarh garrison survived." Tom Vibart sighed disconsolately. "They defended the fort for as long as they could and then tried to get through to Cawnpore by river. They couldn't have been aware of the situation here when they made *that* decision, could they, sir?"

"No," Alex confirmed. "They could not." He wondered whether to tell the boy what he knew of his brothers' fate and decided against it. Now was not the time; the lad was already upset, and no doubt an opportunity would arise later on, when he would be better able to take it in without distressing himself. "Come back to camp with me, Vibart," he invited, "and we'll have a drink together—I think we could both do with one."

They collected their horses and rode through the motley crowd of natives still thronging the approaches to the Bibigarh. The rain had ceased and a watery sun lit the domes and minarets of the city to a soft and lovely radiance, belying the horrors with which now the name of Cawnpore would be associated in the minds of both British and Indian, perhaps for generations to come. Alex shrugged off his depression and, anxious to change the subject, questioned his companion about the mutiny in Benares and the disarming of the 37th. The boy was anxious to talk and replied readily to his questions.

"General Neill had just arrived with a small party of the Fusiliers when we received news of the mutiny of the Seventeenth at Azimgurh. The Brigadier commanding in Benares, General Ponsonby, who, with our Colonel Spottiswoode, had been reluctant to disarm our men, finally agreed that it would have to be done. He was ill—indeed, sir, I don't think the poor old man was really aware of how badly disaffected our fellows were—and he wanted to put off the disarming until the following morning but . . ."

"But General Neill insisted that it must be done immediately, did he not?" Alex suggested.

"Yes, sir. And I'm sure he was right." Tom Vibart spoke with conviction. "We didn't have above two hundred Europeans, apart from the Fusiliers General Neill brought with him, who were quite done up. That is to say, we had a hundred and fifty men and two officers of the Tenth Queen's and Captain Olpherts' nine-pounder battery, with thirty gunners. The Loodiana Sikhs were believed to be loyal, though, and they, with a squadron of the Thirteenth Irregular Cavalry, were ordered to stand by in case they were required to back up the Europeans. The trouble began when our regiment, which had been ordered to muster without muskets, refused to do so. They gathered round the bells of arms, giving every sign of insubordination. Colonel Spottiswoode lectured them and they seemed prepared to obey the order when General Ponsonby turned out the Tenth and, as they approached the parade ground, our men, believing themselves threatened, broke open the bells of arms. They seized their muskets and opened fire on the Tenth, killing four of them. Well, of course, the Tenth returned their fire and so did the Artillery." Young Vibart shrugged helplessly. "It was all tragically mistimed, sir. Our men started to retire toward their lines, firing wildly at any officer they saw. General Ponsonby fell—or dismounted, I'm not sure which—from his horse, and General Neill assumed command. He was directing an attack on our regiment by the Europeans and the Sikhs when the Cavalry shot down their commander, Captain Guise, and their *rissaldar* galloped to the front, yelling that they had mutinied and calling on the Sikhs to join them. The Cavalry were to the rear of the Sikhs and they started to loose off with their carbines. The Sikhs were confused. They turned to fire on the Irregulars and some of them fired on Captain Olpherts' gunners who, of course, poured a hail of grape into them. It was a truly appalling shambles, sir, and that's the truth."

"Do you think the Sikhs intended to remain loyal, then?" Alex asked.

The boy nodded. "Yes, I think they did. Those who were on treasury guard and other duties didn't mutiny. But when those on the parade ground suddenly found themselves attacked from both front and rear, they tried to defend themselves. Colonel Gordon, their commandant, said afterwards that he owed his life to the loyalty of his native officers and, when it was all over, quite a substantial number of his men formed up round him and, under his orders, aided the British troops in clearing the mutineers from the lines. But it was done with fearful slaughter, sir . . ." He talked on, describing how the sepoys of his regiment had barricaded themselves in their huts, from which they had only been driven when Captain Olpherts' battery took up a raking position and fired round after round of grape into them, at a range of 250 yards.

He himself had been wounded, together with three other young ensigns attached to the 37th, their British quartermaster-sergeant, and Captain Dodgson, the acting major of brigade, who had been shot down whilst making a gallant attempt to retrain the Irregular Cavalry from throwing in their lot with the mutineers.

"They took us to a fortified enclosure that had been set up on the parade ground, where the surgeons did what they could for us. But there was no further attack and next day we were all removed to the Mint, a strong building with a flat roof situated between cantonments and the city, which had been previously selected as an asylum for the women and children in case of a disturbance. There were about a 150 of us, all crowded into one room; the British troops had been out all night, bringing in families, some of whom had terribly narrow escapes, because the mutineers were plundering and burning and firing on any white face they spotted. Next day, General Neill sent out parties of Fusiliers and the 10th and most of the Pandies fled. Any who were captured were brought back and hanged. But"—Tom Vibart glanced at Alex—"they were simply hanged, sir. And order was very speedily restored. There was nothing like—like the ghastly business we witnessed here today."

"No," Alex said, his voice without expression. He asked a few more general questions and then enquired, smiling, if Vibart had fully recovered from his wound.

"Oh, yes, sir," the ensign assured him. "I was lucky. One of the fellows with me—Hayter, of the 25th, sir—died of his wounds, and Chapman, who was shot in the face, is to be sent home as soon as he is fit to travel. But mine were just flesh wounds and they've healed."

"You came on with General Neill, I suppose?"

"Yes, sir. I was given a temporary attachment to the 84th and I could remain attached, I suppose. But frankly, sir, I'm looking for a chance to join General Havelock's Movable Column. I don't want to stay here if I can help it."

Alex eyed him thoughtfully. Tom Vibart was just the kind of recruit he wanted, and if he proved even half as good as his elder brother had been, he would be worth his weight in gold to the Volunteer Cavalry. "How would an attachment to the Cavalry appeal to you?" he asked, his smile widening. "Barrow's Horse is looking for good men."

"How would it appeal . . . good Lord, sir, it would appeal more than anything in the world! I'd give my eyeteeth to serve with the Volunteer Cavalry! Can you—I mean would you consider putting in a word for me?"

"I'll do better than that, Tom," Alex promised. "If you can obtain your C.O.'s permission, collect your kit, and report to me, with your horse, at the landing place by four o'clock this afternoon, I'll take you with the rest of the new recruits to Captain Barrow, and I'm quite certain he'll accept you."

Tom Vibart stared at him in open-mouthed astonishment and then gave vent to an excited exclamation. "That's simply wonderful! Bless your heart, sir—I'm truly grateful, believe me. I . . . may I know your name, sir? You didn't mention it and I—"

He had earlier avoided making any mention of his name or of his connection with the Cawnpore garrison for the boy's sake, Alex recalled, but he gave his name, expecting a spate of questions, and was relieved to see that his latest recruit appeared to attach no significance to it. They had their drink together in a virtually deserted mess tent, and then Tom Vibart excused himself in order to seek out his commanding officer and obtain the required permission to transfer to the Volunteers.

When he had gone, Alex ordered lunch and the *khitmatgar* was serving his coffee by the time the other members of the mess returned from the Bibigarh. He listened in silence to their comments on the unpleasant spectacle they had all been compelled to witness, thankful that, with three or four exceptions, they condemned the blood-cleansing as barbaric and likely, when the details became known to the populace at large, to do more harm than good. Appealed to for his opinion by a stout, red-faced captain in one of the Queen's regiments who had defended the principle of savage punishment for all mutineers, Alex endeavoured to evade the question, but the Queen's officer persisted.

"Oh, come now, Colonel Sheridan! I'd respect your view. You were with Wheeler's garrison—you were present when the Nana's troops betrayed your friends at the *ghat*. You saw them brutally and treacherously murdered—would *you* advocate mercy for the Pandies, damn it?"

"No, I would not," Alex returned shortly. "But I would advocate justice."

"Justice?" the captain exclaimed. "What do you mean, sir? Wasn't it justice that we saw being done today at that ghastly prison house, where over two hundred of our women and children were butchered?"

"Perhaps justice was done to the *jullad* but not, in my view, to the sepoys."

"Why not to the sepoys, for God's sake? They're all tarred with the same brush, aren't they?"

Several others joined in, and the discussion was becoming heated when the captain, his plump face redder than ever, grasped Alex's arm and said aggressively, "I asked for your opinion, Colonel Sheridan."

Reluctantly and choosing his words with care, Alex said quietly, "The punishment for mutiny is death; the rebels know that and accept it. There's no question of showing mercy to men who betray their salt, and any sepoy who bears arms against us is aware of what he may expect if he is captured. But to go further

—to defile a Brahmin before hanging him is, in my considered opinion, gentlemen, to defile ourselves as Christians and to deny the principles of justice and humanity by which we have sought to govern an alien race. We shall deserve to lose India and our own lives if we permit such things to be done."

There was a stunned silence, and then a dark-faced Fusilier subaltern said angrily, "They are a conquered race! We govern by right of conquest, sir."

Alex was suddenly angry. "Our conquests were made with sepoy armies. The blood they shed gained us India."

"And yet now they've betrayed us," the Fusilier lieutenant objected. "Virtually the whole Bengal Army is disloyal, if not in open rebellion against us!"

"We commanded their loyalty in the past by respecting their religious customs and scruples," Alex told him. "It is the fear that we have ceased to do so that has brought about this mutiny. The fear is real—the sepoys believe that we have set out deliberately to destroy their caste system, thereby compelling them to abandon their own faith and embrace ours. What was done here today will lend credence to that belief and rouse the peasants as well as the sepoys to rebellion. Indeed if—"

"You Company officers are all the same!" the stout captain put in resentfully. "Right up to the moment when the sepoys held their muskets to your heads, you and others of your kidney wouldn't hear of the possibility that they would mutiny, Colonel Sheridan. 'Our men will never betray us,' you said. And 'We must show no mistrust of our loyal sepoys and all will be well.' Poor old Wheeler trusted the swine, didn't he? He was a sepoy general, for God's sake . . . and they hacked him to pieces in flagrant betrayal of the terms of surrender they had sworn to keep!"

He spluttered indignantly and then returned, like an angry bull, to the attack, ignoring all attempts to interrupt him. "Yet when a vigorous and farsighted commander like General Neill repays them in their own filthy coin, you squeal about justice and humanity and try to tell us that we must respect their religious scruples! You blame *us* for causing the mutiny . . . you, sir, whose bones—but for the grace of God—would now be whitening on the riverbank with those of our countrymen and women who did *not* escape!"

Alex faced him, white to the lips and momentarily bereft of words. Of what use was it, he asked himself wearily, to try to explain to Neill or to this man that, simply because he had been in the Cawnpore garrison, he did not want vengeance on any, save those whose guilt was proven? Had the Nana himself been captured—or Bala Bhat or Azimullah or any of the arch-traitors who had plotted the massacre—he would have watched them die unmoved, would even have watched their defilement without a word of protest, considering it justly deserved. And the ordinary citizens of Cawnpore, who had suffered severely under the Nana's tyrannical rule, would have called out also for their blood. They . . .

"Well, sir?" the big captain prompted scornfully.

"You have no need to remind me of whose bones lie here," Alex assured him, with conscious bitterness. "Or of the debt I owe to my Creator."

There was something of an uproar as several of the other officers endeavoured vainly to come to his support, but the stout captain was not to be diverted from his argument. "Then perhaps, sir," he suggested hoarsely, quoting Neill, "you require to be reminded that they were Christians, denied Christian burial?"

"I am not likely to forget that either," Alex said, an icy chill about his heart, "since my wife and son were among them. But my experience here, during and after the siege, leads me to fear for our countrymen and women now under siege in Lucknow. Should we—which God forbid—fail to bring them relief, what was done with such savagery here may be repeated in Lucknow with greater savagery. Reprisals by one side demand still more terrible reprisals by the other. But if we adhere faithfully to the rule of law, if we punish the guilty and spare the innocent, then there's at least a chance that we shall not have to contend with a nationwide rebellion and—"

"Your wife and son . . . good God, man, how can you stand there expressing such—damn it, such weak-kneed, pacifist sentiments? We shall relieve Lucknow—your brave sepoys won't stand up to us. They'll run at the first sight of British bayonets!" The florid face was thrust into his, and Alex, dismayed by the turn the discussion had taken, retreated a pace, to find Jeremiah Brasyer beside him. The white-haired old Sikh commander laid a hand on his arm and said, lowering his voice, "Your Sergeant Mahoney is outside, Colonel, asking for you—on a matter of some urgency, he says."

"Mahoney? Right, I'll go and see what he wants. But I . . ." Alex hesitated and Brasyer grinned, jerking his head in the direction of the Queen's officer.

"Don't worry about *that* gentleman. It will be my pleasure to join battle with him. He was one of the leaders of the Allahabad necktie party—amateur hangmen, who boasted of how many black swine they'd sent to eternity without the formality of a trial. I've been awaiting an opportunity to cut him down to size, so you may safely leave him to me."

Judging by the sound of raised and angry voices which followed him to the entrance of the mess tent, Brasyer was not alone in this desire, Alex realised, his own anger evaporating. He halted in front of the open tent flap and the tall Mahoney, who was standing to his horse's head a few yards away, came smartly to attention at the sight of him, looking relieved.

"What is it, Mahoney?" Alex asked. "Is there something wrong?"

The sergeant nodded. "It's Cullmane, sir—he's been drinking."

"Drinking?" Corporal Cullmane's conduct had been exemplary since his promotion but, recalling General Havelock's stern order governing the supply of liquor to the men of the column, Alex's heart sank. Each man was permitted a daily issue of grog or porter from the commissariat, a ration so small that, even if he hoarded his entire week's supply, it would be insufficient to render him intoxicated. "Do you mean that he's drunk, Sergeant?"

"As full as the Boyne, sir," Mahoney said glumly. "I noticed he was looking—well, a trifle flushed when we went to the cookhouse for our meal but I didn't think anything of it. He's been running a temperature with that arm of his and, beyond asking him if he was suffering any pain, which he denied, I didn't trouble him. I wish to God I had, sir, but I was busy getting our kit packed for the crossing and it never occurred to me that he'd got hold of any liquor."

"It's not your fault, Mahoney," Alex interrupted impatiently. He shouted for his syce and asked, as the man came running with his horse, "Where is he now?"

"I put him under arrest, sir," the sergeant answered, to his relief. "I was afraid the provos would pick him up or those new civil police. They caught a native gunner trying to steal from the commissariat stores a couple of days ago and they say—I don't know if it's true, sir—that he's to be hanged."

It was probably only too true, Alex thought grimly. The order had been clear enough . . . He swore under his breath and swung himself onto his horse. "Where did Cullmane get his liquor, do you know? He didn't steal it, did he?"

Mahoney shook his head. "He told me he bought it from one of the Sikhs, sir. And I believe him—I don't think he'd be such a fool as to risk stealing it." They put their horses to a trot and he added, glancing at Alex anxiously, "Cullmane's a good N.C.O., sir, one of the best I've served with, but I suppose he'll have to lose his stripes now, won't he, sir?"

"Yes, he will," Alex confirmed. "Unfortunately . . . and he'll be lucky if that's all he gets, because I shall have to report him to Captain Barrow. If he'd still been with his own regiment, he would have been flogged." Mahoney's attitude puzzled him a little. British Army discipline was harsh, even in peacetime; on active service it was, of necessity, harsher still and Mahoney, as senior N.C.O., was only doing his duty in reporting Cullmane's misconduct. On the other hand, he could have dealt with it himself and if he liked Cullmane, as he appeared to, by so doing could have avoided making an official issue of the matter. "Where have you got him, Mahoney?" he asked.

"In the horse lines, sir, out of sight. I . . ." The sergeant again looked anxiously across at him, as if seeking to read his thoughts, and Alex waited without impatience for an explanation. Finally it came; red of face, Mahoney said unhappily, "I would not have brought you into it, sir, if I could have helped it, you understand . . . but Corporal Cullmane was seen. Seen and heard, sir."

"Seen and heard—doing what, Sergeant, for heaven's sake?" Alex demanded. "And by whom?"

The young sergeant swallowed hard. "He mounted his horse, sir, and galloped around like a madman, shouting out 'Tally-ho' and making out he was following hounds. When he wasn't hollering and hallooing, he was singing 'God save Ireland' at the top of his voice. It was the white-bearded officer who saw him, sir—the Sikhs' Commanding Officer. He was riding past and I spotted he was making for your mess tent, sir, and I knew he'd tell you about it, so I came after him. I had to, sir, or you'd have thought I was failing in my duty."

Jeremiah Brasyer, Alex thought, relief flooding over him. The Sikhs' commander had had more than his share of trouble over his own men's drinking and, since he had not mentioned the incident in the mess just now, it seemed probable that be had deliberately turned a blind eye to it. He found himself smiling at the droll picture Mahoney's description had conjured up; after the horror of the Bibigarh executions and the unpleasant scene in the mess, it was good to have reason for amusement, however short-lived.

He said, with careful gravity, suppressing the smile, "You did the right thing, Sergeant Mahoney. I—er—I'll have a word with Captain Brasyer as soon as I can. If he's willing to overlook Cullmane's misconduct, I will overlook it also—*this* time. But it will be up to you to make sure that nothing of the kind happens again. Deal with Corporal Cullmane yourself and as you see fit. Officially I know nothing about his behaviour, so he'll keep his stripes, but you can warn him, unofficially, that if he takes another drop above his daily grog ration, I'll have the hide off him."

"Thank you very much, sir." Mahoney responded. He added grimly, "I'll deal with him—there won't be a next time I can promise you that, sir."

Alex reined in; the sergeant saluted and cantered on toward the Cavalry Lines. By three-fifteen, the troop was lined up by the landing stage, a very sober and chastened Corporal Cullmane among them, his red and blistered face and the chafe marks on his wrists mute evidence of the "pegging out" by means of which he had been restored to sobriety. In silence but with his accustomed efficiency, he prepared to supervise the embarkation of the first six horses, as the pontoons which were to carry them were hauled close into the bank. At three-thirty an advance party of Sikhs marched down, ready to cross, and at a quarter to four—when Alex had almost given up hope of him—Ensign Vibart made his appearance on a lathered horse, to take his place, a trifle breathlessly, with the Volunteer recruits.

"Down ye get, sorr," Cullmane bade him, taking his rein. "And Oi'll cool t'at animal of yours off for ya. She'll catch her death if she has to swim for ut, so she will, t'e state she's in." He led the sweating mare past Jeremiah Brasyer, his face half-hidden behind her foam-flecked neck but, in spite of this, the white-bearded Sikh commander recognised him and, meeting Alex's gaze, closed one eye in an elaborate wink.

At four-thirty, in a renewed deluge of rain, the *Burrampootra* steamed slowly across the flooded Ganges toward the Oudh shore, towing boats and pontoons behind her. She broke down twice during the hours of darkness, but at dawn the following morning, her overworked engines restored to order and clouds of black smoke pouring from her funnel, the last of the Lucknow Relief Force, a company of the Madras Fusiliers, clambered aboard to huddle damply wherever they could find space on her deck. The men were cold and dispirited; they did not cheer when their late Commanding Officer mounted the battlements of his newly constructed entrenchment at the river's edge to watch their departure, and by the time the little river steamer reached the Oudh shore, half a dozen of them were prostrate and writhing in the terrible agony of a cholera attack.

CHAPTER FIVE

⋙ • ⋘

ON THE EVENING of Tuesday, 28th July, in the mud-walled native hut at Mungalwar, six miles from the river, in which he had established his battle headquarters, Brigadier-General Henry Havelock issued orders for the advance on Lucknow.

His Movable Column, a bare twelve hundred Britons and three hundred Sikhs, had a formidable task before of them, as Havelock was well aware. Forty-three miles of hostile, flooded countryside separated them from their objective; a river—the Sai —a canal, and a number of fortified villages and towns constituted the main physical obstacles, and an army of mutineers, estimated at between 25,000 and 30,000, was besieging Lucknow itself. In addition, the Nana Sahib, with a force of several thousand, was reliably reported to be hovering in the Oudh jungles, with the avowed intention of harassing the rear of the Column and, when it advanced, cutting off its communications with Cawnpore.

In a despatch to the Commander-in-Chief, Sir Patrick Grant, Havelock did not minimise the odds against him. He wrote:

> The difficulties of an advance to the relief of Lucknow are excessive. The enemy has entrenched and covered with guns the bridge across the Sai at Bunni and has made preparations for destroying it if the bridge is forced. I have no means of crossing the canal near Lucknow, even if successful at Bunni, where a direct attack might cost me a third of

my force. I might turn it by Mohan, unless the bridge there were also destroyed. I have this morning received a plan of Lucknow from Major Anderson, Engineer in the garrison, and much valuable information in two memoranda, which escaped the enemy's outpost troops and were partly written in Greek characters. These communications and much information orally derived from spies convince me of the extreme danger and difficulty of any operation to relieve Colonel Inglis, now commanding in Lucknow.

It shall be attempted, however, at every risk. Our losses from cholera are becoming serious and extend to General Neill's force as well as my own. I earnestly hope that the 5th and the 90th Regiments can be pushed on to me entire and with all despatch and every disposable detachment of the regiments now under my command be sent for. My whole force only amounts to 1,500 men and ten guns, imperfectly equipped and manned.

In spite of these misgivings, Havelock sent the brave courier Ungud, who had delivered Major Anderson's letter, back once more on his perilous way to Lucknow, with a note which ended optimistically,

We hope to meet you in five or six days.

To Colonel Tytler, who had penned his orders for the advance, he said. "Every mile we can win on the way to Lucknow will afford them *some* relief, I think. And if Grant will only send on those two regiments he has promised me—or even if he'll make our strength up to two thousand immediately, with a battery of horsed guns, we'll smash every rebel force, one after the other . . . and the troops coming up in the rear can settle the country."

Left alone with his son Harry, now acting as his Deputy Assistant adjutant-general in place of Stuart Beatson, General Havelock was silent, his eyes closed in prayer. Opening them at last, he said quietly, "Our force is woefully inadequate for the task it must undertake. But if the worst comes to the worst, Harry my dear lad, we can but die with our swords in our hands. God, in His infinite goodness, has enabled us to come thus far and I would not have it written as my epitaph that I had failed to put my best endeavours into bringing relief to Lucknow. If with God's help and guidance it is possible, then we will do it . . . because there must not be a second Cawnpore!"

"Morale is high, Father," Harry Havelock reminded him. "You could not ask for better or more willing troops. Whatever you demand of them, they will carry out—you need have no fear on that score. They've seen what you can achieve and they have complete faith in your invincibility."

Indeed, throughout the small force, morale had never been higher, in spite of the discomfort caused by heat and the incessant rain. Havelock had won the respect of his officers for his tactical skill and military efficiency. Even those who had at first doubted his ability, or who had resented his appointment to the command over Neill's head, were willing now to follow him anywhere. His soldiers, to a man, admired and trusted their stern little general, who had led them to victory against seemingly impossible odds. He imposed an iron discipline and would not tolerate drinking, but he concerned himself personally with their welfare. On the march from Allahabad, he had driven them to the limit of their endurance, but always he had been there in the thick of the fight, taking his own life in his hands and teaching them, by example, not to flinch in the face of enemy fire. He never swore, but his voice carried above the sounds of battle, urging them on, praising them when their valour earned his approbation and reproving them when it did not. Aware that he had come through twenty-eight engagements without a scratch, they believed him not only invincible, as his son Harry had claimed, but also indestructible.

Whenever he made his appearance in camp, an erect, white-haired figure in a faded blue frock coat, the men flocked round to cheer him, and in the field hospital, where he was frequently to be found, the wounded and the dying were grateful both for his presence and his prayers. Small and old though he might seem, his keen eyes missed nothing, and there was a wiry toughness about him that made light of hardship and privation. Neill and some of his officers might continue to mock Havelock's orations and the services and prayer meetings he conducted, but the men did not, and in the new atmosphere of disciplined sobriety he had created, even the most hard-bitten of them flocked in increasing numbers to hear him preach or read passages from the well-worn Bible he always carried with him. His faith, like his courage, never wavered, and both became a byword, for to the unlettered men he commanded, Henry Havelock was not only a symbol of the devout, if somewhat puritanical type of Christianity in which most of them had been reared; he was also a soldier whose record was a source of pride to them, and they gave him their wholehearted devotion.

They were in high spirits when the advance began at five o'clock next morning. The weather was clear and they marched forward to the stirring sound of the pipes, led by the 78th Highlanders and the Fusiliers, with the leading companies spread out in skirmishing order and a small cavalry piquet scouting the road ahead. Alex, commanding the piquet, sent back word by Tom Vibart that opposition awaited them at a village straddling the road near the town of Unao, three miles from their starting point. The village was typical of hundreds more in Oudh, where each hamlet was frequently at feud with its neighbours—a collection of mud-walled huts, loopholed for defence, the whole surrounded by a high mud wall. It was a strong position, protected on the right by a swamp, with three guns covering the approach from behind a walled enclosure and a large body of rebel troops posted in and behind the village. The town itself lay three-quarters of a mile to the right, but the flooded state of the country precluded the possibility of turning in that direction.

Havelock rode up and, sweeping the scene with his glass, ordered the Enfield skirmishers to open the action, while two field pieces were brought forward. The main body of the Highlanders were drawn up in expectation of being ordered to lead the assault, but, finding themselves under fire from the guns in the walled enclosure, Colonel Hamilton, their commander, cantered back to report.

"Remove them out of range until our guns arrive," Havelock told him.

"Pray, sir," Hamilton pleaded. "They are ready—let them go at the place and have done with it!"

Alex, waiting with his small party—a few yards away, saw a fugitive smile light the face of the little general as he gave his assent. Five minutes later, when the two guns under Lieutenant Crump had unlimbered and placed some well-aimed shots amongst the enemy gunners, he saw the Highlanders and the Blue Caps rush forward with a concerted yell at the walled enclosure. They were met by a withering fire. A scarlet-jacketed Highlander clambered up and fell back, shot through the head; a Fusilier followed, only to be flung back, a bayonet wound in his throat. Three times they charged, three times they were thrown back with heavy losses, and then they were in, the guns abandoned by the rebel gunners and the thatch of the mud-walled huts ablaze.

Lousada Barrow, commanding the main body of the small force of cavalry, led some of his men in to pick up wounded. To Alex he said breathlessly, "They've fired the whole village—men are burning to death in there, ours as well as theirs, and the matchlock men are contesting every hut. But we've been ordered out. Crommelin of the Engineers says there's a large force of the enemy—infantry, cavalry, and guns—advancing on Unao from the other side." He pointed with a blood-smeared hand. "Take your piquet forward, will you, and if he's right, report the position to the general."

Alex needed no second bidding. Spurring forward, their horses over their hocks in the glutinous mud of the swamp, he and his half-dozen men emerged from the smoke of the burning village to see that Captain Crommelin's warning was indeed correct. A force of about six thousand rebels, a large proportion of them cavalry, with twelve or fourteen guns, was debouching onto the road from behind the outskirts of the town. They were still a considerable way away and making a great deal of noise, with trumpets sounding and drums beating, and Alex watched them from behind the shelter of a grove of mango trees, studying them and the lie of the land ahead with the aid of his glass. The road, he saw, ran through the centre of the swamp, but there was what appeared to be a firm tongue of land, about half a mile or so in width, ahead of him and to his right. He scanned it with his telescope and, satisfied that his eyes had not deceived him and that the bright green of the swamp grass gave way, at this point, to dry, sandy soil, he told his piquet to remain under cover and galloped across to make assurance doubly sure. Five minutes later, he was making his report to General Havelock, who acted upon it with swift decisiveness.

Leaving the Sikhs under Jeremiah Brasyer to clear up the village, he ordered the rest of his force to disengage and advance by the narrow passage between the village and the town. Reaching the tongue of dry ground was no easy matter, particularly for Francis Maude's bullock-drawn guns, which were frequently stuck fast in the reddish-brown mud under a galling fire of matchlocks. The Volunteer Cavalry, endeavouring to cover their advance, had several times to hitch their horses to the traces in order to drag them clear, but the road was reached at last and Alex guided them through a series of screening mango trees to the position he had reconnoitred.

Here General Havelock drew the infantry up in line, with four guns in the centre and two on each wing, to await the rebels' attack. The Sikhs rejoined the main body and, in anticipation of an artillery cannonade, the infantry were ordered to lie down and the Volunteers posted behind the guns on either flank. The rebels came forward confidently, even arrogantly, in a long, tightly bunched column, with elephants drawing three heavy-calibre field pieces behind a strong body of cavalry. Still drumming and trumpeting, they held their green Islamic banners on high, yelling defiance and clearly believing that so puny a force as the one that was facing them could offer little opposition to their own overwhelming numbers.

Havelock made no attempt to check their advance. The British line waited in silence, the Colours of the Fusiliers in the centre hanging limp in the hot, still air and Maude's gunners, portfires glowing, crouched expectantly behind their double-shotted 9-pounders. When they were within a thousand yards, the rebels halted and opened fire. Maude's gunners, who had the sun behind them and a perfect sight of their target, replied with devastating effect. Within ten minutes they had silenced the enemy's leading guns and scattered their supporting infantry, and Havelock bade his line rise and move forward, as his opposing commander—realising the mistake he had made—endeavoured to deploy, only to lose a number of guns, which were engulfed by the swamp. Although still very heavily outnumbered, the British advanced steadily, Enfield and Minié rifles and the flank guns playing viciously on the dense mass of rebel infantry, which wavered, broke, and then rolled back. Seeing this, Havelock ordered his own left flank to advance through the morass, led by the Enfield skirmishers of the 64th. Knee deep in mud at the edge of the swamp, the riflemen poured volley after volley into their shattered foe; the saddles of the cavalry began to empty, and as Maude's four guns in the centre unlimbered and sprayed them with grape, they beat a panic-stricken retreat in which the infantry, after a momentary hesitation, chaotically joined. Only the rebel gunners—crack Company troops—maintained the conflict. Deserted by their supporting infantry and deprived of their cavalry screen, most of them perished beside their guns, bayoneted where they stood by the Fusiliers and the 78th.

Fifteen guns were taken and, in undisputed possession of the road, the British swept across the causeway. At 2 P.M. Havelock ordered a two-hour halt to enable them to cook and eat their belated midday meal, while tumbrils picked up the wounded and the dead were buried.

"Look at them!" Lousada Barrow exclaimed disgustedly, waving a hand in the direction of the fleeing rebels. "I've begged to be allowed to pursue them but the general won't have it. The flooded state of the country would make pursuit hazardous, he says, and we are too few for him to take any risk of losing us."

He slumped down beside Alex at the bivouac fire, mopping at his smoke-grimed face. "So we lose the fruits of our victory!"

"What the general says—alas—makes sense," Alex pointed out mildly. "And we've taken fifteen guns, I'm told."

"But without beasts to draw them, we cannot use them; they're to be spiked and thrown into the swamp." Barrow gulped down a long draught of porter, shaking his head at the mess of under-cooked meat someone offered him. "No, thanks—I'll confine myself to wet rations until this evening." He consulted his pocket watch. "The general intends to push on, so we're to reconnoitre ahead with Fraser Tytler as soon as we've eaten. I'll go this time, Alex. Your troop is to be divided, half to act as escort to the artillery and the other half to accompany the wounded to the rear and serve as baggage guard." He gave brief instructions and then added, smiling, "You've done well with those recruits, my dear fellow, damned well! They handle themselves like cavalry-men born and that sergeant of yours is an acquisition—not to mention young Vibart. How did you get hold of him?"

Alex explained, and Lousada Barrow's smile widened. "Ah, one of those Vibarts, is he? And living up to the name, it would appear. I'm sorry he's to be given no chance of glory, but blame that on the floods and the general's reluctance to lose us. I'll take him with me on the reconnaissance—it will be good for his edu-cation, if nothing else." He rose, stretching his cramped limbs. "If my wife could see me now, she wouldn't believe her eyes! But thanks be to God, she's in England with the family. Our last child, a boy, was a sickly little fellow and we had to take the inevitable but painful decision to separate, for his sake."

"It was the right decision, in these circumstances, Lou," Alex said. He thought of his own efforts to persuade Emmy to go to Calcutta and bit back a sigh.

"Yes," Barrow agreed. "Undoubtedly it was, Alex. Young Charlie is now five years old and Piercy writes that he's a fine little chap—as sturdy as anyone could wish. Odd that I should think of them now, though, isn't it? Could it be a premonition, perhaps?"

"God forbid!"

Lousada Barrow grunted. He said, as he swung himself onto his horse, "It's not for one's own sake that one worries, but for theirs. A Government pension for one of my rank won't suffice to keep a widow and six children, I fear, so no doubt I should be grateful for the general's wish to preserve us intact. But . . . if anything should happen to me, I can count on you to do what you can for my family, can't I?"

"Of course you can, Lou," Alex assured him.

The bugles sounded, half an hour later, and the advance continued.

Lucknow was still thirty-seven miles away and the next obstacle was the town of Busseratgunj, five miles on. This was a walled town, situated at the rear of an extensive *jheel,* with deep, water-filled ditches encircling the walls which, as usual in Oudh towns, were loopholed and strongly defended. In addition, the gate was defended by a round tower, on which four guns were mounted. A causeway, 150 yards long, crossed the swamp to the rear of the town and Havelock, on receiving the report he had asked for from Fraser Tytler, decided that, after a preliminary bombardment, he would send the 64th on a turning movement to the left, for the purpose of cutting off the defenders' escape route to the causeway. As they did so, the 78th and the Fusiliers were to assault the gate and the town, with the Sikhs and the 84th in support, in order to catch the enemy between two fires.

The battle opened in fine style, Maude's guns throwing a hail of accurately placed shots, limbering up and pushing forward to resume the bombardment, supported by the Fusiliers skirmishing and the Highlanders and 64th in line. Alex, on the right flank of the advancing artillery, although able to take no active part in the action, had a grandstand view. Francis Maude, a lean, dapper figure in his grimy white uniform, was in his element, laying a gun here, waving his gunners on there, and, bringing them up to his favourite 700 yards' range, finally silencing the enemy's answering cannonade.

Havelock ordered the 64th off on their turning movement and the Fusiliers and the Highlanders hurled themselves against the earthworks with great gallantry, forced the gate at the point of the bayonet, and were into the town, driving all opposition before them. Unhappily the 64th had delayed to exchange shots with the defenders of a small building which they should properly have taken in their stride, and the main body of the defeated rebels was already streaming out, in a confused and jumbled mass of men and horses, across the causeway. Seeing this, Havelock despatched his son Harry—who had just remounted, after having his horse shot under him—with a brusque message to the 64th's Commanding Officer: "If you don't go at that village, I will send men that will, and put an everlasting disgrace on you!"

That morning at Unao the 64th had shown some hesitation in advancing to the attack; they had remained lying down under heavy fire until a big Irish private named Cavanagh had gone forward alone and died, cheering them on, and Havelock had expressed his dissatisfaction with them. Now, stung by his message, they made a dash for the causeway but reached it too late to cut off the rebels' retreat. The sepoys who had garrisoned the town made off, carrying their wounded with them, and leaving the inhabitants to their fate.

Disappointed, although their second victory had been gallantly and decisively won, the line was halted at the edge of the *jheel* and the exhausted men bivouacked where they stood, many of them on the causeway itself. Havelock rode across to inspect the piquets posted on the far side and, as he returned in the fading light, his horse having to step over the recumbent forms of sleeping soldiers, one of them roused himself and, recognising the horseman, jumped to his feet shouting, "Clear the way for the general!"

The cry passed down the line and, worn out though they were, the men started to cheer. "Clear the way for the general! It's the general, boys—give him a cheer and clear the way there!"

General Havelock beamed at them. "You've done that *well* already, men!" he answered. "You've done that very well."

"And we'll clear it all the way to Lucknow, sir," a husky young corporal promised. "God bless you, sir!"

Touched, the general thanked them and continued across the causeway. For him there was to be no sleep, however. In the building his staff had taken over as their headquarters, he pored over the list of killed and wounded and sick, appalled by the figures Harry set before him. He dictated an Order of the Day which was characteristic of him:

> Soldiers, your general thanks you for your exertions today. You have stormed two fortified villages and captured nineteen guns. But he is not satisfied with all of you. Some of you fought as if the cholera had seized your minds as well as your bodies. There were men among you, however, whom he must praise to the skies. Private Patrick Cavanagh, 64th, was cut literally in pieces by the enemy, while setting an example of distinguished gallantry. Had he lived I should

have deemed him worthy of the Victoria Cross. It could never have glittered on a more gallant breast.

This done, the general made a full report on the day to the Commander-in-Chief, ending:

> The loss during the day's fighting was heavy—namely 100 men killed and wounded. They, with the sick, took up the whole of the sick carriage of the force. The loss of the enemy in killed and wounded was over 400, as nearly as can be estimated, but as I have no cavalry I can risk in pursuit, they carried off both dead and wounded and, though abandoning their guns, their horses, bullocks, and equipment generally, if not always, have escaped me.

He pleaded again for reinforcement by the two European regiments he had been promised and a battery of horse artillery, and continued:

> We are now reduced to 1,000 European infantry and can place only 850 in line, our numerous sick, wounded, and baggage requiring strong guards in this country, where every village contains enemies, and we are diminishing daily from cholera, dysentery, and fighting.

All night, Havelock wrestled with the problem of whether to retire to his starting point at Mungalwar to await the necessary reinforcements or to take the risk of going on. To go on would, in all probability, mean leaving his sick and wounded by the roadside and this he could not contemplate; in addition, as his son Harry pointed out, every *dhoolie* and sick cart was in use, which meant that none would be available for future casualties. To stay where he was, less than halfway to Lucknow, was out of the question, since his communication with Cawnpore would almost certainly be cut. He had barely men enough to hold the little town, and none at all that he could spare to guard the road. Prudence, humanity, and military experience alike told him that his only course was to retire—his Movable Column was too small, too poorly equipped, too vulnerable to go on. His men had fought with great tenacity and courage; they had been victorious and none would want to retire, now that they had come so close to their goal. Probably they would think him wrong if he ordered them to abandon the ground they had won and, in far-off Calcutta, he knew, there would be many all too ready to criticise his decision—to accuse him, even, of faint-heartedness. But he could not let such considerations weigh with him, the general told himself, and, his own mind made up at last, he sent for Colonel Tytler soon after dawn.

"Tytler," he said, coming to the point without preamble, "In your opinion, what chance have we of effecting the relief of Lucknow if we push on at once?"

"In my view, General," his Chief of Staff answered, without hesitation, "we have none at all, with our present resources. To make the attempt and fail would, I feel sure, seal the fate of the garrison. Colonel Inglis has said that he can hold out until the fifth of August; we have to some extent relieved the pressure on him by drawing troops away from the siege, and if we return to Mungalwar, they will almost certainly follow us. Provided the reinforcements reach us within the next few days, we shall still be in time to save Lucknow, and by going back now, we shall save our own sick and wounded."

"My view is the same as yours," Havelock told him. "Although whether it will be shared in Calcutta or, for that matter, in England is by no means certain!" He shrugged with weary resignation.

"And our own men won't like it, poor fellows."

"True, sir," Tytler conceded. "But it would be no use attempting to fight our way into Lucknow with eight hundred Europeans when Inglis himself has warned that we shall require two or three thousand, if we are to have any chance of reaching the Residency at all! And even that supposes that we could cross the Sai at Bunni without loss, by a bridge we're told has been destroyed . . ." his smile was wry. "Shall I give the order to retire, sir?"

Havelock shook his white head. "No, I will give it myself, since the decision is mine. Fall the Column in at four o'clock this afternoon, if you please, and I will break the news to them then."

At four, the Column was formed up, facing towards Lucknow, and Havelock, after a brief explanation of his reasons, gave the order to retire. The men's faces fell; there were murmurs of surprised and angry protest, and Alex, sitting his horse with the twenty of his troop who had been detailed to act as escort to the guns, heard several of them swearing in disbelief. But the order had been given and must be obeyed; dejected and sullen, they marched back across the battlefield they had contested the previous day and, after bivouacking overnight at Unao, reached Mungalwar in a deluge of rain, to find what shelter they could in the mud huts of the village. They were unmolested by the rebels but with every mile more men fell out, suffering from sickness and exhaustion, and when the Column finally halted, casualties from these causes outnumbered those inflicted in action against the enemy.

General Havelock, as weary and dispirited as the men he commanded, received a message from the Commander-in-Chief, sent by electric telegraph and forwarded from Cawnpore by Neill. This contained the heartbreaking news that the Dinapore sepoys were now in open revolt, for which reason the two British regiments he had been promised, the 5th Fusiliers and the 90th Foot, could not yet be sent to reinforce the Lucknow relief column. He had believed them to be already on their way upcountry, and the information that they were not coming was a shattering blow to him. It was followed by another. Late on the evening of 1st August, a personal letter from Neill was delivered to his Headquarters by a staff officer and he read it with growing anger.

I late last night received yours of yesterday,

his second-in-command had written, in a hasty, almost illegible scrawl.

I deeply regret that you have fallen back one foot. The effect on our prestige is very bad indeed. Your camp was not pitched yesterday before all manner of reports were rife in the city—that you had returned to get more guns, having lost all you took with you. In fact, amongst all the belief is that you have been defeated and forced back. It has been most unfortunate your not bringing any guns captured from the enemy. The natives will not believe that you have captured one. The effect of your retrograde movement will be very injurious to our cause everywhere.

White with fury at such gross insubordination, Havelock turned the page, to read that reinforcements—in the shape of a half-battery of Horse Artillery and a company of the 84th—had left Allahabad on their way to join him.

When these reinforcements reach you,

Neill's final paragraph read,

you ought to advance again and not halt until you have rescued, if possible, the garrison of Lucknow. Return here sharp with them for there is much to be done, between this and Agra and Delhi.

Young Lieutenant Hargood of the Fusiliers, who had replaced Lieutenant Seton as his AFDC after Seton had suffered a severe wound at Unao, eyed his Chief apprehensively, fearing, from his expression, that an outburst was imminent. But General Havelock was not given to futile loss of temper in front of his subordinates, and, to Hargood's surprise, he said in a flat, controlled voice, "Be so good as to tell my son that I wish to see him, if you please." When the AFDC had hurried off on his errand, the general turned to Lieutenant Simpson, who had brought the letter, and bade him wait outside. "There will be a reply. Kindly wait for it."

Simpson saluted and withdrew. Left alone, Havelock reached for pen and paper and, his hand perfectly steady, wrote his answer.

There must be an end to these proceedings at once. I wrote to you confidentially on the state of affairs. You send me back a letter of censure of my measures, reproof, and advice for the future. I do not want and will not receive any of them from an officer under my command, be his experience what it may.

Understand this distinctly, and that a consideration of the obstruction that would arise to the public service at this moment alone prevents me from taking the stronger step of placing you under arrest. You now stand warned. Attempt no further dictation. I have my own reasons, which I will not communicate to anyone, and I alone am responsible for the course which I have pursued.

When his son Harry arrived breathless, the general placed both letters in his hand. "Read these," he invited.

Harry read them, unable to contain his indignation.

"He'll communicate these—these entirely false accusations to Calcutta, Father," he warned.

"I know it," the general admitted. "But I can do nothing, save advise Patrick Grant of the true situation and let him judge for himself. If I take this Column—even with the paltry reinforcements they have sent me—to Lucknow I shall, in all probability, lose every man. If that is what Government requires of me, then I'll do it, Harry. But inevitably, if I do, the loss of this force in a fruitless attempt to relieve Colonel Inglis will bring about *his* fall."

"Wait, Father," Harry pleaded. "Wait at least until we hear when the regiments from Dinapore *are* to be sent."

Next day a second telegraphic message from the Commander-in-Chief added to the general's despair.

Events in Bengal make it impossible to send up the 5th and 99th regiments, and it is certain that no other European regiments can reach Allahabad for two months . . .

this starkly informed him, and then, influenced, it seemed probable, by the opinion Neil had expressed to him, Sir Patrick Grant ended his message by urging an immediate attempt to relieve Lucknow.

The "paltry reinforcements"—a hundred men of the Queen's 84th, two 9-pounder guns of Captain Olpherts' battery, under Lieutenant Smithett, and two 24-pounder howitzers from Cawnpore—reached Mungalwar on 4th August. Havelock paraded them and congratulated them on having come into a camp of heroic soldiers, who had six times met the enemy and each time defeated him and taken his cannon, but, learning from Smithett that his native gun lascars had shown signs of disaffection, he had them disarmed and sent back to Cawnpore to work as labourers in

Neill's entrenchment. That evening he despatched Ungud to Lucknow with a message saying he would make a second attempt to bring about the garrison's relief, and the Column marched to Unao. Receiving intelligence that Busseratgunj was again occupied in strength by the rebels, the advance was continued at first light.

Employing similar tactics to those which had been so successful on the previous occasion, Havelock once more drove a vastly superior force of rebels from their stronghold. This time the 84th were entrusted to perform the turning movement, and they did so with dash and courage, leading the British column in a gallant bayonet charge which took them across the causeway at the heels of their fleeing foe. The Horse Artillery galloped forward with a slender escort of Volunteer Cavalry and, unlimbering well ahead of the infantry, pounded a number of enemy camps situated in the plain beyond the causeway with grape and shrapnel. As their occupants abandoned their tents and took to flight, led by a large body of irregular cavalry, both Alex and Charles Palliser pleaded to be allowed to give chase with the Volunteers, only to receive a regretful refusal. Disconsolately they sat their horses, watching their enemy escape, and Lousada Barrow, who had conveyed their plea to the general, confessed to his own frustration.

"Lucknow is our goal, my friends," he said. "We cannot afford to lose men or expend all our ammunition on the way . . . or so Colonel Tytler informs me." He sighed. "There's to be a council of war now, which I'm ordered to attend, to decide whether we continue the advance or not. In the meantime, the orders are for you to retire, with Smithett's guns, to the causeway."

Palliser cursed, loudly and angrily, as they rode back. "I know you're a Havelock man, Colonel Sheridan," he told Alex. "But this is too much! God's teeth, we win victories and then retire, as if we'd suffered defeat! And for us in the cavalry, it's a choice of baggage guard or escort to the artillery, with the occasional reconnaissance from which, on sighting the enemy, we are commanded to beat an inglorious retreat. Let's go on to Lucknow at any price, I say, and have done."

But it was not to be. The recapture of Busseratgunj had cost ten men killed and over a hundred wounded or stricken with cholera and, with a quarter of the gun ammunition expended—although enemy casualties exceeded 400—the officers whom General Havelock had summoned to discuss the situation agreed unhappily that their desperate gamble had little chance of succeeding.

Colonel Tytler summed up. "The worst is yet to come," he said, weighing his words carefully. "We are still thirty miles from Lucknow. Every village is held against us; the *zamindars* have risen to oppose us, and they are all round us in bodies of five or six hundred strong, waiting for an opportunity to fall upon the wounded and the baggage train. The bridge of boats at Bunni is strongly entrenched and defended by cannon. According to our spies' reports, the Pandies will blow it up on our approach. How, then, can we cross the Sai?"

"There will be some boats, surely, Colonel?" Harry Havelock put in. "And the bridge could be repaired."

"That would take too long, Harry," Captain Crommelin objected. "And we should have to work under fire. We might lose half our force, on that crossing alone. Boats remain a possibility, but—"

"Even if we contrived, by some miracle, to seize sufficient boats," Tytler said flatly, "we would still have to get across the canal at the Char Bagh and then fight our way through a mile and a half of Lucknow streets in order to gain the Residency. Colonel Inglis can promise only a diversion in our favour and some flank fire with his guns. And if we fail to reach the Residency, he says he cannot cut his way out to join us. His letter's here . . ." Unfolding the crumpled scrap of paper Ungud had delivered from the besieged garrison that morning, he read it aloud, "'It is quite impossible with my weak and shattered garrison that I can leave my defences . . . that's it, in black and white, gentlemen.' And he adds that he is hampered by 350 women and children and nearly half that number of sick and wounded, for whom he has no carriage whatsoever! In my considered view, we have no chance of relieving Lucknow or of evacuating the garrison to Cawnpore, as the Commander-in-Chief requires, until we are reinforced by at least two more regiments of Europeans. We should be sacrificing this force, without a chance of benefiting the garrison, if we attempted now to go on."

General Havelock, who had contributed no view of his own, looked from one to the other of them in mute, reluctant question. All, with the exception of his son Harry, agreed with Tytler's assessment.

"*I* think," Harry Havelock said hotly, "that we must advance at all hazards. Even if only a handful of us succeeds in reaching the Residency, honour demands that we make the attempt."

"Of what use will a handful of exhausted men be to Inglis?" Lousada Barrow asked. "They will simply be more mouths for him to feed, Harry."

"It must not be said of us that we failed in our duty," Harry objected. "And you know who will say it, do you not, Lousada! My father's reputation is already compromised by our earlier retreat. Calcutta has been told of it by a man who believes he could do better and—"

"Are you," Tytler demanded, "prepared to sacrifice this whole force and the interests of British India, rather than compromise your father's reputation? However galling it is for you—and, as I am fully aware, for the general himself—to retire, this is not a personal question, Harry. If this Force were annihilated in an unsuccessful attempt to reach Lucknow, for how long do you suppose General Neill could hold out in Cawnpore? Not only Lucknow would be lost but Cawnpore also . . . and then Allahabad would be attacked! Our presence here in Oudh, as a fighting force, will aid Colonel Inglis's resistance, but we are too few and too poorly equipped and supplied to bring him relief and, for this undeniable fact, your father cannot be blamed."

"But he will be," Harry Havelock retorted bitterly. "That, too, is an undeniable fact, Colonel." He looked across at his father and, observing that the faded blue eyes were filled with tears, jumped up impulsively to put an arm about his shoulders. "I am thinking only of you, Father," he said, and added softly, "In the eyes of the world, a good soldier dies with his sword in his hand."

"I know it," the general answered. "But I must, nevertheless, agree with Tytler . . . although with great grief and reluctance. God knows I would gladly lay down my life to prevent another Cawnpore, Harry my dear boy. But from a military viewpoint, the loss of this Force would be a greater calamity, at this time of grave crisis, than the enforced surrender of the Lucknow garrison. Colonel Inglis may yet hold out and I pray that he will." He rose wearily to his feet. "We retire to Mungalwar, gentlemen. Issue the necessary orders, if you please. Oh, Captain Barrow—a moment, if you please."

"Sir?" Barrow halted expectantly.

"I received a message from General Neill which will be of interest to Colonel Sheridan of your Volunteers," Havelock told him. "I should have passed it on before this but my mind"—he smiled apologetically—"has been somewhat over-exercised of late. Inform Sheridan, would you, that four more of the Cawnpore garrison have survived and have been sent in safely by the friendly rajah who gave them shelter, following their escape. I have a note of their names somewhere and—"

"They're here, sir," Harry Havelock supplied. He read from the note. "Lieutenants Mowbray Thomson and Henry Delafosse of the 53rd Native Infantry, Gunner Sullivan of the Bengal Artillery, and Private James Murphy of Her Majesty's 84th."

"Thank you," Barrow acknowledged. "Sheridan will be overjoyed, I know." He saluted and went in search of Alex, who received the news with a heartfelt, "Oh, praise be to God! They were in Eddie Vibart's boat with me and . . . where were they found, Lou, do you know?"

Barrow shook his head. "I only know that they were given shelter by a friendly rajah. But they're in Cawnpore now and you may be seeing them before long." He sighed and glanced at Charles Palliser, who was standing nearby, consuming the last of his midday meal. "We're going back to Mungalwar." Palliser swore disgustedly but the Volunteer's commander cut him short. "The alternative would be our annihilation, Charlie, in the carefully considered opinion of the general and his staff, with which, having weighed up our chances, I fully concur." He repeated some of the points which had been made and then said crisply, "Baggage guard, gentlemen, if you will be so good. We shall be moving in half an hour."

Back, once more, at Mungalwar, General Havelock found much to cause him concern. An urgent note from Neill warned him that a trusted Sikh spy had brought word that a concentration of rebel troops, numbering at least 4,000 with five guns and believed to be commanded by the Nana, had assembled at Bithur and posed a threat to Cawnpore. Neill wrote:

> I cannot stand this. They will enter the town and our communications are gone and if I am not supported, I can only hold out here. I can do nothing beyond our entrenchments—all the country between this and Allahabad will be up; our powder and ammunition on the way up by steamer may well fall into the hands of the enemy, and we will be in a bad way.

In a strange reversal of his initially critical attitude, he begged Havelock to cross back to Cawnpore with his entire force and, in his next letter, he reported that the strong, highly trained, and well-equipped Gwalior Contingent had mutinied against their ruler, Sindhia, and were moving toward the Jumna River. The Maharajah had hitherto kept them in check but now, Havelock was only too well aware, they could, depending on circumstances, pose a grave additional threat to Cawnpore, instead of marching on Agra, which had apparently been their initial intention.

A further appeal for aid from Lucknow, as well as one from Agra, reached him but the general decided that he must first deal with the immediate threat to Cawnpore. Work had already been started on repairs to the bridge of boats by his engineers and now he ordered that these must be completed with all possible speed. By 12th August, Captain Crommelin, who had toiled heroically at the difficult task, reported the bridge restored, and the sick and wounded, together with all stores and spare ammunition, were sent across the river to Cawnpore that night. Learning, however, from his spies that a considerable force of rebels was advancing from Busseratgunj in the hope of impeding his crossing, Havelock told his son Harry, with a smile, "I think we must take the initiative and strike a blow against them, rather than await their attack on our rear, don't you? Perhaps, if we can strike them hard enough, it will suffice to keep them immobile during our withdrawal."

The column of gaunt and war-weary men advanced, for the third time, to Unao, where they bivouacked for the night, the sick carriages and *dhoolies* swiftly filling with cholera victims. In spite of this, the advance was continued next morning and, a mile and a half in front of the earlier battlefield, the enemy were discovered in great strength close to a village known as Boorkiya, which straddled the Lucknow road.

Original reports had put their number at about 4,000, but when Tytler and Barrow returned after reconnoitering the position, it was with the unwelcome news that armed peasants and a body of Oudh horse had almost doubled this number. The enemy's right rested on the village, their left on a ridge 400 yards distant. Both flanks were defended by artillery and a ditch, with a breast-high mud wall lined with infantry connecting the two batteries; the cavalry were massed on their left flank. Along their front lay what appeared to be a level expanse of dry, grassy land but this, Tytler warned, was almost certainly swamp,

Havelock studied the position through his glass and then sent the 78th and the Fusiliers, with four horsed guns, off to the right, to attack the left of the rebels' lines. The heavy guns he directed to the left, supported by the 84th, with orders to turn their right flank and drive them from the village. Keeping his remaining troops and guns in the centre, he ordered the howitzers to open fire with shell.

Due to the ravages of cholera and dysentery, the Volunteer Cavalry had paraded that morning barely forty strong, and Alex was escorting the horsed battery, under Lieutenant Smithett, with a scant twenty men—the majority the now-seasoned cavalrymen of his original troop. Smithett, eager to bring his guns into action, forged ahead of his supporting infantry and, as he unlimbered to the right of the swamp, the rebel nine-pounders opened a furious fire on him from their entrenched and elevated position on the ridge. Smithett returned their fire but could make little impression on the well-protected and well-served enemy guns. Half his gunners were killed or wounded and he had lost four of his horses before, at Alex's urgent instigation, he limbered up and took ground to the right.

As Smithett was leading his depleted battery to their new position, the enemy gunners turned their attention to the advancing Highlanders and Smithett was out of their line of fire. But he was moving slowly, and the rebel cavalry, observing his predicament, started to move forward with the obvious intention of cutting him off from his support and seizing or disabling his guns before he could again bring them into action. There were about seven or eight hundred of them, all Oudh irregulars and well mounted; with the sun glinting on their *tulwars* and lance-tips, they looked formidable enough, but they were coming cautiously and at a trot, with a wary eye on the line of advancing High-landers. Watching them, Alex decided that a charge by his own men—if carried through resolutely and in close formation— might disperse them long enough for Smithett to gain his objective and again unlimber his guns.

His tactic succeeded better, even, than he had dared to hope. His small troop, bunched round him in a single line and with the advantage of the downhill slope, charged into the loosely packed right flank of the Oudh horsemen who, anticipating no opposition and with the sun in their eyes, reeled back, startled, from the unexpected assault. They were given no time to determine how few their attackers were. Alex, thankful now for the hours of patient training which had welded his recruits into a disciplined body, wheeled and halted them and then, his knotted reins loose on his horse's neck and his sabre in his left hand, spurred back into the mêlée to hack his way through, Mahoney and Cullmane on either side of him, the rest close on their flying heels, yelling like banshees.

As they emerged, miraculously still twenty strong but with blown horses and aching arms, he saw that Smithett's guns were in position and, leading his troop off at an angle to leave them a clear field of fire, he left the final rout of the Oudh cavalry to the gunners. Aided by a handful of volunteers from the Fusiliers, Smithett's men completed it.

Minutes later, with a cheer that woke echoes even above the roar of the guns, the Highlanders hurled themselves onto the ridge and, with the Blue Caps challenging them for the honour, entered the battery at its summit without firing a shot. They bayoneted the gunners and then, still cheering, turned two of the 9-pounders they had captured onto the rebel infantry below. It was impossible to see, through the smoke, how the 84th had fared but, as the Highlanders and the Fusiliers drove on toward Busseratgunj, a dense mass of armed peasants and sepoys came pouring out of the village in headlong retreat. A shower of grape from the captured guns sped them on their way and, from the centre of the British line, the Sikhs and the 64th joined the pursuit.

The general was delighted. His centre and his heavy guns had been impeded by the swamp but, once again, his small "force of heroes" had defeated a vastly superior enemy for the loss of thirty-five killed and wounded. The pursuit was halted, as before, at the end of the Busseratgunj causeway and, as the tired infantrymen tramped back toward Mungalwar, followed by the laden sick carts and *dhoolies,* he counted the cost and found it, if high, at least in his favour. The rebels had lost over 300 killed and six guns captured, and this, their third defeat in less than three weeks, had left them beaten and cowed. He could now, Havelock thought, safely cross back to Cawnpore and deal with the Nana's force at Bithur. Since entering Oudh, the British column had suffered a total of 335 killed, wounded, and sick, of whom by far the greater number were cholera victims.

After resting his men for a day at Mungalwar, Havelock sent his heavy guns across the newly repaired bridge of boats and then, with the Volunteer Cavalry and the Fusiliers acting as rear guard, the whole force—now numbering 750 Europeans and 250 Sikhs —returned to Cawnpore on Friday, 14th August, blowing up the Oudh end of the bridge behind them. They were worn out by the constant fighting, suffering from the ill effects of exposure, and many—who, until then, had held out—collapsed with cholera, against the ravages of which they now had little resistance.

Soon after Havelock's arrival in camp, James Neill waited on him and reluctantly gave him a letter he had received from the Commander-in-Chief, instructing him to discuss the feasibility of an immediate advance on Lucknow. The tone of the letter was proof of the disloyalty with which he had communicated his views on the advance during his Chief's absence, and Havelock told him, with some relish, "If his Excellency requires it absolutely —or if *you* now think it practicable, General Neill—I will order my bridges over the islands in the Ganges to be restored and march immediately. But of course, if I do so, you will have to deal with the insurgents at Bithur with the resources at your com- mand—I could give you no assistance."

Describing this interview a little later to his son Harry, the general said, permitting himself a wry little smile, "He replied that he conceived the attempt without reinforcements could only terminate in disaster, without the possibility of relieving the garrison, which would be injurious to our interests in this part of India. I, as might be expected, my dear Harry, concurred in this opinion. He then asked me when I intended to march on Bithur."

"And what did you tell him, sir?" Harry enquired.

His father sighed. "Since the medical experts had just informed me that, at the present rate of deaths from cholera, the whole force will have disappeared in six weeks . . . I said we would march at first light on Sunday."

"Neill has done you irreparable harm," Harry said. He swore softly and then, meeting the general's reproachful gaze, apologised. "Forgive me, Father . . . for many things. You were right not to go on from Busseratgunj. If we had gone, Cawnpore would have gone too—and probably Allahabad after it. But if the people at Lucknow perish before we can relieve them, the guilt of their blood will not be on *your* head. It will be on the heads of those who, for the mere wish to be able to say that three regiments of the Bengal Army had remained staunch, refused all advice to disarm them at Dinapore and cut the means of relieving them from under our feet! If only they would send us those two European regiments they insist on retaining there, we could still save Lucknow."

"Pray God they will be sent before it is too late," Havelock answered gravely. "Neill tells me that they *may* be here early next month, and Olpherts is on his way from Allahabad. But in the absence of any definite word, I must write again to Colonel Inglis."

"You are worn out, sir. Let me write for you," Harry offered, but his father shook his head. "This is a letter I must write myself, my dear boy . . . though I confess it breaks my heart to write it.

But Inglis hints that his native force is losing confidence—he fears they may leave him and says that he cannot man his defences without them—and *I* fear that, like poor Wheeler, he may endeavour to treat with the enemy. He must not do that, Harry . . . before heaven, there must not be a second Cawnpore!"

Harry did not argue. He brought pen and paper and the general sat down at his camp-table. His hand shaking visibly, he wrote:

> I have your letter, and I can only say do not negotiate but rather perish sword in hand. Reinforcements may reach me in from twenty to twenty-five days. As soon as they do I will prepare everything for a march on Lucknow.

He let his head fall onto his outstretched hands when the brief missive was written, praying silently, and then, from sheer exhaustion, fell asleep.

His A.D.C., William Hargood, entering a few minutes later to inform him that Ungud had not yet returned from his last perilous mission to Lucknow, gave his message, instead, to Harry. He added grimly, "And rumour in camp has it that Archdale Wilson is likely to abandon the siege of Delhi—should not the general be told?"

"Let him sleep, Willie. God knows he has enough to bear already." Gently Harry Havelock pulled a cloak about his father's thin, bowed shoulders. Pausing to read the letter to Colonel Inglis, which—as in all communications with Lucknow—was written partly in Greek characters, he expelled his breath in a long-drawn sigh. "This can't go with anyone but Ungud, obviously. I'll take charge of it until our courier returns."

"*If* he returns," Hargood qualified.

"You might say that of any of us," Harry retorted. "For God's sake, is there no good news?"

"You may consider it good news, Harry, when I tell you that the police *thanadar* chosen by General Neill to hold office at Bithur—one Aitwurya ..." Hargood was smiling—"returned precipitately therefrom after a raid by Oudh irregulars on his *thana* and was denounced by the relative of a man he had mistreated. His house was searched and large quantities of European clothing—ladies' clothing—and jewels were found, all taken from the poor captives in the Bibigarh. Aitwurya, under questioning, confessed to have taken a leading part in the massacre and—" he paused.

"Well?" Harry prompted, his mouth a tight, hard line.

"Neill had him flogged, taken to the Bibigarh for some revolting form of retribution he's devised, and then hanged him from a gallows set up in the courtyard."

"The Mills of God grind slowly," Harry quoted. "But they grind exceeding small ... Let us hope, Willie my friend, that time is also running out for the Nana. We march on Bithur at first light on Sunday morning, the dear old Governor told me, and if the reports are true and the Nana *is* there ..." his tired, unshaven face relaxed in a smile which echoed Hargood's. "I'd give my right arm to take *him* prisoner!"

"You'd be trampled down in the rush," Hargood told him. "Our Colonel Sheridan has now been joined by four more of General Wheeler's garrison, and Sheridan has already given his right arm. I think you will have to allow him the prior claim."

"Gladly," Harry Havelock conceded. "Very gladly, Willie. I'd allow it to any one of them."

CHAPTER SIX

➳➳➳ • ⋲⋲⋲

IN MOWBRAY THOMSON'S tent, pitched on the *glacis* of the new entrenchment overlooking the river, Alex sat with the two men he had never expected to see again. It was, for all three of them, a poignant moment and, after the first eager exchange of questions and explanations, they lapsed suddenly into silence, still not quite able to believe that it was happening and hesitating to put their emotions into words.

"You're looking tired, Alex," Mowbray Thomson said at last, breaking the silence when he had replenished their glasses. "It's been an exhausting fourteen days in Oudh, by all accounts."

"Exhausting and desperately frustrating," Alex admitted. "I have a better understanding now of what Neill was up against, when he was endeavouring to relieve us with no transport and only a single regiment. We faced very similar problems, but the one single factor that has defeated General Havelock's attempt to relieve Lucknow has been an enemy we can't fight—cholera. Our force was decimated by it."

"It's bad in camp," Henry Delafosse said grimly. "And I don't know of a more ghastly way for a fighting man to meet his end. We were fortunate in that respect, at least, in poor old Wheeler's entrenchment. Cholera was the one thing we didn't have to fight against." He sighed. "The camp is one vast hospital and the surgeons are at their wits' end. I visited Jim Sullivan—Gunner Sullivan—earlier this evening. The poor chap got several musket balls in him when we were swimming downriver. Rajah Drigbiji

Singh did all he possibly could for us whilst we were under his protection but, of course, there's no hospital at Moorar Mhow, so there wasn't much his native doctor could do for Jim Sullivan. Dr. Irvine took his right leg off this afternoon—above the knee. He came through the amputation fairly well, but Irvine doesn't hold out much hope for him."

Remembering the grey-haired veteran gunner, who had shared more than one vigil with him in Vibart's overloaded boat, Alex was conscious of a pang. To have survived the siege of the Cawnpore garrison, the three-day-long ordeal in the boat, and the six-mile swim to Drigbiji Singh's territory and then to die in hospital was tragic. "How about the Irish lad, Murphy of the 84th?" he asked.

Mowbray Thomson's face—looking absurdly boyish without the red-gold beard which had sprouted during the siege—was lit by a smile of singular warmth. "He's a fine lad, that . . . and his regiment gave him a hero's welcome, by all accounts. I should imagine he's gloriously drunk by this time, in spite of Garrison Orders!"

"Will he be sent back to his regiment, Tommy?"

"He volunteered to go back. But General Neill took him into his garrison force." Thomson shrugged. "He's a very odd sort of fellow, the brigadier-general. There's nothing he won't do for the men under his command and his Blue Caps—officers and men— simply worship him. But . . . he offered me an appointment as assistant-provost-marshal, under Herbert Bruce."

Alex flashed him a quick, searching glance, puzzled by his tone. "Have you accepted it?"

Mowbray Thomson refilled their glasses. "Frankly, Alex, I'm in two minds as to whether I should. I like Bruce and the civil magistrate, Sherer, very much indeed, and they're the ones I'd be working with but . . ." he hesitated. "We heard rumours, even in Moorar Mhow, about General Neill's reprisals in Allahabad and Benares and in the country districts. We heard of whole villages being burnt to the ground, frequently with the inhabitants inside them. We heard of innocent peasants being strung up from trees along the Trunk Road, having first been defiled, and we . . . well, we thought our informants were exaggerating and we took the stories with a pinch of salt, didn't we, Henry?"

Henry Delafosse inclined his shaven fair head. "You can't take those stories with a pinch of salt here, Alex. They weren't exaggerated. General Neill has embarked on a truly savage campaign of vengeance—every day he flogs and hangs any man who is even remotely suspected of complicity in the mutiny or of having supported the Nana's usurpation. Perhaps you've heard of how he compels both Muslims and Hindus to break caste before he executes them?"

"I witnessed two examples of that," Alex confessed. "Before I crossed into Oudh."

"And do you hold with it?" Thomson asked.

"No, very decidedly not . . . which appeared to surprise the general. He took it for granted that, as a survivor of poor old General Wheeler's garrison, I would be thirsting for revenge." Alex frowned. "I want to see retribution against the Nana and Azimullah and the rest of the leaders who betrayed the surrender terms and ordered—or connived at—the massacre. I shouldn't be human if I did not . . . They robbed me of all I held dear, my wife, my child, my friends, my comrades in arms. They defeated us with broken promises and by treachery, they . . ." He gulped down the contents of his glass and Thomson rose, without being asked, to refill it. "I want to see mutinous sepoys punished, but simply and solely by the forfeit of their lives, Tommy. Neill's reign of terror, far from stemming the revolt, is causing the Oudh *zamindars* to rise against us. Thousands of them are supporting the rebels—we saw them at Unao and Busseratgunj."

"The rumours were having that effect in the area we were in," Delafosse said. "So much so that, before he would let us leave, Drigbiji Singh insisted on our writing a letter for him to keep, so that he could prove he had helped and sheltered us, in case Neill Sahib's soldiers came to Moorar Mhow." He spread his hands helplessly. "If a genuine friend and loyal subject is afraid, small wonder the Oudh *zamindars*—who have no reason to love us-feel they've nothing to lose by throwing in their lot with the rebels. Alex . . . tell me, General Havelock's supposed to be a devout Christian, isn't he? Does he agree with what Neill is doing?"

"He most certainly does not," Alex asserted with conviction. "An Order of the Day was issued when we first entered Cawn-pore, in which General Havelock clearly stated that—and I quote—'whilst mutineers, civilian traitors, and other miscreants will be brought to swift and merciless justice, barbarism is *not* to be met with barbarism.' It was a very necessary Order, particu-larly after what had been done in the Bibigarh became known to our troops. But I assure you, it was strictly adhered to, so long as General Havelock was in command here." He quoted the rest of the Order and saw relief reflected in both the anxious young faces opposite him.

"Then do you suppose he'll put an end to General Neill's wholesale executions?" Mowbray Thomson asked. "If I could be sure of that, I'd jump at the assistant-provost-marshal's job."

"I'm quite certain he will, Tommy," Alex assured him. "There's been a good deal of friction between them—mostly caused by Neill—and when the general learns what's been going on in his absence, he'll be horrified, because his orders were most explicit and Neill has deliberately flouted them. Havelock's not the man to stand for that."

"Good. Then I shall contact Herbert Bruce tomorrow." Thomson smiled. "I'm sickened by all this fighting and killing. I know it has to be done but, for a while at least, I'd like to forget I'm a soldier and try, instead, to construct something out of the ruins this revolt has left in its wake. I . . ." He reddened. "I'm humbled, I suppose, by the miracle of my own survival and by Drigbiji Singh's loyalty and kindness. I often ask myself why, Alex. I mean, why did God save *us,* out of the whole garrison? When we made our last sally from Eddie Vibart's boat, we thought it would be our last . . . None of us expected to live, did we? Yet four of us did—five, if poor Sullivan pulls through. When we staggered ashore it was because we couldn't swim any farther and we expected the villagers who were waiting for us to cut us to pieces . . . but instead they fed and helped us and then took us to Drigbiji Singh for protection."

"And he refused several demands from the Nana to hand you over, I believe," Alex said.

Thomson nodded. "Yes, he did. I've put in an official request that he should be rewarded, but that won't pay our debt to him." He sighed. "And still I ask myself why God chose *us* to live on, when there were so many others more deserving. John Moore, for example, or Georgie Ashe or Vibart . . . even the poor old general. Your wife, Alex, who spent herself caring for the sick and wounded, Amelia Wheeler, Caroline Moore . . . dear heaven, any of them had a better claim to life than I have. And as for those poor souls who perished in the Bibigarh . . ." He shuddered. "I have nightmares about them."

"Yes," Alex confessed. "So do I." He looked at Delafosse. "What about you, Henry—have you had enough fighting?"

"No, not yet." Henry Delafosse spoke gravely, without bravado. "Like you, my dear Alex, I shall soldier on. It's all I know how to do and, I must admit, I have a deep and bitter longing to hit back at the Pandies. But in battle, on more even terms than they permitted us in that ghastly entrenchment on the plain. Everyone's now saying it was indefensible, and it *was*." The other two nodded in agreement and Delafosse went on, "I want, if it's humanly possible, to save the poor people in Lucknow from the fate our people suffered. My conscience plagues me, as Tommy's does, because they're dead and I'm alive but, for as long as God sees fit to spare me, I'll fight their killers. Do you remember what Eddie Vibart said in the boat, when we were just about at the end of our tether? 'Some of us must live,' he said. 'Whatever it costs. Our betrayal *has* to be avenged.' He was right . . . and our archbetrayer, the Nana, is said to be at Bithur, so I'm joining the column, Alex."

"We'd welcome you in the Volunteer Cavalry," Alex offered. "Eddie Vibart's young brother is with us, by the way—Tom. As might be expected, he's a splendid youngster."

"Thanks, but no. I'm a shocking horseman. And I've found myself a niche." Delafosse laughed, with something of his old spirit. "Jack Olpherts has just arrived in camp, with the other half of his battery. He was at the hospital, visiting Francis Maude—who was in, having treatment for a crushed foot—and when I mentioned that I'd been one of poor old General Wheeler's gunners, Olpherts said he could find employment for an experienced officer. So I shall be attached to the Bengal Artillery for the duration of this campaign and I'm glad. It would have been a pity to waste all the knowledge of gunnery I acquired during the siege."

"It would indeed," Alex agreed. He answered Thomson's questions concerning Tom Vibart and added, "We march, or so I'm told, for Bithur on Sunday morning . . . and your guns will probably see more action, Henry, than we shall in the cavalry. The Nana is said to have four to five thousand troops, mainly regulars, and to be strongly entrenched, with five guns."

"So long as he is commanding in person," Henry Delafosse said, his blue eyes bright. "I shall be satisfied. He is the one man I would hand over, without a qualm, to General Neill. I would even have him blown from the muzzle of a 9-pounder, which, God knows, is a messy and revolting business as practiced here on some of the captured native officers! But if the Nana were to be condemned . . . quite honestly, I believe I'd volunteer to be his executioner. It's a Mahratta punishment, anyway, isn't it, Alex?"

"Yes . . . and one reserved, usually, for those who betray their salt."

"Then it would be no less than justice for the self-styled Peishwa of the Mahrattas!" Delafosse claimed jubilantly. "God, I pray he'll fall into our hands on Sunday!"

"There was a very strong rumour going about," Alex said thoughtfully, "when we reentered the city a month ago, that he had drowned himself in the river. But—"

"He appears to be very much alive now," Mowbray Thomson put in. "Neill's spies insist they have seen him several times. So let us drink to his final demise, shall we?" He opened a fresh bottle of champagne and grinned when Alex accused him of being too generous a host. "Nonsense, my dear fellow—this is an occasion! Like the Nana, we three have returned from the dead. And in any case. I received a draft for my back pay and a gift of six bottles of this stuff from General Neill, of all people. He says he keeps himself alive on it and recommends it against the cholera, dysentery, and a host of other ills. So charge your glasses, my very dear friends, with the Cawnpore elixir." He poured lavish measures of the bubbling liquid into each of their glasses and then raised his own. "I give you a toast . . . success to our arms at Bithur and eternal damnation to the Nana and all who conspired with him against us!"

They drank the toast, and Alex, who had touched no liquor except watered-down rum or porter during the campaign in Oudh, set down his glass and got to his feet. "I'm loth to break up our reunion while the night is still young," he said regretfully. "But my head's not proof against your hospitality, Tommy. I'm woefully out of practice and there are very strict orders concerning the need for sobriety in Havelock's Column, in case you haven't heard. The men are not permitted to drink more than their daily ration and, although the officers are not so restricted, they *are* required to set an example."

"Havelock's Saints, eh?" Thomson suggested. "Don't tell me you've joined them?"

"Well, one can hardly order a man fifty lashes for an offence one commits oneself," Alex defended. "And the proof of the effectiveness of the General's ban on drunkenness is the fact that no excesses have been committed by the men under his command since the column left Allahabad."

"Touché, Alex!" Thomson acknowledged. "Henry and I will sign the pledge tomorrow. We're no more accustomed to strong drink than you are, if the truth be known. We've existed on a liquid diet of buffalo milk and sherbert during our stay at Moorar Mhow; although we were offered *bhang* to smoke more than once, we didn't try it. It kept poor Sullivan alive and reasonably free from pain, so we gave him our share, poor devil." He picked up the champagne bottle and held it poised above Alex's empty glass. "One more toast and then we'll call it a night, Colonel sir, I promise you. But this toast we have to drink, don't we, Henry?"

"We do indeed," Henry Delafosse confirmed solemnly. They rose and lifted their glasses. "To you, sir," Thomson offered. "And to the award of the Victoria Cross you so richly deserve. You—"

"Victoria Cross?" Alex stared at them in dismay. "But how did you know . . . oh, for heaven's sake, you can't drink to that! I'm not getting it, I—"

"Henry Simpson told us you were!" Delafosse exclaimed. "He knows you or so he said—he was with the Irregular Cavalry and then with your Volunteers and now he's on Neill's staff. We thought he'd know, if anyone did. But—"

"But there *was* a rumour," Thomson put in. "A rumour that General Havelock intended to recommend you for a Cross but that General Neill somehow scotched the notion. We pooh-poohed it, of course. I mean, there's no truth in it, is there, Alex?"

"There's a certain amount" Alex admitted. He was suddenly quite sober, all the carefree ebullience induced by half a dozen glasses of champagne evaporating, like the tiny, pricked bubbles on the surface of the last, and he set it down untasted. "It's a long story and my weary bones are crying out for the first comfortable night's sleep I've had since crossing into Oudh. So, if you'll forgive me, I'll postpone the telling of it to a more appropriate moment. Suffice it now to say that I myself requested that no recommendation should be made on my behalf—if, indeed, it was ever General Havelock's intention to put my name forward. It may not have been—I only had General Neill's word for it and he—"

"Yes, but for God's sake, Alex!" Delafosse broke in indignantly. "They must give a Cross for Cawnpore, surely, and if they do, we'd all of us like to see you get it."

Alex shook his head. "Let's leave the matter for the time being, shall we? in no circumstances is my name going forward, but if a Cross it given for Cawnpore, it should go to one of you, and I shall do all in my power to see that it does. There may not be one given, you understand, but—"

"May not be one given?" Mowbray Thomson echoed in surprise. "I confess I don't understand, Alex—why not?"

"When have you known the Horse Guards or the Indian Government to acclaim a military disaster or reward defeat?" Alex countered wryly. "Our siege was a disaster. Whatever the reasons or the excuses—and we can offer a great many—we were compelled to surrender and British prestige has suffered an enormous setback in consequence. That is the concerted view of everyone who took no part in it. You should hear them when they go to inspect our entrenchment—Neill in particular."

"I have heard them. They look at the crumbling perimeter and are astounded that we held out as long as we did. So am I, when I look back."

"But we were defeated, Tommy—not by the enemy but because our preparations were inadequate. Medals and honours are for the victorious, not for the defeated. And we're the only ones left of the Cawnpore garrison." Alex shrugged. "I don't think, somehow, that the Indian Government will want to be reminded of us. By the same token, I don't expect General Havelock to win any honours for his recent heroic endeavours in Oudh, because he has failed to relieve Lucknow ... but we shall see. If you want an example of courage of the highest order, you can find it in his decision *not* to go on with a totally inadequate force."

"You're not being cynical, are you?" Delafosse questioned uncertainly.

Alex shook his head. "No. Disillusioned, perhaps, because I'm facing facts as they've been revealed to me since I joined the Movable Column—but not cynical." How, he wondered, could he explain to them, how make them understand? "Listen," he bade them. "We blamed Neill, did we not, for his failure to come to our aid? But he never had a chance, I know that now . . . less chance even than Havelock has been given to bring aid to Lucknow. Each will be blamed for his failure to achieve the impossible—just as we've been—but the real blame lies at the door of those who deprived India of British troops and of the means to transport such as we have to the places where they are needed."

"That's true," Thomson affirmed. "My God, yes, that's true! If we'd had the one British regiment we were promised, we could have held Cawnpore."

"And with the two *he's* been promised but hasn't yet received, General Havelock could relieve Lucknow," Alex said. "That's been the tragic story of this mutiny—Government wasn't prepared for it and local commanders took no heed of warnings, with the honourable exception of Sir Henry Lawrence, God rest his brave soul! He *did* make what preparations were possible for a siege and, because of that, I dare to hope that the Lucknow garrison may hold out until we can reach them . . . if no more promises are broken concerning reinforcements." He smiled into their two bewildered young faces and clasped each of their hands in turn. "Don't despair, my boys! If we succeed in taking the Nana on Sunday, all the failures will be forgotten—even ours. We shall be showered with decorations! Thanks for the champagne, Tommy . . . and goodnight, both of you. I cannot tell you how much it means to me to be with you again."

"It means a great deal to us, Alex," Mowbray Thomson returned warmly.

They stood in front of the tent flap, watching him mount his horse, their faces still a trifle bewildered, and Alex felt his throat tighten as he turned to take his leave of them. They had gone through so much together, he thought, that for as long as they lived there would be a bond between them . . . and only death would break it. They appeared, standing there in their makeshift cotton uniforms, two ordinary, undistinguished young officers, whose thin, newly shaven faces revealed little of what they had endured, little of the heroism both had shown throughout their long ordeal, or of the courage and resourcefulness it had taken for them to survive. He wished, passionately and despairingly, that he could obtain for them the reward each had earned, not once but a hundred times when their crumbling entrenchment had been besieged, and knew, with the sharpness of disillusion, that it was unlikely that he would succeed. He had told them the truth and, perhaps, prepared them for what they might expect but . . . it had hurt him to have to do it. He smothered a sigh and kicked his tired horse into a canter. As senior surviving officer of the Cawnpore garrison, he was entitled to submit a recommendation on behalf of his two juniors, and tomorrow, after he had slept, he would do so.

And the following day, God willing, would see the Nana's defeat at Bithur . . . .

At first light on Sunday, 16th August, the 78th's five pipers played the column of gaunt, war-weary men on their way through the city to the Bithur road. The total force that could be raised was now under a thousand, of whom a bare 750 were Europeans, but the Highlanders marched with heads held high, singing the words of their Regimental March, as the pipes skirled it proudly from the front of the column.

Pibroch o' Donuil Dhu! Pibroch o' Donuil!
Wake thy wild voice anew—summon Clan Connel!

Leave the deer, leave the steer, leave nets and barges,
Come with your fighting gear, broadswords and targes!

General Havelock watched them, tears in his eyes. They were, he knew, about to face the strongest force the enemy had yet gathered to oppose them. His spies had been explicit; the Nana was defending his town and Palace of Bithur with 4,000 picked troops, all of them regulars—the 31st and 42nd regiments of Native Infantry from Saugor; the 17th from Fyzabad; and portions of the 34th, disbanded at Barrackpore the previous March. With them were portions of three regular cavalry regiments, including the 2nd Light Cavalry, a battery of five guns, and a horde of Mahratta irregulars.

As the day advanced, the sun rose and men fell out, struck down by sunstroke and cholera; the singing ceased and the column marched in grim silence, rifles shouldered and bearded faces grey with dust. After an eleven-mile march, a halt was called and the general himself rode forward, with Colonel Tytler and an escort of Volunteer Cavalry, to reconnoitre the position. In front lay a wide plain, dotted with villages and dense plantations of sugar cane, through which flowed a tributary of the Ganges, too flooded to be fordable by troops of any arm. The only access to the town, which lay behind it, was by a narrow stone bridge, defended by a breastwork and armed with artillery. The road ran across the plain to the bridge, and the rebel troops could be glimpsed behind the loopholed walls of villages and moving amongst the trees on either side of it, whilst others were occupying entrenched enclosures recently constructed to cover the approaches to the bridge.

As Havelock studied the Nana's depositions, his glass to his eye, a strong body of native cavalry emerged from the trees to his right; calmly moving across to the opposite side of the road, the general called for the leading guns of his artillery to open fire on them. The horsemen swiftly dispersed and galloped out of range, and two of the enemy guns—whose position had, until then, been masked by the vegetation by which they were surrounded—returned the fire. Smiling as he trotted back to the column, Havelock directed Captain Olpherts to silence them and, whilst this was being done, he deployed his column to right and left of the road.

Alex, riding as escort to Maude's battery, found himself still on the road as the advance was ordered. To the right, the 78th and the Fusiliers made a rush to attack a village, from which a heavy fire of musketry was impeding the advance; they made short and bloody work of it and, as the defenders were driven out at the point of the British bayonets, Francis Maude unlimbered his heavy guns and opened fire on the main entrenchment at a range of 1,000 yards. To the left, Olpherts' horsed battery moved gallantly forward, supported by the Sikhs and the 64th and the 84th, meeting with a punishing fire from rebel troops concealed amongst the trees. They were soon lost to sight in the smoke of battle but, as Francis Maude again limbered up to bring his guns to within canister range of their objective, Alex glimpsed one of Olpherts' teams dashing from the trees a long way ahead of the supporting infantry and thought he recognised Henry Delafosse leading them. They were halted by one of the general's A.D.C.s, but, undeterred by this, unlimbered without losing a yard of ground and poured a heavy infilading fire into the redoubt which barred their path to the bridge.

On the right, the Fusiliers and the 78th kept pace with Maude's bullock-drawn guns; the rebels, waiting behind their breastwork, held their fire until the advancing line was five hundred yards from them and then, displaying an unusual measure of disciplined courage, poured volley after volley into the British ranks. Major Stephenson, commanding the Fusiliers, led both regiments into a field of sugar cane, and emerging from this to the left of the breastwork, they stormed and entered it. Hand-to-hand fighting ensued, of which the onlookers could see little, and then, to the cheers of his men, the 78th's adjutant, Lieutenant Macpherson, mounted the parapet and waved his sword high above his head to signify that they had taken the position.

The rebels were retreating across the bridge into the town now, and as Lousada Barrow cantered up to join him, Alex begged, in a fever of impatience, "Can't you get the general's permission for us to pursue them? If the Nana is here, he can't be allowed to escape—he must not!"

"I'm sorry, Alex," Barrow answered with bitterness. "A pursuit has been ordered, but by the infantry. We're to cover the bridge, in case any of them break back or the cavalry threaten our rear."

The Highlanders and the Fusiliers, who had borne the brunt of the attack, flung themselves down exhausted in such shade as they could find, and Alex watched, fuming, as the bridge and the road beyond it filled with fleeing mutineers. They were so close that he could distinguish their uniforms; he saw a company of the 42nd Native Infantry, carrying their Colours, go running across the bridge without a shot being fired after them until Lieutenant Crump galloped up with a 9-pounder and, at his behest, sprayed their retreating backs with grape. The rebel cavalry were nowhere to be seen—which, he reminded himself wryly, was typical of the Second, who had not distinguished themselves during the siege, and he wondered whether *Subedar* Teeka Singh was still commanding them.

"Ah, here are the Sikhs at last!" Barrow exclaimed. "I gather that they and the 84th were held up by a loop in the stream. The general's orders are that they are to lead the pursuit."

Led by Jeremiah Brasyer and supported by the two Queen's regiments which had been with them on the left flank, the Sikhs charged eagerly across the bridge, yelling their battle cry, but, to their evident disappointment, meeting with little opposition. The weary Highlanders and the Blue Caps dragged themselves to their feet and prepared to march in after them and the *dhoolie*-bearers and sick carts went about the melancholy task of picking up wounded. The sun was sinking before the last of these were borne in the wake of the infantry into Bithur, and Alex, once again consumed with impatience, called Tom Vibart over to him.

"Ride in, Tom," he ordered. "Find out what's happening and whether or not the Nana has been taken prisoner. If he hasn't, ask Captain Barrow's permission for me to take a patrol to make a search along the riverbank."

"Right, sir." Vibart hesitated. "Do you—do you suppose he *has* been taken?"

"No, I do not!" Alex answered explosively. "But I'm hoping against hope that he has."

He waited, a prey to conflicting emotions, as the light faded and the sick carts returned, with a burial party, to pick up the dead, and Lieutenant Crump led half a dozen of his gunners into the rebels' entrenchment to spike the 24-pounder they had left behind them there. The artillery officer was cursing as he rode back across the bridge.

"They saved their field guns, blast them to hell! Must have taken them out under cover of the smoke while our fellows were coming up. And the infernal Sikhs kicked up such a shindy that about two hundred Pandies, who were in the Palace garden plundering anything they could lay their hands on, managed to get clean away. They were cavalry, regulars, too, and they'd evidently been camping in the garden—their tents are still there and a few of their horses as well."

"What about the Nana?" Alex demanded.

"Neither sight nor sound of him, alas!" Crump answered regretfully. "The devil take him!"

Young Vibart cantered up a few minutes later to confirm this disappointing news. "Captain Barrow obtained the general's permission for you to make a search of the riverbank, sir, but he told me to tell you that he fears it will be too late. On very reliable information, he said, sir, the Nana fled from the town two or three hours ago."

"Alone, Tom?"

"No, apparently he had some of the women of his *zenana* with him and an escort of several hundred of his own troops. They rode out toward the river, where there were boats waiting, Captain Barrow said."

Alex concealed his chagrin. As Lousada Barrow had feared, his search of the riverbank proved abortive, but some frightened fishermen, at a village half a mile beyond Bithur, confirmed that the Nana, with his escort, had crossed to the Oudh shore some two hours previously. It was useless to prolong the search and, with darkness over taking them, the patrol rode back to Bithur to bivouac for the night in the grounds of the Palace.

Receiving an urgent message from Neill, who had been left to hold Cawnpore with barely a hundred fit men, warning him that a large detachment of rebels was advancing from the south, General Havelock led the column back next morning, leaving the Nana's defences in ruins behind him. He had achieved his ninth victory, for the loss of 49 killed and wounded—against the rebels' 250—but he felt little elation, for the Nana had once again eluded him, and reports coming in from Oudh confirmed his worst fears. His withdrawal across the Ganges had had a disastrous effect; where, initially, local rajahs and *zamindars* had refused to join in the revolt, now, encouraged by his retreat to Cawnpore, virtually all of them had done so, and spies brought reports of rebellion and anarchy throughout the province. This augered ill for Lucknow but, with only 700 of his column still capable of fighting, there was nothing Havelock could do until reinforcements reached him, save wait with what patience he could muster and rest the men who had served him so well.

Returning to his old Headquarters, he found a copy of the official *Calcutta Gazette* awaiting him. It was dated 5th August and contained the announcement that Major-General Sir James Outram, under whom he had served in Persia, had been appointed to command the Dinapore and Cawnpore Divisions, which were to be combined in one command. Havelock read it, at first conscious of bitter disappointment; his independent command was ended and his task of relieving Lucknow would now fall to his new Chief.

"Neill will say that you have been superseded, Father," his son Harry told him indignantly. "And if you have, it will be thanks to the reports he has been sending behind your back to Calcutta. A plague on him for his disloyalty!"

"No," General Havelock said. "This is not intended as supersession, Harry. After all, it is dated the fifth of August, when Government—and, indeed, we ourselves—still had hopes of being able to fight our way to Lucknow. James Outram is the first senior general to become available; I'm still only a brigade commander, don't forget, not of sufficient seniority to be appointed to the combined command. In any case, my dear boy"—his smile, like his tone, held genuine warmth—"James Outram and I are old friends. There is no one in the British or Indian Army under whom I would rather serve . . . and he'll get things done, he'll see to it that we are sent the two Dinapore regiments. And when Sir Colin Campbell arrives to take over from Pat Grant as Commander-in-Chief, we may confidently expect an improvement in the allocation of reinforcements and supplies, to enable us to go forward into Oudh once more. What matters it who is given the honour and glory of saving Lucknow? What is essential is to save the garrison, and Sir James Outram will do it, if anyone can."

"Yes, but—" Harry began, still angry. His father shook his white head in reproof.

"We have no cause for resentment, Harry—even against General Neill, because this is *not* his doing. It might have been kinder, perhaps, had General Grant written to me personally concerning the appointment, but he, too, has been superseded by Sir Colin, so . . ." He spread his small, neat hands in a gesture of resignation. "Our task is now to restore our brave fellows to health and fitness. They must be rested, but their fighting powers must not be impaired by any lapse of discipline and, above all, there must be no drunkenness. The first thing I want to do is tell them how splendidly they have fought, because every man deserves the highest praise a commander can bestow on him."

He seated himself at his table and, when Harry brought him pen and paper, set to work to compose the last Order of the Day he would issue as Force Commander.

The brigadier-general congratulates the troops on the result of their exertions in the combat of yesterday. The enemy was driven, with the loss of 250 killed and wounded, from one of the strongest positions in India, which they obdurately defended. They were the flower of the mutinous soldiery flushed with the successful defection at Saugor and Fyzabad; yet they stood only one short hour against a handful of soldiers of the State, whose ranks had been thinned by sickness and the sword. May the hopes of treachery and rebellion be ever thus blasted! And if conquest can now be achieved under the most trying circumstances, what will be the triumph and retribution of the time when the armies from China, from the Cape, and from England shall sweep through the land?

Soldiers, in that moment your labours, your privations, your sufferings, and your valour will not be forgotten by a grateful country! You will be acknowledged to have been the stay and prop of British India in the time of her severest trial.

Harry read the Order when he had done. "I believe, Father," he observed, "that you may have written your own epitaph. Did you intend to?"

The general smiled. "Yes, my dear boy," he admitted. "I rather think I did . . . and indeed, I think I'm entitled to, don't you?" He did not wait for Harry's answer but, pulling out a fresh sheet of paper, took up his pen again. "Now," he said, his smile fading. "I will make a few notes concerning recreation and the maintenance of discipline. We need a Chaplain at one end of the scale and more cavalry at the other; I want band concerts organised as soon as possible and . . . yes, why not some horse racing, to raise the men's spirits? Can you think of anything else we could do, Harry?"

"We could end the custom of having the Last Post sounded at funerals, sir," Harry suggested practically. "Constant repetition becomes somewhat depressing. And how about General Neill's reprisals at the Bibigarh? From what I can gather they, too, are constantly repeated and they're not doing us much good in the eyes of the native population."

A steely glint lit General Havelock's grey eyes. "Yes, indeed— those are most timely suggestions. Perhaps, dear boy, you would be so good as to send General Neill a request that he present himself here at his earliest convenience?"

"With great pleasure, sir," Harry Havelock acknowledged. "And by the way, my cousin Charley writes that he and Johnson have 40 loyal cavalry sowars, who aided their escape to Benares when the rest of the regiment mutinied. Their behaviour has been exemplary and Charley is most anxious to offer you their services, sir, with his own. Shall I tell him they may join us?"

General Havelock's hesitation was brief. "By all means, Harry. But to be honest, when I mentioned more cavalry I had Europeans in mind . . . men of the calibre of Barrow's Volunteers and those infantrymen Sheridan trained so well. We could give him another forty or fifty, perhaps. On every occasion, I have felt the lack of cavalry. We beat the enemy in the field but are never able to follow up our victories by determined pursuit, and we shall require to do so, if we are to relieve Lucknow. Ask Captain Barrow and Colonel Sheridan to come and see me also, would you please?"

"Sheridan was very frustrated yesterday evening at Bithur," Harry said, "because we failed to lay the Nana by the heels, and I'm damned if I blame him, in the circumstances. We *ought* to have had the fellow."

"We never had a chance of taking him," Havelock said, with asperity. "He took to his heels soon after we fired our first shot. I'm thankful, though, that he went into Oudh. I was very much afraid he might go to Calpi, in the hope of urging the Gwalior

Contingent to launch an attack on us here. So far they appear not to have committed themselves, but if they *do* come here—"

"It will be an end to the Cawnpore Horse Races," Harry finished for him, his tone flippant. "And the band concerts and the rest for our men."

"It might well be an end to Cawnpore," the general returned sharply. He bent again over his papers and Harry went in search of William Hargood, whom he despatched to summon General Neill.

For Alex Sheridan, the respite which followed the return of the column from Bithur came none too soon. A heavy downpour had succeeded Sunday's blazing heat, and man after man had fallen out during the march back, gripped by dysentery or shaking with fever. By the exercise of all the will power he possessed, Alex contrived to sit his horse, head down against the driving rain, but when he dismounted outside the tent he shared with Lousada Barrow, he found it impossible to stand upright.

Barrow and his old bearer, Mohammed Bux, assisted him into the tent and he collapsed on the bed, shivering uncontrollably. "Lou," he urged, through chattering teeth. "I may have the cholera and I don't want to infect you with it, for God's sake! Have me moved, will you please?"

"I'll get one of the surgeons to have a look at you," Barrow evaded. "Just lie where you are, Alex, there's a good fellow. Time enough to worry about me when we find out what's wrong with you. In any case, I'm immune to infection now—I must be, I've been exposed to it so often."

When Dr. Irvine, the Artillery's surgeon, appeared some two hours later, Alex was barely conscious. The doctor's examination was brief.

"It's not cholera . . . yet," he said, his voice harsh with weariness. "But it could turn to that all too easily. My diagnosis is exhaustion, coupled with exposure and malnutrition—and what everyone in this force is suffering from, chronic dysentery. I'd have Colonel Sheridan moved to the Hotel, where we've set up an officers' hospital, but it's overcrowded and his resistance is so low that he would almost certainly catch the infection if I did. He'd be better off here, quite honestly, Captain Barrow, if he can be looked after."

"He can be looked after, Doctor," Barrow assured him.

"Then I'll leave you some medicine for him," Irvine promised. "What he needs is rest, as much nourishing gruel as he can swallow, a dry bed, and no exertion. If you can see that he has these, then he should pull through. I can't guarantee it, though; he's in a pretty weak state. The after-effects of the siege, undoubtedly, have caught up with him." He rose and stood for a moment looking down at his new patient with eyes red-rimmed and swollen from lack of sleep. "I wish to God there were more we could do for poor fellows like this, but damn it, there isn't. We lost another of the survivors of General Wheeler's garrison last night—the gunner, Sullivan. He put up quite a fight, but the shock of having his leg taken off proved too much for him. I'm sorry; he was a brave man." He added some more instructions for Alex's care and then said grimly, studying his scarred face, "What astounds me, Barrow, is that he kept going for so long. Look at that head wound, for heaven's sake! It would have killed most men, but Sheridan's been campaigning with it and it's healed perfectly. You wonder, sometimes—especially in my profession—what makes some men survive and others die."

"Will power?" Lousada Barrow suggested, smiling. "Mind over matter? Or are these just other words for courage?"

"I don't know," Dr. Irvine confessed. "All I can tell you is that the majority of the fellows we're losing from cholera and other sicknesses are the young and seemingly healthy, who arrive with fresh drafts from Calcutta. They go down like ninepins, almost as soon as they get here, and they're dead in a few hours. But the seasoned campaigners, the veterans, pull through . . . and, so far as the cholera is concerned, there are more cases in camp than you had during your fortnight in Oudh, without tents and on reduced rations—taking total numbers into consideration, that's to say."

"The ground between the lines in camp is being fouled," Barrow said. He frowned. "Perhaps if the whole camp were moved to fresh ground it might reduce the spread of infection."

"They tried that in the Crimea," Dr. Irvine answered, "without conspicuous success, but . . . we're requesting that it be considered and we're increasing the number of latrines in the hope that the dysentery cases will use them. Another possibility is that water can be infected and we're trying to ensure that all drinking water, at least, is boiled. Try it with Colonel Sheridan . . . he's going to need a lot of fluids and it just might help."

Alex's fever continued for the next week, and he lay, frequently delirious and sometimes deeply unconscious, on Lousada Barrow's camp bed, cared for by the faithful Mohammed Bux and, when he was free of his duties, by Barrow himself. He was dimly aware of them by his bedside, but it was not until his fever abated and consciousness returned that he began to realise how much he owed to them both. His old bearer's anxious, bearded face was the first he recognised, as the servant knelt beside him, holding a cup to his lips; later, when Barrow came in, tired and soaked to the skin, he, too—before changing his clothes—enquired as to Alex's welfare and opened a bottle of champagne which he instructed Mohammed Bux to give him, drop by drop.

Alex greeted both of them by name the following morning; by evening, as his temperature sank, he was able to raise his head from the pillow and hold a glass for himself. He improved steadily after that but, although his mind was now clear, physically he was as weak as a child and Dr. Irvine, calling to ascertain how he was progressing, found him making his first shaky attempt to walk and ordered him sternly to return to his bed.

"You've made a remarkable recovery, Colonel Sheridan," he said. "But it's taken more out of you than you realise. We must concentrate on building up your strength. If you'll take my advice, you'll stay where you are for at least another week—then we can think about getting you on your feet again."

Alex, perforce, obeyed these instructions, but the days of inactivity began increasingly to irk him and Lousada Barrow, sensing the reason underlying his impatience, told him consolingly that he was missing little of importance.

"You chose a good time to be ill, my dear Alex. Lucknow continues to hold out, thank God, and although we're making preparations, no reinforcements have yet reached us, nor has Sir James Outram. There can be no advance into Oudh until both arrive . . . but he and the new Commander-in-Chief, Sir Colin Campbell, are not letting the grass grow under their feet. General Outram is already on his way to Benares, old Lloyd has been relieved of the Dinapore command, and both the Dinapore Queen's regiments are to be sent to us, almost certainly by mid-September. Also Major Eyre's battery and some loyal native cavalry—40 of them, I'm told, under General Havelock's nephew."

"Sir James Outram—Sir Colin Campbell?" Alex stared at him, mystified. "I thought Outram was in Persia and Sir Colin, surely, is retired and in England?"

Patiently, Barrow explained the circumstances which had dictated both appointments. "Sir Colin Campbell has come overland—he reached Calcutta last week. You should be pleased . . . damn it, he was one of your best Crimean generals, wasn't he? And you know his reputation here."

"I'm more than pleased, Lou," Alex assured him. "But General Outram's appointment to a combined Division is less easy to understand. If he commands Cawnpore as well as Dinapore, what of General Havelock? Surely *he's* not being relieved, is he?"

Again Barrow explained, and added, smiling, "Harry Havelock showed me the telegraph his father received from General Outram this evening. I can't quote it verbatim, but he told Havelock that he was expecting both the 5th Fusiliers and the 90th to reach Benares sometime today and that he intended to push on with them to Allahabad. Then he stated that he would leave 'the honour of relieving Lucknow' to General Havelock and would accompany him in his Civil capacity as Commissioner, serving under him as a volunteer. The dear Old Gentleman was moved to tears, Harry said . . . not that he doesn't deserve it. But Outram is making a considerable sacrifice, you know he's not a rich man and, if Lucknow is relieved, and the twenty-three *lacs* of rupees in the Treasury are saved, the general in actual command of the relieving force stands to gain a fortune in prize money. Apart from that, if Outram were commanding, he could expect a baronetcy, since he's already a K.C.B. But as a civilian volunteer, he'll get little or nothing. Less, even"—Lousada Barrow gave vent to his booming laugh—"than I shall!"

Alex listened in astonishment. He knew General Outram by repute and had met him once at a dinner in Lucknow, when— newly promoted—he had been British Resident in Oudh. He remembered the general as a small, black-bearded man, with a deceptively hesitant manner and an addiction to Manilla che-roots, which he had puffed at continuously throughout the evening. As a young captain, he had served with distinction on Sir John Keane's staff in the Afghan war and, after reaching Cabul with Pollock's avenging army, had then served under Sir Charles Napier in the Scinde campaign. Napier, who was not given to paying fulsome compliments to junior officers, had called him "the Bayard of India"—*chevalier sans peur et sans reproche*—a title which had stuck to him ever since. Although senior to Havelock, whose lack of money and influence had retarded his promotion, Outram was eight or nine years younger, but they had, Alex recalled, served together in the recent Persian campaign and were said to be close friends.

"Who was it that first called him the Bayard of India, Alex?" Barrow asked, as if reading his thoughts. "Sir Charles Napier, wasn't it, at a farewell dinner at Sakhar, when Outram was leav-ing his command?"

Alex nodded. "Yes, if my memory serves me aright, it was. He seems to be living up to it, does he not? How many people in his position would make such an extraordinarily chivalrous ges-ture to a subordinate? I'm not surprised that our little general was moved to tears by that message."

"No, nor am I. Indeed, I . . ." Barrow broke off, as old Mohammed Bux came in with a bottle of champagne and glasses on a tray. "What's this, Bearer—more of General Neill Sahib's *bubble-pani?*"

"Neill's *bubble-pani,* Lou!" Alex exclaimed. "Don't tell me that General Neill sent this?"

"Not only this, my dear Alex, but most of the other bottles we've spooned into you to aid your recovery." Lousada Barrow poured out two brimming glasses and offered one to his patient with an amused grin. "You've had numerous visitors and a great many gifts and enquiries concerning your health. Neill came in person one evening while you were still semiconscious, to advise champagne as the best cure for you. And your two fellow-sur-vivors, Thomson and Delafosse, came several times. So did Charlie Palliser and Willie Hargood, on behalf of the Chief. Well . . ." he raised his glass. "Here's to your very good health, Alex, my friend—may your shadow never grow less!"

Alex thanked him warmly as he drank the toast. "If it hadn't been for you, I doubt if I should have remained a survivor, Lou. I owe you more than I can ever repay and—"

"Nonsense, my dear fellow!" Barrow brushed his thanks aside. "In the words of General Havelock, when the men cheered him after Bithur—'Don't cheer me, my men, you did it all yourselves!' And talking of men, Alex, the lads you trained have besieged me with enquiries about you. One in particular—your ex-whipper-in from Tipperary, Cullmane—asked me to tell you that he'd vowed on his mother's grave not to touch a drop of liquor until your return to the troop."

"Then I'd better delay my return, if it'll make a reformed character out of Cullmane," Alex said, laughing.

"Don't do that, " Barrow besought him, in mock dismay. "We need you—there are another batch of volunteers from the infantry to be licked into shape and none of us has your touch."

"Square it with the surgeon and I'll report for duty tomor-row, Lou."

Barrow shook his head. "You'll take whatever time Dr. Irvine says you need, Alex. That's an order and be damned to that brevet of yours!" He rose, setting down his glass. "I must go. We're mount-ing a reconnaissance in the Calpi direction at first light tomorrow —the usual scare about the blasted Gwalior Contingent, who appear to be mercifully inactive—but the general wants a report, so I must select who's to go on it." He stumped out, shoulders wearily bowed, and Alex cursed his own weakness. But his recovery continued and three days later Dr. Irvine permitted him to return to light duties in camp. By 10th September, he was once again training the last batch of recruits for Barrow's Volunteers, and the whole Force was cheered by the news that General Outram expected to reach Cawnpore on the 15th, with reinforcements numbering nearly 1,300 men, in addition to Major Eyre's battery and two howitzers.

On the 12th, the engineers started to prepare the pontoons and boats required to repair the bridge across the Ganges, and at dusk on Tuesday, 15th September, General Outram marched in at the head of his column, having decisively defeated a rebel force which had attempted to dispute his passage from Allahabad.

The following morning, he issued his first Divisional Order to the Cawnpore column, which began:

> The important duty of relieving the garrison of Lucknow had at first been entrusted to Brigadier-General Havelock, C.B., and Major-General Outram feels that it is due to this distinguished officer, and to the strenuous and noble efforts which he has already made to effect that object, that to him should accrue the honour of the achievement.
>
> Major-General Outram is confident that the great end for which General Havelock and his brave troops have so long and so gloriously fought will now, under the blessing of Providence, be accomplished.
>
> The Major-General, therefore, in gratitude for and admiration of the brilliant deeds of arms achieved by General Havelock, will cheerfully waive his rank on the occasion and

will accompany the force to Lucknow in his Civil capacity
—as Chief Commissioner of Oudh—tendering his military
services to General Havelock as a volunteer.

Havelock's reply ran:

> Brigadier-General Havelock, in making known to the
> column the kind and generous determination of Major-
> General Sir James Outram, K.C.B., to leave to it the task of
> relieving Lucknow and of rescuing its gallant and enduring
> garrison, has only to express his hope that the troops will
> strive, by their exemplary and gallant conduct in the field,
> to justify the confidence thus reposed in them.

The men cheered their little general when they read these
Orders. Awaiting them, on the Oudh side of the river, were an
estimated force of 7,000 rebel foot, 1,000 cavalry, and 18 guns.
The British column, consisting of 2,300 Queen's infantry and
250 Sikhs, with 80 Volunteer Cavalry, two 9-pounder batteries,
one heavy battery of four 24-pounders, and two howitzers, began
to cross the river on the 19th. By dusk on the 20th, Major Eyre's
heavy guns, which had covered the crossing, and the rear guard
passed over the bridge of boats into Oudh, and General Havelock with his son Harry left the bungalow on the riverbank—once
owned by a Prince of Oudh—which they had occupied since
August, to join the column. In the entrenchment, 300 men were
left to hold Cawnpore, under Colonel Wilson of the Queen's
64th; Brigadier-General James Neill commanded one wing of
the Lucknow relief column and Colonel Hamilton of the 78th
the other, whilst Sir James Outram, mounted on a mottled roan
horse, joined the ranks of the Volunteer Cavalry.

At daybreak on 21st September, in a deluge of rain, Havelock
gave the order to advance once more on Lucknow.

CHAPTER SEVEN

❧❧❧ • ❧❧❧

DURING THE RIVER CROSSING, the rebels had attempted, with skirmishers and some horsed 9-pounder guns, to impede the British column, but the attacks had not been pressed home and a few rounds from Francis Maude's well-trained gunners served effectively to discourage them. They retired to General Havelock's old camping ground at Mungalwar where, some seven to eight thousand strong, they waited for the expected attack, firing on the Volunteer Cavalry when they rode forward to reconnoitre.

At first light on 21st September, when Alex and Lousada Barrow went with Colonel Tytler and General Outram's Chief of Staff, Colonel Napier, to report on their position, they came under so heavy a fire from sepoys and matchlock men, concealed in the breast-high corn bordering the road, that they had themselves to take cover until their assailants were dispersed. Trotting forward again, they saw that the enemy had positioned infantry to defend the fortified mud huts of the village and a newly constructed walled enclosure to the left of the road. To the right, a line of breastworks had also been built, behind which six guns were sited to cover the road—one of them a 24-pounder, mounted to the rear of a separate stockade of interlaced brushwood and timber, which was lined with sepoy musketeers.

As the British column advanced in drizzling rain to the attack, with Major Eyre's heavy battery in the centre, covered by the 5th Fusiliers in skirmishing order, the rebel guns opened an accurate fire. A round-shot wounded one of the battery elephants, and the great beast turned, trumpeting in pain and fury, to charge and scatter the British gunners. The remaining elephants in the battery, sensing danger, held their ground but refused to drag the guns any further and, when all attempts to goad them on had failed, bullock teams had to be brought up to take their places.

After some delay and confusion, Vincent Eyre was able to deploy his cumbersome pieces across the road and engage the rebel front with great effect, and Havelock, after studying the position, decided to employ his favourite turning movement. He sent his main force, with Olpherts' horsed battery, to the left, leaving the 90th Light Infantry to clear the village, which they did in dashing style, eager to show themselves the equal of the column's veteran regiments. The Highlanders and the Blue Caps, not to be outdone, surged forward and stormed the breastworks and, as the enemy line started to waver and break, Havelock cantered over to where the Volunteer Cavalry were drawn up in two lines, with Outram and Barrow at their head.

He bowed to General Outram and said, addressing Lousada Barrow, "Be so good as to pursue the beaten enemy with your squadron, Captain Barrow!"

"With pleasure, sir," Barrow acknowledged. It was the moment for which the Volunteers had been waiting, and they took full advantage of the opportunity to show their mettle. Led by their commandant with their Volunteer general beside him, they charged furiously into the mass of rebel infantry, wielding their sabres mercilessly. Outram, on his big Australian waler, was in his element, his gold-topped Malacca cane doing duty in place of the cavalry sabre he lacked, and the rebels' retreat became a rout. Havelock himself rode with the second line, which Alex was leading, but his horse sustained a number of wounds, which compelled him to pull up, and he waved them on as he coaxed his limping animal from the fray.

"Close up and take cover!" Barrow yelled, as a bend in the road disclosed a body of mutineers, who had rallied under the command of a mounted *subedar* into a loosely-knit square. They fired a volley at over-long range; the Volunteers closed ranks and continued their charge. The sepoy riflemen did not wait to receive it but scattered without attempting to fire a second volley, diving desperately for cover in the tall-growing corn or seeking refuge in flight along the open road.

To the right, Alex saw, two 9-pounder guns mounted in a well-constructed entrenchment barred the way and, as the gunners tried frantically to bring their guns to bear on the charging cavalry, he wheeled his line to take the battery in flank. The tall Mahoney beside him, yelling like a fiend, he put his horse at the breastwork and, before the gunners could get off a shot, he and his troop were inside, cutting them down. He saw, out of the tail of his eye, that Outram was with him, using the battered and bloodstained cane like a flail and yelling as loudly as any of the rest. Some of the men had been unhorsed, and when they dashed up to enter the battery on foot, the general bade them stay with the guns.

"They're our prizes!" he shouted and, digging spurs into his bony waler, galloped on after Barrow, whose line was spread out across a cornfield on the far side of the road, in hot pursuit of the fleeing foe. Alex was about to follow him when he noticed that shots were coming from his left. Turning to ascertain the cause, he saw that fifty yards from him, in an entrenched enclosure, a company of sepoys in regulation scarlet full dress uniforms had gathered about their Colour and, with more courage than the majority of their comrades had shown, were firing into the advancing ranks of the 5th Fusiliers as they emerged, in extended order, on the far side of the village.

Mahoney shouted something he could not catch, and the next moment he was making for the enclosure, intent, it seemed, on taking it single-handedly. Rallying his troop, Alex cantered after him, delayed by the necessity to form them into line, and then watched, in astonished admiration, as the tall young sergeant, bearing a charmed life, leapt his horse over the breastwork of the enclosure and fought his way through the scarlet-clad defenders. The next moment, he had seized the Colour and was bearing it away in triumph, its gilt-embroidered folds draped over his horse's quarters.

With the loss of their Colour, the sepoys' resistance petered out. A few spasmodic shots were fired at the approaching horsemen, but when they reached the enclosure, the mutineers did not contest it with them. They ran from behind their breastwork as Mahoney rejoined the troop with his trophy, his horse bleeding from several bayonet wounds but he himself grinning broadly and miraculously unscathed. Leaving the scattered sepoys to be rounded up by the Fusiliers, Alex shouted a breathless "Well done!" to his sergeant and, observing that Lousada Barrow had returned to the road to rally and reform his command, led his troop back to join them.

After a brief halt to deal with casualties and rest their blown horses, the Volunteer Cavalry resumed the pursuit, augmented by the sixty Irregulars commanded by Captain Johnson and Lieutenant Charles Havelock. They tore past the village of Unao—now a deserted cluster of blackened, burned-out huts—through the narrow passageway, and out onto the Busseratgunj road, to see the bulk of the fleeing enemy streaming along it toward the town.

Hitherto, although defeated by Havelock's small column, they had never suffered pursuit in any previous engagement, and now, following their usual practice, they were endeavouring to take out their guns and ammunition, with the evident intention of making a stand when they gained the walled defences of the town. Outram and Barrow allowed them no time and showed them no mercy and, as the British cavalry fell on their rear, sabring them down, the ammunition tumbrils were abandoned or upended into the swamp. A third gun was captured, intact and with its gun-cattle, when Lousada Barrow led a spirited attack on the gunners, whose escorting infantry made a panic-stricken bid for escape, leaving the *golandazes* to their fate.

Only when Busseratgunj was as empty of rebel troops as Unao had been did Barrow regretfully call a halt to permit the infantry to catch up with them. Their casualties had been amazingly light—ten wounded but still mounted and six men missing. The mutineers', by contrast, were estimated at approaching 200, the majority of these killed; but the horses of both Volunteer and Irregular squadrons were quite done up and the men in little better state. Thankful for the respite, they dismounted and flung themselves onto the damp ground; only Cullmane and two or three others of his troop, Alex noticed, loosened their girths and rubbed their sweating animals down before taking their own ease. But they were all happy, and when General Havelock rode up on a fresh horse, accompanied by James Neill, to congratulate them on their achievement, both officers and men cheered him enthusiastically. Mahoney, very red of face at being singled out, was brought up by Neill and invited to display the Colour he had taken. On this being identified as having belonged to one of the original Cawnpore regiments, the 1st Bengal Native Infantry, Havelock shook him warmly by the hand and Outram, his dark, bearded face wreathed in smiles, took half a dozen of his Manilla cheroots from his pocket and presented them to the delighted sergeant.

"These, my lad," he announced, "are the most precious gift I have to bestow, but you've earned them twice over. That was a very gallant action of yours and, if we both survive, I shall see to it that your name is put forward with a recommendation for a Victoria Cross."

Mahoney stammered his thanks and, as he rejoined his comrades, General Neill said, with conscious pride, "The lad's a Blue Cap, you know, sir . . . I lent him to Barrow as a Volunteer."

Sir James Outram grunted. "I hope he lives long enough to get his Cross," he said, and then, holding up his battered cane, demanded the loan of a cavalry sabre in place of it. "There was I," he added, amid laughter, "called upon to charge by Captain Barrow and all I had in my scabbard was a General Officer's ceremonial sword, which wouldn't cut through paper, let alone a mutineer's skull! I want to be prepared for the next occasion."

In a general mood of optimism but in a continuous downpour, the column bivouacked on the plain at the end of the causeway, officers and men sleeping on the damp ground, their weapons beside them. It was still raining next morning when they moved out, but, if uncomfortable and dispiriting, the rain was at least cool, and they covered the fifteen miles which separated them from Bunni by three in the afternoon. Barrow's troop of Volunteers rode ahead to ascertain the state of the crossing and sent back the unexpected but welcome intelligence that the British advance had been so rapid that the last of the defeated rebels from Mungalwar were still straggling over the bridge, which they had made no attempt to destroy.

Havelock himself, with Outram and the two brigade commanders and their staffs, rode up to inspect the bridge, and Alex's troop of Volunteers followed them, escorting Olpherts' horsed field-gun battery. Havelock was all smiles as he lowered his glass. The canal boats—brought with considerable labour from Cawnpore, in the baggage train—were thankfully abandoned. Olpherts' battery and the Volunteer Cavalry crossed the Sai River, meeting with no opposition, and, as the first brigade's infantry were starting to cross, Jack Olpherts fired a royal salute, in the hope that the sound would reach Lucknow and give fresh heart to its beleaguered garrison. The second brigade halted on the Cawnpore side of the river, and the hungry men, unable to light bivouac fires to cook their rations, ate the dry biscuit from their haversacks and lay down once more on the rain-soaked ground to get what rest they could.

In a native hut by the roadside, Outram and Havelock pored over a map of Lucknow, drawn by Lieutenant Moorsom of H.M.'s 52nd, and discussed and finally agreed upon a plan of action. Despite the ease of their victory at Mungalwar, both generals were aware of the formidable task now facing them. Lucknow was besieged by an estimated 25,000 to 30,000 mutineers, with well-entrenched guns, and the most recent letter from Colonel Inglis had warned that the fighting strength of the defenders had been reduced by wounds and sickness to 350 Europeans and about 300 Sikhs and loyal sepoys, all of whom had been on half rations for the past month. Failure to battle their way into the Residency would almost certainly lead to its fall, since the confidence of the loyal sepoys, already shaken by the 11-week-long siege, with no sign of relief, would be destroyed and they would abandon the defences.

On the morning of 23rd September, the rain ceased and the column marched off in high spirits, the men confident that they would succeed in reaching their objective. Even Alex, who had more idea than most of the obstacles which lay ahead, was optimistic, and Olpherts—whom the men had nicknamed "Hellfire Jack"—was in splendid humour, cracking jokes with his teams and making bets on who would be first to enter the Residency. For ten miles, under a cloudless blue sky, the advance continued without a sight of any hostile force. Everyone had eaten that morning at eight-thirty, and no halt was called until two o'clock, when Colonel Tytler rode back with Lousada Barrow to report that the enemy were in sight, three miles ahead, and that the patrol had been fired on by a cavalry piquet, which they had put to flight.

"They're holding the Alam Bagh," Barrow said, as he waited for the generals to accompany him on a final reconnaissance. "About ten thousand of them. Their centre on high ground, covering the road, and their right protected by swamp, in a line which extends for about two miles. They've got well over a thousand cavalry, but their guns are too well masked for me to be able to estimate their number. There are two field-guns covering the road immediately ahead, though."

Alex felt his throat tighten as he listened. He remembered the Alam Bagh as one of the summer palaces of the Kings of Oudh, situated four miles outside the city. It was famous for the magnificence of its shade trees and garden, but, like all such palaces erected by Moslem nobles, it was adapted for defence. A lofty stone wall, with turrets at each angle, enclosed the garden and, within this, the palace and its adjoining buildings offered good cover for sharpshooters and the matchlock men who normally guarded it.

"A tough nut to crack," Charles Palliser said, grinning at the prospect. "But a pound to a penny we crack it before nightfall!"

General Havelock made his inspection and, on his return, A.D.C.s were soon galloping along the column with his orders. Colonel Hamilton's second brigade—the 78th, the 90th, Brasyer's Sikhs, and Olpherts' field battery—received instructions to turn the enemy's right. Owing to the swampy ground and the depth of water on either side of the road, it was evident that a wide detour would be necessary, and General Neill's first brigade was halted in order to allow the second to pass through it to the left. Whilst this manoeuvre was taking place, two rebel guns, well sited on a low hill, opened fire on the head of the column and Eyre's heavy guns and the 8-inch howitzers were ordered up to silence them. It was, however, some time before they could be brought up, since they could only advance by way of the road and the gun-elephants, as always, were reluctant to go forward under fire.

Further delay was caused when Hamilton's brigade encountered obstacles in the shape of deep irrigation ditches and flooded fields, so that Neill's second brigade—consisting of H.M.'s 5th, 64th, and 84th and the Madras Fusiliers, with the Volunteer and Irregular Cavalry and Maude's battery—was compelled to hold the front alone. Under a hail of case and canister, Neill led them toward a patch of dry ground where there would be room for them to deploy, but as he crossed a wide, rain-filled ditch, his horse went down, a round-shot grazing its quarters and passing only a few inches behind its rider's back. He scrambled out, cursing angrily and covered with slime, but, assisted by two of his staff, quickly remounted and continued to lead his brigade forward to the dry ground, where he was able to deploy them.

Growing impatient at the delay, General Outram yelled to Lousada Barrow to take the cavalry to cover Hamilton's turning movement, which was being threatened by a body of rebel horse, and, nothing loth, Barrow gave the order, just as Eyre's heavy guns made their appearance and, unlimbering, started to shell the enemy emplacements to their front. Outram, scorning the detour that Hamilton had made, led the squadron at a gallop across the flooded ground and they took minutes to cross a *jheel* which had held Hamilton's Highlanders up for half an hour as they struggled, thigh-deep in water and mud, to march round it. Olpherts' horsed battery came tearing after the Volunteers at a stretching gallop; a wide, rain-filled ditch—which the men of Barrow's squadron had taken in their stride—lay between the gunners and the road, and seeing this, Alex pulled up, jerking his head to it in warning. With "Hellfire Jack" riding a big rawboned chestnut at their head, the whole battery plunged into the formidable obstacle without a check. For a moment there was chaos—a wild medley of drivers, guns, limbers, struggling horses, and splashing water—and then they were out, carried by their own impetus to the farther side. As they swept past Neill's brigade and back onto the firm surface of the road once more, their guns miraculously intact, the Blue Caps cheered them excitedly and Neill himself doffed his khaki pith helmet in appreciation of their feat.

The rebel cavalry, unnerved, turned tail and fled before Olpherts could bring his guns to bear or the Volunteers come to grips with them; then as Neill's brigade advanced, Hamilton's at last completed its turning movement and attacked the right flank, driving them relentlessly back. A single 9-pounder—one of the two that had first opened fire—remained in position and continued to hurl round shot into the ranks of Neill's Fusiliers, causing casualties and impeding their advance. Well served and bravely worked, it was too far ahead to be taken by the infantry and Alex, whose halt by the ditch had left him some distance behind

Barrow and the Volunteers, found himself beside young Johnson and his small troop of Irregulars.

"I believe we could take that gun, sir," Johnson said breathlessly. "Shall we try?"

"Wait till they're reloading," Alex cautioned. "And then go at it like stink!" He measured the distance with his eye—it was a thousand yards, but Johnson's horses were fresh. "Now!" he shouted and went with them as Johnson gave the order to charge. Twenty of the Irregulars followed him, sabres drawn, spurring their lathered horses into a gallop as reckless and headlong as that of Olpherts' gunners a few minutes before. The Oudh *golandazes* matched them for courage; they struggled frantically to reload, and even though they managed to do so, the firing number had no time to apply his portfire to the touch-hole. Johnson himself cut him down, and the glowing portfire fell, to be trampled into extinction by the sowars' pounding hooves. None of the Oudh men attempted to flee; they stood by their gun, fighting with sponge-staffs and *tulwars,* striking out at the legs of their opponents' horses and wounding several of them.

But they were outnumbered and the struggle did not last long; with the gun silenced and the gunners dead or dying, Johnson slid from the saddle of his disabled mare and, with his pistol, calmly put the poor animal out of her misery. Alex gestured to his own saddle and, with the Irregulars' young commander mounted behind him, they rode back by the way they had come, compelled to abandon the captured gun by the galling fire of sepoy sharpshooters posted on the walls of the Alam Bagh. But the Highlanders and the 5th Fusiliers were now at the gates; they battered their way in and in a savage rush cleared the enclosure, the defenders—who had seen the left and centre of their line broken and in retreat—falling back before the bayonets of the yelling, vengeful British soldiers, who shouted "Remember Cawn-pore!" as they stabbed and thrust at any who opposed them.

With Johnson—both of them remounted on fresh horses—Alex returned to his own troop in time to take part in an exhilarating and triumphant pursuit, led by Outram and Barrow, which took them right up to the heavily defended Char Bagh enclosure and within clear sight of the mosques, minarets, and palaces of Lucknow itself. Six guns—two of heavy calibre—were mounted to cover the bridge across the canal and the approaches to it. On the Lucknow side, men could be seen hard at work constructing emplacements and defensive palisades, and digging trenches that bisected the road that led most directly to the Residency.

The houses and gardens on both sides of the bridge were loopholed and filled with musketeers, who poured such a hail of fire on the advancing Volunteers that, after a swift inspection with his glass, Outram ordered them to withdraw out of range. As they did so, two 9-pounders opened on them from the so-called yellow house, half-hidden by trees at the rear of the Char Bagh enclosure, to which Olpherts requested and obtained permission from Outram to reply. As his first two guns were unlimbering under Henry Delafosse's energetic command, the enemy guns—smartly handled—took up a new position, the movement screened by a high wall. They again fired with telling effect on the British cavalry, who were compelled to fall back still farther. Clear now of the buildings which had obscured their view of the open ground to their right, they saw suddenly that a body of some eight or nine hundred rebel horsemen were advancing towards them from the Bibiapoor road, and Alex gave vent to an exclamation of astonishment when he recognised the white-robed figure riding with drawn *tulwar,* at their head.

"Lou!" he shouted, trotting to the front rank of the Volunteers, where Outram and Barrow had halted, glasses raised, to study the advancing enemy. "Surely that's the Moulvi of Fyzabad, isn't it—on the grey Arab?"

Lousada Barrow swore luridly as he trained his glass on the leader of the rebel cavalry. "You're right, Alex, it *is* the Moulvi! Talk of the devil—I was just telling General Outram of the part he played in the Fyzabad mutiny. By heaven, I wish we could lay him by the heels, he's the most dangerous rabble-rouser of the lot. But the swine will make off back to the city as soon as they see us, I'm afraid. They won't try conclusions with us in the open."

The Moulvi had been the evil genius of Cawnpore, Alex thought, a savage anger catching at his throat. It had been he at the Nana's elbow—prompting, advising, even threatening—who had been largely responsible for the initial betrayal of General Wheeler's trust and friendship. Perhaps he had also been responsible for the final treachery at the Suttee Chowra Ghat, he and Azimullah Khan and the evil Bala Bhat . . . drawing rein at Barrow's side, Alex said urgently, "They haven't seen us yet—look, they're still coming on. Withdraw under cover, Lou, before they do spot us. I believe we might tempt the Moulvi to delay his return to the city."

"How?" Barrow demanded doubtfully. But without waiting for Alex's reply, General Outram gave the order for the Volunteers to withdraw to the cover of a grove of trees on the opposite side of the road. When they reached their new position, he echoed Barrow's question. "They're making for the Dilkusha Bridge—how the deuce do you propose to stop them, Sheridan?"

"By trailing my coat, sir," Alex said. "I'm known to the Moulvi and we have a few old scores to settle." His brain was racing as he recalled an old and well-tried trick of the Bashi-Bazouks in the battle for Silestria. Always outnumbered by the Russians, they had been compelled to resort to cunning, sending forward a few unsupported horsemen on what appeared to be a reconnaissance, and when the Cossacks gave chase, leading them into an ambush. The trick, to be successful, required fading light and the right sort of cover but . . . the light was fading now. There were trees and buildings and the walls of the yellow house compound to serve as the hills and forests of the Danube Valley had served the Bashi-Bazouk horsemen. And if Olpherts' guns could be so positioned as to be out of sight of the Moulvi's cavalry until they approached within range, then . . . Alex outlined the tactics he proposed to employ, wasting no words. Barrow frowned as he listened, but the general's dark eyes were lit by an appreciative gleam.

"You're a man after my own heart, Sheridan," he observed, smiling. "I worked a ploy like this with the Bheels once, and Lake used it—on a grand scale, of course—at Laswaree. He used his cavalry to invite a charge and then wheeled 'em to attack the enemy's flanks, leaving his guns an unimpeded field of fire in the centre. I believe it's worth a try, even on the off-chance of bagging a prisoner of the Moulvi's importance . . . eh, Barrow?"

"It's damned risky, sir," Barrow demurred. "But it might work."

"Everything we've done has carried an element of risk," Outram qualified. "And when have we not been outnumbered?" He glanced about him, shrewdly assessing the position. "Olpherts' guns will have to be carefully placed—send for him, will you please? There's no time to be lost if we're to have a hope of bringing this off. How many men do you want with you, Sheridan?"

"Two, sir," Alex answered promptly. "My two best rough-riders—Mahoney and Cullmane." They settled details of the route he would take, and when Olpherts trotted up, the general said gruffly, "Right, then, Sheridan—off you go and good luck to you. We'll set your ambush for you."

The ruse almost succeeded. Alex rode forward, with Mahoney and Cullmane, making no attempt at concealment. He saw the Moulvi bring his cavalry to a halt, saw him raise a spy-glass to his eye and after careful inspection wave his followers on at a cautious trot, wheeling them so as to face the possible menace of an attack. As the distance between them shortened, he heard Olpherts' guns open fire—apparently on their original target. Glancing over his shoulder, he realised, with a quickening of his pulses, that Outram had been as good as his word.

In addition to the supposed reconnaissance party he himself was leading, two of Olpherts' guns had been brought into view, with twenty of Johnson's sowars as their only support, to act as bait to the trap. The capture of three British cavalrymen might not have been temptation enough but two guns and a scanty escort must, even to the wily Moulvi, seem a wholly desirable prize. Of the other two guns and the hundred-strong Volunteers there was now no visible sign. He grinned at Cullmane,

"Ride for the guns, Cullmane," he ordered "And make all the row you can. You've just spotted the Pandies and you're panick-ing—trying to warn Captain Olpherts of the danger he's in. Go it as if the Gallant Tips were behind you and a fox in view!"

"Or better still as if you'd a bottle of good Irish whiskey inside you," Mahoney quipped, grinning too.

Cullmane needed no urging. He flung back a cheerful insult and rode like the fine horseman he was, heedless of the obstacles in his path, emitting a series of ear-splitting "View Hulloo's," and turning in his saddle to gesticulate wildly in the direction of the Moulvi's advancing horde. The gunners of Olpherts' half-battery played up magnificently to his lead. With Hellfire Jack himself tugging at the traces, they brought their guns round to bear on the rebel cavalry, fired two rounds of grape at extreme range and, failing to reach their target, started to limber up as if in sudden alarm. Then, their escort bunched protectively round them, they made off at a gallop towards the road, guns and limbers swaying perilously as they thudded across the broken, waterlogged ground, seemingly with the intention of retiring to the Alam Bagh. The Moulvi detached two hundred or so of his horsemen in pursuit as the battery vanished from sight behind a high-walled garden. To Alex's chagrin, the Moulvi himself remained with the bulk of his force, which he brought unexpectedly to a halt, spyglass again to his eye as he subjected the surrounding countryside to a prolonged scrutiny.

"The bastard's not going to fall for it, sir!" Mahoney exclaimed, his voice harsh with disappointment.

"He's being cautious," Alex returned impatiently. "The devil take him!"

The moment had come when he would have to trail his coat to some effect, he knew, or lose forever the chance of enticing the Moulvi of Fyzabad into the trap so carefully prepared for him. Some of the rebel cavalrymen were taking matchlocks from slings and saddle-holsters, and he winced involuntarily as a fusillade of shots whined overhead, a few coming unpleasantly close. The range was long, but most Oudh Irregulars were good marksmen, even when mounted, and he heard Mahoney swear as a spent musket-ball struck his horse, causing it to rear and whinny. It would behoove them to retire; no ordinary reconnaissance patrol would stay under fire from so large a force in normal circumstances. He glanced around and saw that a second and slightly larger body of Pandy sowars, armed with lances, had also been detached and was now cantering off to the right of where he and Mahoney were waiting, for the obvious purpose of cutting off their retreat to the Alam Bagh. Theirs and Olpherts' . . . he rose in his stirrups, checking their position in the vanishing glow of the sunset, measuring the distance with his eye.

"Is your animal all right, Sergeant?" he asked. Receiving Mahoney's assurance that it was, he added crisply, "Then ride like hell back to the road! Don't wait for me."

"But, sir, you—"

"I'll be right behind you," Alex promised. "On your way, lad."

The sergeant obeyed him, driving spurs into his horse's flanks and heading, at an oblique angle, for the road. Half a dozen of the Moulvi's sowars went after him with yells of derision, but the Moulvi continued to sit his motionless grey Arab, the spy-glass still to his eye, the main body of his followers equally motionless at his back. Clearly their suspicions had not been allayed. Alex bit back a sigh. He swung his own borrowed charger right-handed and then, as if only now aware that the way back to the Alam Bagh was about to be contested, he changed direction, succeeding—as he had hoped he would—in drawing the detached body of horsemen in pursuit.

Like Mahoney, he headed back towards the road at an angle, taking a line that would bring him well within the Moulvi's vision. It was now or never, his mind registered, as he drew level, his horse fully extended. Would hatred and the memory of old scores as yet unsettled overcome suspicion? He glimpsed the grey as it made a sudden surge forward and then he was past, listening for the thud of hooves pounding after him as he jerked his sweating animal into a second swift change of direction which almost brought it to its knees.

Ahead of him he could see Mahoney, well in advance of his pursuers and, at the road verge, the Volunteers coming from concealment and making their expected move forward in an extended line, to invite the enemy's charge.

He was within less than a hundred yards of them when, without warning, his horse stumbled and went crashing down, flinging him over its head. Winded, he lay where he had fallen, facedown on the rough ground, momentarily expecting to be ridden down by the Moulvi's horsemen as they charged in answer to the challenge. He heard the guns open and the sound of galloping hooves and realised, dazedly, that both sounds were receding. They had faded into the distance—and the guns to silence—when, bruised and shaken but otherwise unhurt, he finally picked himself up.

Outram himself, with Palliser leading a spare horse, came to meet him as he stumbled across the damp, sandy space that separated him from the road. The light had almost gone and it was difficult to read the expressions on their faces. Alex let Charles Palliser assist him to mount and then, looking down at him, saw that he was smiling. "We failed, didn't we?" he asked uncertainly.

"We failed to bag the Moulvi," General Outram admitted. "But I wouldn't say the ambush was a failure, my dear Sheridan . . . and you played your part magnificently! So did the Volunteers. Damn, they went out and routed close on six hundred Pandy!"

"But surely they didn't charge, sir? If they had, I shouldn't be here."

Outram laughed. "No, we charged them as planned, from either flank, leaving the guns in the centre. And they turned tail and fled. We chased them as far as we could. Knocked quite a few of them down, too. The light's gone, so it's impossible to say how many, but Olpherts' gunners accounted for at least fifty from the detached squadron." He clapped a friendly hand on Alex's shoulder. "We'll call it a day, shall we? And not a bad day, Sheridan, not a bad day at all, my dear fellow."

They rode back to the Alum Bagh, to find the British column already occupying both Palace and walled enclosure, with bivouac fires springing to life on all sides of the newly captured stronghold. As they neared the battered gateway, a staff officer galloped up with a despatch for Outram.

The general read it by the light of a lucifer, frowning; then his expression changed.

"Thanks be to God!" he exclaimed, his voice not quite steady. "Thanks be to God . . . My friends, Delhi has fallen! General Archdale Wilson has retaken Delhi! Make it known to your commands, gentleman . . . for what better inducement could we be given to succeed in our own task than this wonderful news?"

He put spurs into his weary horse and dashed off in search of General Havelock, the cheers of the Volunteer Cavalry, as the news was made known to them, echoing behind him in the swiftly falling darkness.

"The tide is turning in our favour at last," Lousada Barrow said. "For which I, too, say thank God."

Rain started to fall again, as piquets were posted and guns mounted to guard against any possible night attacks, but in spite of the rain, more cheers rang out as the news that Delhi was once more in British hands reached regiments and batteries. Since only a few of the tents had come up, most of the men were compelled to spend their third night on the waterlogged ground, but the intelligence from Delhi had put them in good heart, and there was general disappointment when they learned the following morning that no immediate attack on Lucknow was to be made. General Havelock, showing his accustomed consideration for the men he commanded, ordered that tents were to be pitched and the day spent in rest and recuperation. An attack by rebel cavalry on the baggage train delayed the arrival of the tents until just before midday. It was beaten off by the baggage guard from the 90th Light Infantry but not until Olpherts' battery, with the Volunteer Cavalry, had gone to their aid.

Throughout the day, the roar of guns could be heard from Lucknow—the defenders, evidently, were being subjected to a heavy bombardment, to which they replied with spirit. Not all the rebel guns were turned on them, however; those mounted behind a screen of trees near the Char Bagh bridge fired continuously at extreme elevation on Havelock's Force, and round-shot ricocheted among the tents, causing a number of casualties. All Eyre's efforts, with his howitzers and 24-pounders, failed to silence them, but he kept at it tirelessly, refusing to rest. For the Volunteer and Irregular Cavalry also there was little time to rest; patrols had to be sent out and a lengthy reconnaissance made to ascertain enemy gun positions covering the approaches to the Residency.

Alex went out, with Lousada Barrow, on a final reconnaissance ordered by General Outram, late in the afternoon. All day, he and General Havelock had been debating plans for the attack, which was to be launched next morning, and it was rumoured that the two generals were not in complete agreement as to the best route to follow. Outram, who knew Lucknow well, having been both Resident and Chief Commissioner for several years before the mutiny, was not in favour of the plan which Havelock had put forward and he said so forcibly, as he trotted toward the city with his staff and escort.

Alex, who was also reasonably familiar with the geography of the sprawling, densely populated city, listened with interest to the snatches of conversation he could hear, conscious that whichever route was finally chosen would, inevitably, present hazards none of them could foresee.

The most direct route was by the road they were now on, crossing the Char Bagh bridge and thence straight through the heart of the city for a mile and a half, entering the Residency through the Bailey Guard gate. This being the route the rebels were expecting the British force to take, it was strongly defended, and spies told of palisades and trenches across the road and every house loopholed and filled with riflemen. Havelock considered that it would prove impossible or, at best, cost the lives of half his force. His own plan was to move across the open ground to the southeast, seize a building known as the Dilkusha Palace, bridge the River Gumti under cover of its walls, and then move round the city to its northwest angle, recrossing the river by an iron bridge immediately in front of the Residency and under the protection of its guns. Near the iron bridge and on the north bank of the Gumti, a palace with a walled garden—the Padshah Bagh—offered an excellent defensive position for his troops to assemble in before crossing the five hundred yards of open ground which separated it from the Residency.

In theory, this was an admirable plan, Outram conceded.

"But how the devil," he demanded, of no one in particular, "does General Havelock imagine he can move his artillery—and the elephant battery in particular—across country so waterlogged it's virtually a morass? It can't be done, can it, Cooper?"

Major Cooper, newly appointed to command of the column's artillery, hesitated. "General Havelock asked my opinion, sir," he answered finally. "I said I believed we could manage well enough with Maude's and Olpherts' batteries. But, of course, Eyre's *is* a different proposition. It will take time and—"

"Too much infernal time!" Outram growled. "But General Havelock won't move without his heavy guns." He pulled up and subjected the distant Char Bagh bridge and enclosure, and the yellow house behind, to a lengthy scrutiny with his field glass. The rebel guns were still throwing their round-shot into the British camp and puffs of white smoke, rising above the trees, revealed their position to the watchers. "On the other hand, Major," Outram said thoughtfully. "If we brought Eyre's 24-pounders along the road at first light and mounted them there"—he pointed—"he could knock out those two and the guns in the yellow house before our main body began the advance. Then once across the bridge, the assault brigade under General Neill could advance along the left bank of the canal until it reaches open ground, then swing left by the Sikander Bagh and advance to the Residency by the plain between the river and the Kaiser Bagh. Maude's battery could cover the crossing and Olpherts' accompany Neill."

"There's a well-entrenched 24-pounder sited directly across the Char Bagh bridge, General," Fraser Tytler reminded him. "And another five or six covering the approaches from the Lucknow side. Our batteries will have no cover if they're brought up to engage them and there will only be space for two field guns . . . The road is narrow."

"They'll have to be taken at bayonet point by the infantry," Outram agreed. "But Maude can have a crack at them first." He puffed at his cheroot, dark brows furrowed. "Whatever route we decide on will entail heavy losses, I fear, Tytler . . . but it's got to be done. Our people have taken Delhi, which was held to be impossible, but I'll warrant *that* wasn't done without loss. I'm in favour of the shorter way. General Havelock's plan simply isn't feasible after all this rain and we cannot afford to delay until the ground dries out. The assault has to be made tomorrow and it has to be completed in daylight. Havelock is in command, of course, until we enter Lucknow. But he must be persuaded that, in conditions like these, no detour round the city, with heavy guns, is possible. You can see that, can't you? Take your horse off the road, for God's sake, and you'll be over his hocks in water."

"I know that, sir," Fraser Tytler conceded. "But all those palaces near the Kaiser Bagh will have batteries in them. We shall have to fight every foot of the way."

"We shall in any case, my dear Colonel—every infernal foot. We can't take the most direct way in—we're all agreed that would be suicidal. The long way round might cost fewer lives, but it would take too long—the guns would be held up, if they made it at all, and the infantry exhausted by wading through swamp. So we haven't much choice, have we?" He sighed and swung his horse round in the direction of the camp. "Come back with me, Tytler, and help me to convince your Chief that his plan is unworkable."

"Very well, sir." Tytler exchanged a rueful glance with Barrow and the reconnaissance party returned to the Alam Bagh.

That evening the wounded and sick, together with the baggage and the tents, were moved into the Alam Bagh, with a guard of three hundred men. The two assault brigades were ordered to parade at first light; they were to cook breakfast and to take with them 60 rounds of ammunition per man and 48 hours' rations. Spare ammunition was to be carried by camels and the only camp followers to accompany the force were cooks, *dhoolie*-bearers, and officers' *syces*.

The morning of 25th September dawned clear and fine. Havelock, after inspecting the force, sat down to breakfast with his son Harry at a table set out in the open beneath the Alam Bagh wall,

where Outram and his staff joined them, at a little before eight.
With a map spread out between them, the two generals were
making their final depositions when a 9-pound round-shot from
the battery near the Char Bagh bridge, a thousand yards away,
struck the ground a few feet from them, bounded over their
heads, and killed a gun-bullock, already limbered and standing a
short distance away.

Havelock smiled and gestured to the map. "I agree to your
route, Sir James, but my heavy guns I must and will have!"

"So be it, my dear Henry." Outram held out his hand. "You
are in command . . . Permit me to wish you success."

At eight-thirty Neill's brigade, with all the artillery and accompanied by Outram, moved off. It was to be followed by the second
brigade, with Havelock in personal command, the plan being for
Neill to force the Char Bagh bridge and then for Hamilton's
brigade to pass through it and lead the advance to the Kaiser
Bagh. The Volunteer and Irregular cavalry formed the rear guard,
covering the ammunition supplies and the baggage.

Firing was soon heard from the Char Bagh. Barrow and Alex,
sitting their horses at the rear of the baggage train, as the long
column made yet another of its frequently inexplicable halts, listened and wondered, unable to make out much through the
smoke. The firing and the crackle of musketry redoubled in volume and became continuous; they looked at each other anxiously
and Lousada Barrow said, "It sounds as if they are meeting with
even more opposition than we anticipated. Pray heaven they get
through!" He cursed as a small body of camp followers attempted
to leave the train and sent Mahoney and Cullmane to round them
up. "If we fail today, it will be all up with the garrison . . . and
possibly with us as well. Dear God, I wish I knew what was happening!"

It was half an hour before news began to filter through to them, mainly from wounded being carried back to the Alam Bagh in *dhoolies* and tumbrils. The first brigade had met with an inferno of fire and Maude's gunners had been virtually wiped out as he had sought vainly to put the enemy battery defending the Char Bagh bridge out of action.

"It was fearful." a young Fusilier officer confided, as Alex and Lousada Barrow bent over his *dhoolie* to give him the lighted cheroot he had asked for. "The round-shot and grape literally tore up the road, cutting our brave fellows to pieces, while the bullets fell among us like a shower of hail. How I escaped I do not know." He looked down at his shattered legs and shuddered. "Maude's guns are being served by volunteers from the infantry— his sergeant-major, a fine fellow named Lamont, had the whole of his stomach carried away by a round-shot, and two of his other men were decapitated. The general—Outram—was wounded in the arm. But he was very cool, just asked someone to bind his arm with a neckerchief, to stop the bleeding, and carried on. He took the 5th to see if he could find a way to enfilade the bridge."

"Are we across the bridge?" Alex asked.

The injured boy nodded. "I think some of us are. Harry Havelock came up with orders for General Neill to charge and carry the bridge, and Lieutenant Arnold, with about a dozen of our Blue Caps, went at it, led by Colonel Tytler and young Havelock. The enemy 24-pounder opened on them at point-blank range. Poor Arnold lost both legs, Colonel Tytler's horse was killed under him, and all the rest killed or wounded, except Havelock and a corporal of ours called Jakes. Those two stayed on the bridge, Havelock on his horse, with bullets flying round him, waving the rest on with his sword. And they went at it, sir. It was the finest thing I ever saw—our Blue Caps and some of the 84th went over the bridge and took the enemy battery with the bayonet, before they could reload. That was when I was hit, so I don't know any more. But all the guns were taken, the ones in the yellow house too."

The wounded Fusilier subaltern had scarcely finished his account when an A.D.C. galloped up with orders for the baggage train to advance and cross over the canal.

"The 78th are to form your rear guard, sir. It's imperative that you hurry—ammunition is running short and the men must replenish their pouches as soon as you can get the spare ammunition to them."

With the Volunteers harrying them, the camelteers and waggon-drivers made reasonably rapid progress. They came under musketry fire from loopholed houses on the Lucknow side of the canal and found the road and the approaches to the bridge littered with bodies, but all the buildings on the Alam Bagh side had been secured and, when the Highlanders of the rear guard had replenished their ammunition pouches, the whole train negotiated the narrow bridge without suffering more than a dozen casualties. When they started to move along the lane which followed the canal to the right, however, they ran into a hail of musket balls, which only ceased when two companies of the 78th carried and occupied the houses from which the fire had been coming, hurling the occupants out through doors and windows on the points of their bayonets.

It had taken almost two hours for the baggage train to cross and enter the lane and, as the last tumbrils were toiling up a steep incline beyond the bridge, a fierce attack was launched on them from the Cawnpore road. A large force of rebels—mutineers and Oudh troops—advanced with drums beating and banners flying. Dividing, as they neared the canal, one section with two brass guns seized a small temple overlooking the lane, from which they subjected the hapless baggage train to a withering fire of grape.

The second and larger section flung themselves with suicidal courage upon the Highlanders, and the Volunteer Cavalry, with no room to charge, could only go to their aid in ones and two, hacking at the fanatical Oudh men with their sabres and losing half a dozen men and a number of horses in the melee. Alex saw young Graham Birch cut down and with Cullmane beside him, went to try and hold off the sepoys who were stabbing at him with their bayonets. He managed to do so for long enough to enable Cullmane to rescue the wounded subaltern and then his good little mare, which had carried him thus far so bravely, died from a musket-ball in the chest. He had no time to mourn her; as he picked himself up, badly shaken, two sepoys came at him and he had to fight his way back to the lane with the High-landers, hard put to it to preserve his own life when a fresh wave of attackers issued from a nearby building, to drive a wedge between the men he was with and the rest of their company. But the Highlanders were doughty fighters and, as he charged breath-lessly after them, the newly arrived rebels turned tail and fled, several of them flinging themselves into the muddy waters of the canal rather than face the menace of the line of levelled bayonet.

Back in the lane once more, Alex saw that the temple had been cleared and he stood watching and struggling to regain his breath as the Highlanders dragged out the two brass cannons and dumped them unceremoniously into the canal, cheering deri-sively as they did so. Order was restored and the attack finally beaten off, the Highlanders sending a well-aimed volley into the retreating backs of their assailants. Alex sheathed his sabre and, still breathing hard, limped across to rejoin Lousada Barrow, who was organising the collection of wounded. Only then could the baggage train reform and continue on its way, the ammunition tumbrils serving to carry some of the wounded. Preceded by a melancholy line of laden *dhoolies,* the tumbrils rolled slowly down the narrow, rutted lane under the escort of Johnson's faithful Irregulars, many of whom had wounded men on their cruppers or clinging to their stirrup-leathers.

The Volunteers' casualties had been light in comparison with those suffered by the hard-pressed 78th, but six men had been wounded, Barrow said, including Charles Palliser, young Birch and Cullmane—all three of whom had insisted on remaining with the squadron. He added, tight-lipped, that Lieutenants Grant and Brown and a civilian volunteer, John Erskine, had lost their lives. At his suggestion, Alex took over Erskine's horse, a handsome grey Arab, and rode with him to the rear to aid the Highlanders' withdrawal.

From their commander, Captain Hastings, they learnt that Harry Havelock had been wounded in the street fighting beyond the Char Bagh Bridge.

"He took a musket-ball in the arm," Hastings said, mopping his red, smoke-grimed face with the back of his hand. "Sergeant Young, of ours, picked him up and put him into a *dhoolie.*" He gestured to the baggage train, dimly seen in the smoke of battle as it wound its way along the narrow, circuitous lane of General Outram's chosen route, in the direction of the Dilkusha road and the still-distant Kaiser Bagh. "His orderly went with him but his father should be told, I think—if you can spare a man to take the message, Captain Barrow. I can't, I've few enough as it is with whom to effect our withdrawal. The minute we leave this street, the infernal Pandies will be into it like the bloody jackals they are. If you can help to cover our rear guard, Colonel Stisted will be grateful, I know. He's still down there somewhere."

Lousada Barrow glanced at Alex. "Will you find the general and tell him?"

Alex nodded and set off after the main column. Its pace was slow, the delay, he thought, almost certainly due to the difficulty of dragging Eyre's heavy guns along the waterlogged sand of the road. But, because the rebels had expected Havelock to follow the direct route to the Residency, his detour to the right along the bank of the canal had taken them by surprise, and opposition—judging by the lack of bodies—had been slight, and most of it had been concentrated on the Highlanders left to hold the street leading from the Char Bagh bridge.

Reaching a more open area, Alex was able to quicken his pace. The Kaiser Bagh was, he knew, about a quarter of a mile to his left, hidden from him by the intervening buildings, but he could see the cupolas of the Begum Koti directly ahead. He followed the road to the Sikander Bagh until it made a sharp turn to the left and, riding toward the city again, glimpsed the magnificent, pearl-shaped dome of the Moti Mahal and the river ahead and to his right. The baggage train held him up as he made for the Moti Munzil Palace and the sound of very heavy cannon fire warned him that the column must be approaching Kaiser Bagh.

"They've run into trouble," Johnson told him, as he reined in beside the baggage escort. "The Thirty-Second's Mess house seems to be occupied in great strength and they must have a heavy battery in the Kaiser Bagh. I've never heard such fire . . . listen to it, for God's sake! It's hard to make out what's going on but I think a halt has been called under cover of one of the palaces. I hope to heaven it has . . . I want to get the wounded to a place of safety as soon as I can. There's only us and a few walking wounded to guard them and it's taking us all our time to stop the *dhoolie*-bearers from running off."

Alex asked for Harry Havelock but Johnson shook his head regretfully.

"I haven't seen him, sir. He may be in one of the *dhoolies* but, as you can appreciate, there are the devil of a lot of them. I'll make a search as soon as I can and send word if I find him. You're on the way to inform the general I take it?"

Alex nodded. He said, with a wry smile, "It's a pity you and your sowars can't repeat your exploit of the other day and take those guns at the Kaiser Bagh—but I fear they'll be too well entrenched. The Pandies have been preparing to receive us ever since they realised we'd changed direction at the bridge—and they've had plenty of time, alas to dig in and wait for us."

He rode on, running the gauntlet of musketry fire from loop-holed buildings and rooftops and guided by the ceaseless roar of cannon fire ahead and to his left. He passed a few *dhoolies* and picked up a wounded Fusilier, who was gallantly struggling along, using his Enfield as a crutch, but of Harry Havelock there was no sign. He found the column halted behind the sheltering walls of the Moti Munzil Palace and, in a narrow passage-way, at the centre of a confused circle of staff officers, soldiers, guns, wounded men, bullocks and ammunition waggons, he saw that the generals were conferring.

Outram, on his big roan waler, had his arm in a sling and his Malacca cane grasped in his sound hand, the inevitable cheroot clamped between his teeth, at which he was puffing more from habit than enjoyment. Havelock—whose horse had been shot under him, an A.D.C. said—was on foot, pacing up and down displaying the first signs of agitation Alex had ever known him to reveal in public throughout the campaign. They were too far away for him to hear what they said but it was evident, from the expressions on both their faces and the restrained courtesy with which their discussion was being conducted that, once again, the two commanders were far from being in agreement as to what course to pursue. Captain Moorsom had his survey map spread out on the ground a short distance from them and, from time to time, Havelock raised his voice to ask for information concerning the position of some of the buildings which still separated them from the Residency.

Colonel Tytler, his uniform mudstained and his face grey with fatigue, was sitting his horse in silence on the edge of the group of staff officers and Alex reined in beside him and started to make his report. Seeming almost as if he had not heard, the Deputy-Judge-Advocate-General told him, in a tired voice, that General Outram had advocated remaining in one of the Palaces for the night and resuming the attempt to reach the Residency next day, when the fighting troops were fed and rested, the sick and wounded taken care of and the scattered column reformed.

"Sir James thinks we should advance no further than the Chutter Munzil and halt there."

"It would seem prudent," Alex suggested uncertainly

"General Havelock, on the hand, believes that we should push on," Tytler said. "He fears that, if we do not, the garrison may fall to a night attack . . . and it's on the cards that they might. They're under a cruel bombardment now, as you can hear, Sheridan—and from all sides, not only this. We're within less than a quarter of a mile of the Bailey Guard gate and can advance under cover through Martin's House and the King's Stables to the Chutter Munzil, once those heavy guns outside the Kaiser Bagh are silenced. Eyre's trying to knock the Kaiser Bagh battery out now and Olpherts is engaging the Mess House." He sighed. "The general proposes to halt only long enough to enable the baggage train and the rearguard to catch up with us and then go on.

We've only about three more hours of daylight left, so a decision must be reached very soon."

Alex listened, frowning. The Chutter Munzil Palace—so called from the gilt *chutters* or umbrellas which crowned its summit—was, he knew, a large, rambling building surrounded by a high brick wall. Built originally for a seraglio, it would afford shelter and protection to the harassed column . . . he hesitated and then asked bluntly, "What do you think the final decision will be, Colonel? "

Tytler answered with a shrug. "General Havelock," he said flatly, "is still in command until we reach the Residency. The street leading to it is reported to be entrenched and heavily defended by batteries and thousands of rebel infantry—and we shall not be able to bring the guns in that way. All the same, I think we must go on." He sighed and then asked sharply, as if suddenly awakening to the fact, "Weren't you and Barrow with the rearguard, Sheridan? What the devil's happened to them? And what about the baggage train, for heaven's sake? I've had a detachment of the 90th standing by to go in search of them—they're not in serious trouble, are they?"

"The Highlanders were being very hard pressed, sir, and had suffered heavy casualties," Alex told him. He made his report and Colonel Tytler winced when he mentioned Harry Havelock's wound. "Dear heaven, this will break the poor old man's heart! Is Harry badly wounded?"

Alex had perforce to shake his head. "I can't tell you that, I'm afraid," he said apologetically. "All I know is that he took a musket-ball in the arm and Hastings of the 78th had him put into a *dhoolie*. I was unable to find him but Johnson has a large number of wounded with the baggage train. He should be almost in sight by now—he wasn't far behind me, but he had been separated from the rearguard and he could do with help to bring the wounded in, Colonel. His *dhoolie*-bearers were in a state of panic and he had his hands full keeping them with the train. I'll go back with the detachment of the 90th, if you wish, and look for Harry Havelock."

"No, wait," Tytler bade him. "The general may want to speak to you. I'll go and have a word with him now." He started to thrust a way through the assembled officers but, before he reached Havelock's side, there was a sudden hush as somewhere near at hand the roar of a heavy gun faded abruptly into silence and, rising above the incessant crackle of musketry and the thunder of more distant guns, came the sound of British cheers.

"The Kaiser Bagh battery has been put out of action! " the general exclaimed. "We *must* go on." He appealed to General Outram. "The street will be the worst but we know what to expect. At most it will be five hundred yards from the Chutter Munzil to the Bailey Guard, Sir James. We shall be slated but we can push on and get it over."

General Outram reddened angrily but he controlled himself. "In God's name," he returned, "Let us go on, General Havelock!"

There were a few subdued cheers from the officers grouped about them but Colonel Hamilton cut them short. " My regiment is not yet here, sir," he reminded Havelock; then, seeing Alex, he called out above the hubbub, "Colonel Sheridan, how fare the 78th? Have you brought news of them?"

Alex crossed to his side. He repeated what he had told Tytler. "Captain Barrow's squadron is with them, sir, assisting their withdrawal. It took longer than anyone anticipated because of the severity of the attack launched against them from the Cawnpore road." Colonel Hamilton asked a number of questions concerning the 78th's position and casualties, which Alex answered to the best of his knowledge and, with a brusque nod of thanks, the Highlanders' senior Colonel went to confer with the two generals. They were still discussing the situation, out of earshot of their staffs, when word came that the baggage train, with the wounded, had rejoined the column.

Orders went out swiftly and, Alex's mind registered, Havelock was showing something of his old decisiveness and fire at last, undeterred by the presence of the man who had relinquished command to him. The 90th Light Infantry, under Colonel Campbell, were ordered to take up defensive positions with Vincent Eyre's two heavy guns remaining where they were, in the Moti Munzil Palace, into which the wounded, the baggage and all the ammunition tumbrils were brought and placed under cover. The 90th sent out its detachment to search for and aid the 78th and, with ammunition pouches replenished, the rest of the column was ordered to advance, with Olpherts' battery and a cavalry escort, through the enclosed garden of Martin's House and under cover of the wall of the King's Stables to the Chutter Munzil Palace.

All went well until the head of the column emerged from Martin's garden and struck one of the main roads, when it was met by artillery and musketry and found its way barred by a massive gate at the entrance to the King's Stables. The skirmishers of the 5th Fusiliers, who were in the van, scattered into cover and Olpherts—as always, in his element when the situation called for dash and daring—galloped up with two of his field guns, unlimbered and opened fire on the gate. Alex, who was with Johnson and the scanty escort of his Irregulars, twice charged and dispersed large bodies of rebel infantry attempting to outflank the gunners. Johnson's sowars fought like tigers with lance and sabre but, inevitably, saddles were emptied and each time those who were left returned with wounded comrades mounted behind them or clinging to their stirrups.

At last the great gate sagged and then crashed down under the impact of Olpherts' round-shot and James Neill, commanding the leading brigade, led his Blue Caps in a bayonet charge and carried the building, cheering wildly. They continued, driving all opposition before them, and had vanished into the smoke when Olpherts limbered up and guns and cavalry clattered after them into a long, narrow passage-way which led to the Chutter Munzil Palace, the walls of which offered adequate protection for the whole column.

The order came to halt and bring in wounded. As it was being obeyed, the two generals, with Hamilton, Tytler and a number of staff officers gathered round Moorsom's survey map, and Outram again urged a halt until daylight. Havelock, grim faced and determined, shook his head firmly to the suggestion.

"The poor old general! " Jack Olpherts observed, with feeling. He slid wearily from his horse beside Alex and Henry Delafosse, who had also taken the opportunity to stretch their cramped limbs. "There's been no word of his son, apparently, and he's nearly beside himself with anxiety . . . but, in spite of that, he's for pushing on to the Residency to finish the job. Look at his face, for God's sake! No power on earth could stop him now, with less than five hundred yards to go to his goal!"

"They may be the hottest five hundred yards we've ever had to face," Delafosse said. His face was blackened by gunsmoke and he looked exhausted, the sweat tracing a score of tiny rivulets across cheeks and chin but he grinned in Alex's direction. "Hotter even than it was at the Suttee Chowra Ghat, Alex my friend! They say there are thousands of the swine out there in that street, just waiting for us to show ourselves, and they've got a battery in the Clock Tower, Moorsom thinks, covering the Bailey Guard gate. All the same, I'm for going on to finish the job, aren't you? Those poor devils in the garrison have waited three months for us to come to their relief—we can't fail them now."

"The more you look at it, the less you'll like it, my men," Alex quoted and Jack Olpherts laughed in genuine amusement.

"Very true," he agreed. "Whose words of wisdom were those? They sound like the general's."

"Yes, they were . . . they referred to a twenty-four-pounder howitzer on the road to Cawnpore, which he wanted the Sixty-Fourth to charge."

"And did they charge it?"

Alex nodded. "Yes, indeed they did—led by young Havelock because none of their own officers were mounted. That was the occasion when Harry didn't get recommended for the Victoria Cross. He—"

"Haven't you heard the latest?" Delafosse put in.

"The latest?" Alex eyed him blankly, too tired to be interested in gossip or rumour. "The latest what, pray?"

"Incentive to heroism on the part of the Company's soldiers," Delafosse answered, his tone unexpectedly dry. "The general told Jack earlier today that he would recommend him for a Victoria Cross. Provided . . ." he paused, and added with emphasis, "*provided* the award of the Cross is opened to the Company's officers and men! Did you know that it wasn't?"

Alex shook his head and Jack Olpherts laughed his deep, booming laugh. "I don't think the general did, until quite recently. Must be an official pronouncement but, like so many of these damfool rules and regulations, Alex, I don't suppose it's intended as a slight against the Company's officers, do you? Anyway, what the hell? We're not fighting for bloody Crosses are we? *I'm* certainly not—I just want to show the thrice-damned Pandies what it means to betray their salt . . . and put the fear of God into them for what they did at Cawnpore. To be honest, I enjoy being in action with my guns—it's what we're trained for, dammit, and it beats peacetime soldiering into a cocked hat. And talking of guns, I wonder if Henry Moorsom can find us a route that would enable us to take that battery in the Clock Tower when they're not expecting it? I think I'll have a word with him."

"Hold on, Jack," Alex warned him. "Here comes Neill. Perhaps he's got news—he seems in an almighty hurry."

General Neill jerked his sweating, dust-covered horse to a standstill close to where his fellow generals and their staffs were waiting. "Your gallant Highlanders have covered themselves with glory, Colonel Hamilton! " he announced in ringing tones. "They took a providentially wrong turning and advanced by the Hazarat Gunj road, instead of following our route to the Sikander Bagh. It brought them out, with Barrow's Volunteers, at the rear of the Kaiser Bagh and they took and spiked the four guns at the gate—charging the gunners from the rear, whilst they were engaged in replying to Eyre's battery on their front. The 78th have now rejoined the column, General Havelock, with Barrow's Volunteers . . . and they've brought your son in."

Cheers greeted this heartening announcement and grew in volume, as the news spread from man to man. Havelock smiled briefly and congratulated Colonel Hamilton; then, his face deathly pale he raised a hand for silence. "The wounded and the baggage train will remain in the Moti Munzil, with the rearguard, covered by Major Eyre's guns. The rest of the column will reform, with the 78th leading. We shall move out through the courtyard and make straight for the Bailey Guard gate of the Residency— the guns will be guided to it by Captain Moorsom, using a different route. God grant that we may succeed in gaining our objective!"

This time the cheers were deafening and Alex felt his heart lift with them, as even the wounded added their voices to applaud their general's decision. Five hundred yards lay between Havelock's Force and the beleaguered Residency . . . what mattered it if those five hundred yards should demand the utmost in courage and sacrifice of the men who had fought for so long and against such desperate odds to gain this one objective? What mattered it if, as Henry Delafosse had said they proved to be the hottest five hundred yards which any of them had yet been called up on to face? The men were still cheering and, from the far end of the passage-way the 78th's Pipemajor was playing *Pibroch o'Donuil Dhu* as, nearer at hand, Jeremiah Brayser yelled to his Sikhs to fall in and the Blue Caps and the 5th Fusiliers replenished their ammunition pouches. They were ready to continue the advance . . .

Alex took leave of his two companions and was about to go in search of Lousada Barrow and the Volunteers when James Neill called out to him to wait.

"You are familiar with this part of Lucknow, are you not, Sheridan?" he asked.

"Yes, sir, reasonably so," Alex replied readily. "Is there any way that I can serve you?"

"You can ride with me," Neill said. "And assist me to find a way in for the guns when they rejoin the column. Two companies of my Blue Caps have been relegated to the rear to cover them. Tell me . . . what lies at the end of this passage we're in?"

"A courtyard, sir, surrounded by houses, with an archway that leads out into the Khas Bazaar. I imagine that Moorsom will direct the guns right-handed through the Paen Bagh and bring them up by the road from the Furhut Baksh and the Terhee Kothee Palace . . ." Alex described the terrain and Neill nodded.

"Then Olpherts had better post one of his guns in front of the archway." He snapped an order to one of his staff and went on thoughtfully, "Young Havelock's badly wounded, I'm afraid. This morning at the Char Bagh bridge, when he took it upon himself to lead my Blue Caps against the battery on the other side of the canal, I told him—none too kindly—that the Blue Caps had their own officers, who were more than capable of leading them. And I meant it, damn the boy! 1 wasn't going to have a repetition of that business with the Sixty-Fourth outside Cawnpore. But the young devil chose to ignore my order and he went with them in spite of it. He and Tytler, who's old enough to know better, devil take him! "

"Harry did pretty well, by all accounts, sir," Alex said.

James Neill smiled, with unexpected warmth. "Yes, damn his eyes, he did! I hope he survives to get the Cross which the Old Gentleman wants for him so much. He earned it on the Char Bagh bridge, Sheridan, I'm bound to admit. He and Fraser Tytler too . . . though I still don't hold with staff officers superseding regimental officers in the heat of battle." His smile widened and he laid a hand on Alex's knee. "You don't press your claims, do you? A brevet-lieutenant-colonel and you've served under Barrow all this time, without a word of complaint."

"I've had no reason to complain, sir," Alex returned, a trifle stiffly. "As you reminded me—my command is there." He gestured ahead of them, in the direction of the Residency. "I shall be satisfied if I live to resume it."

"I respect you for that," Neill told him, still smiling. "So ride to the Residency with me, at the head of my Blue Caps, will you? I shall be honoured by your company, Colonel Sheridan."

Alex's throat was suddenly tight. "And I by yours, General Neill," he responded huskily. "And I very greatly by yours."

The long day was nearing its close and the light beginning to fade when the order came to advance. The reformed column was led by Generals Outram and Havelock and, with the 78th Highlanders and the Sikhs of the Ferozepore Regiment at its head, started to move towards the shadowed courtyard of the Chutter Munzil Palace, sheltered briefly by the surrounding walls.

Emerging from the courtyard into the glow of the setting sun, the Highlanders entered an inferno of cannon and musketry fire. The narrow street was studded with all manner of obstacles —deep trenches, intended to impede the passage of the guns, palisades lined with musketeers, wooden barricades—and every house was a fortress. From rooftops, doors and loopholed walls poured a tempest of shot and from each trench and cross-street well-sited guns unleashed a deadly rain of grape and canister and round-shot, scything down the ranks of the advancing Highlanders.

But they came on, a single piper playing them home, the Sikhs and the Blue Caps—their comrades throughout the long campaign—close on their heels, the 64th and the 84th preparing to follow them, the 5th Fusiliers acting as rearguard. The leading regiments could not reply to the fire of their enemies, could not wait even to succour or pick up their wounded—their orders were to advance to the Residency and not to halt until the gate was reached and they obeyed these orders to the letter. At times, so narrow was the street and so close the barricaded houses that the rebels' muskets were being discharged at pointblank range, and stones and roof tiles were hurled viciously down on them, as sepoy mutineers spat into their faces, shrieking abuse at them above the tumult of battle

Havelock and Outram, exposed at the column's head, sat their horses with inspiring calm. Colonel Tytler was the first of the mounted staff officers to go down but young Charles Havelock, riding behind him, with Napier and Hargood, was off his horse in an instant. With Hargood's help the bleeding, barely conscious Tytler was lifted back into his saddle and the three continued on their way, the A.D.C.s on foot, with their arms round him, holding him upright.

Alex, at Neill's side, with Major Stephenson and Lieutenant Grant, rode through the worst of the fire unscathed, though men were falling all around them. The Bailey Guard gate was in sight now. Dimly, through the pall of smoke which filled the Khas Bazaar, they glimpsed the dull red stone bastion, its heavy, iron-bound door riddled with round shot. Above it, on the ramparts, figures were dancing and leaping in an excess of joy and voices hoarsely cheered them on. The door, barricaded since the start of the siege, could not at first be opened. Outram—who had dashed heroically after the leading company of the 78th, which had overshot their objective—joined Havelock, moments later, his mission successfully accomplished, and the two generals were assisted into the Residency, having to scramble over a low mud wall and the embrasure of a 9-pounder gun guarding the entrance. Then the earthen barricade was cleared, the great door creaked open and they were at the centre of a milling throng of cheering, exultant defenders who sallied forth, rifles at the ready, to bid them welcome. In the momentary confusion, three loyal sepoys of the 13th Native Infantry were mistaken for mutineers and bayoneted but the rest, under the Bailey Guard commander, Lieutenant Aitken, made a gallant rush into the street to aid some wounded, whom they brought in on their backs.

The Highlanders, led still by their single piper and with a

young assistant-surgeon carrying their Colour, marched up to the gate and, as they reached it, man after man turned to yell defiance at the rebels with the words they had used all day as their battle cry, "Cawnpore! Remember Cawnpore!"

Beneath a tall archway, a hundred yards or so from the Bailey Guard, James Neill halted. The guns had gone, under Moorsom's guidance, along the route Alex had predicted so as to avoid the yawning trenches dug across the road taken by the main column, but Olpherts' single gun—which Neill himself had posted in front of the Chutter Munzil courtyard—had somehow been delayed. Cursing, Neill sent an aide to ascertain its whereabouts and waited, waving his Blue Caps on.

"For the Residency, my boys!" he shouted, as the Fusiliers surged past him under Stephenson's lead. "On you go, Blue Caps—follow your officers!"

The men, bayonets gleaming in the rays of the dying sun, gave him a ragged, breathless cheer as they passed. Neill drew in his breath sharply as he saw their depleted ranks.

"To think," he said, a note of sadness in his voice. "To think that less than three months ago they were untried recruits—boys, who had never been under fire! Look how they bear themselves now like heroes, every last one of them. By God, I'm proud of my regiment, Sheridan!" Then, with an abrupt change of tone, "Where the devil's that gun? The infernal thing ought to be here by this time!"

He sat his horse, head turned to watch for the appearance of the missing gun and, through a loophole in the archway above him, a sepoy took aim and fired. The ball struck the left side of his head and, to Alex's shocked dismay, he slumped forward as if poleaxed and fell heavily to the ground, as his horse took fright and galloped off. The gun appeared, as Alex was kneeling beside

James Neill's lifeless body and Captain Spurgin, his brigade major, who was commanding the gun escort, flung himself from his horse and ran to where he lay. Between them, he and Alex lifted the body on to the gun limber and thus it was borne into the Residency.

Alex entered in the wake of the Blue Cap escort, dazed but elated, the cheers of Lucknow's defenders ringing in his ears. There had been no second Cawnpore, he thought. The brave garrison, which had held out for three long and weary months was saved from the hideous fate his own garrison had suffered and he thanked God, breathing his prayer silently as he slid from his horse and a pale young woman came to take him by the hand and lead him to shelter. She was a stranger but her gaunt pallor made her seem curiously familiar, her ragged dress and close-shorn hair reminding him suddenly, heartbreakingly of Emmy.

She held a cup of water to his lips and said, with gentle solicitude, "Drink this—you must be very thirsty. I will clean your wound for you and then you can rest." Unaware that he had suffered any hurt, Alex thanked her and, as he drank the water in great, eager gulps, she added softly, "We are so glad to see you, sir. You are the answer to all our prayers, you and the rest of your valiant company."

Alex let her tend him, still dazed and only dimly aware that there were other wounded men on either side of him. Then, worn out but conscious of no pain, he slept and only roused himself when—hours later, it seemed—he heard Lousada Barrow's voice, thankfully calling his name.

EPILOGUE
⋙ • ⋘

ON THE MORNING of 26th September, the leaders of the rebel host were summoned to a council of war by the Begum-Regent of Oudh, Hazrat Mahal, and a room was prepared for the meeting in the Padshah Bagh, the elegant small palace built in 1830 by King Nasir-ud-Din, on the opposite side of the river to the British Residency.

First to arrive was the Moulvi of Fyzabad, Ahmad Ullah, newly appointed by the Begum as her chief military adviser. He had paused on his way at the camp of Man Singh, in the hope of persuading the powerful Hindu chief to attend the council, and his failure to do so had left him in no pleasant humour. As he listened to the thunder of the guns across the river, he imagined that he heard the cheers of the besieged British, still ringing out in welcome to Havelock's relief force. He turned on the two grey-bearded old *subedars* who came to join him in the council chamber a few minutes later, cursing them for cowardly bunglers and sparing them nothing in his bitter contempt.

"The accursed *feringhis* should never have been permitted to reach the Residency!" the Moulvi raged, eyes blazing beneath their beetling brows. "They were but a handful, ill-equipped, exhausted by their long march in the heat—outnumbered by more than ten to one. Yet they are there, they are inside the Residency walls and you, who call yourselves generals, failed to stop them!"

"They left over five hundred dead behind them," Mirza Guffur Bey, the general of artillery, pointed out sullenly. "And whilst they may have entered the Residency, Moulvi Sahib, they will not leave it alive—have no fear on that score."

His fellow general, a Hindu of Brahmin caste, whose bemedalled scarlet tunic testified to his years of fighting service in the company's army, came swiftly to his support. Normally, they were rivals, warily mistrustful of one another, but the Moulvi's reproaches had been levelled at them both with equal vehemence and had angered him by their injustice.

"Not all the British have reached the Residency," he stated coldly. "Their wounded, their heavy guns and all their baggage remain as yet in the Moti Munzil, guarded by fewer than a hundred *lal-kote* soldiers. They are surrounded, and we shall not let them escape us. I promise you that, Ahmad Ullah."

"Then see to it!" the Moulvi bade him harshly. "Both of you . . . go, as soon as this council is over, and prove your brave words. Show me by your deeds that you are worthy to hold the commands to which the sepoys elected you. If you do not, then as Allah is my witness, I shall have you blown from cannon for the incompetent fools you are . . . and, though I am no professional soldier, I shall myself assume command of the army in the name of the brave Begum, to whom I have sworn allegiance."

"The Begum comes now," Mirza Guffur informed him. Resenting the Moulvi's arrogance, but not daring to show his resentment, he crossed to the window overlooking the street and peered downward with narrowed, short-sighted eyes. Even in the old days, when King Wajid Ali had ruled in Oudh, this upstart rabble-rouser from Arcot had wielded great influence, he reflected. Now, fresh from the victory at Cawnpore, the Begum had been deceived into appointing him to the highest rank in her army and the Moulvi had made it clear that he intended to use the power she had given him ... and woe betide anyone who dared to stand in his way.

Times had changed, the old general of artillery reminded himself regretfully. Instead of a king, he must serve a woman who had gained her present rank and title by way of the king's bed. A dancing girl, a courtesan, Hazrat Mahal had not even been acknowledged as a wife whilst the old Padshah Begum lived, but now her son, the ten-year-old Birjis Quadr, had been crowned king of Oudh, and she was regent, the only member of the royal household left to do battle against the hated British. He sighed, looking down as the palanquin approached the palace in regal style, its escort of cavalry clearing the way through a mob of cheering people. Certainly the citizens of Lucknow had taken her to their hearts, forgetful of the loyalty they owed to Wajid Ali, unjustly deposed by the British and, since the annexation of Oudh, their exiled prisoner in Calcutta.

So enthusiastic was the crowd's welcome that the four giant eunuchs marching beside the litter in the silk ceremonial uniforms with the fish emblem of the royal house emblazoned on them—hitherto reserved for state occasions—were compelled to use the flat of their *tulwars* to hold back the jostling throng. But many ignored the *tulwars,* pressing forward eagerly for a sight of their new ruler, and Hazrat Mahal, in the manner born, waved a languid, bejeweled hand from behind the parted curtain in acknowledgement.

Yesterday, Mirza Guffur recalled, she had led her troops—also in the manner born—from the *howdah* of a fighting elephant. Despite his misgivings, his proud old heart warmed to her. Of humble birth she might be, but now that her chance had come, she was behaving like a queen, with dignity and courage, seeking to save the throne which the British had stolen and which

Wajid Ali—to his eternal shame—had not lifted a finger to preserve. True, she wanted it for her son, but he was of the blood royal, even if she was not, and a Muslim king of Oudh was infinitely preferable to domination by the Hindu Nana of Bithur. The old general watched Hazrat Mahal descend from the palanquin and mount the palace steps, assisted by Mammu Khan—a dissolute courtier, who was said to be her lover—and once again found himself approving the regal presence she assumed.

The one-time dancer was not young. Seen at close hand, her face was lined and coarsened by age, but she had painted out the blemishes very skillfully and her figure, in its richly shimmering silk robe, was that of a mature woman, still holding more than a hint of the beauty for which she had once been famous. And— a touch of genius, this—on her head she wore a warrior's plumed steel helmet adorned, as her eunuchs' resplendent uniforms were, with the fish emblem of the ruling house of Oudh.

"She makes a fine show," the Moulvi observed with grudging admiration. He came to stand at the general's side, an odd little smile playing about his bearded lips as he watched the Begum turn at the head of the steps to wave farewell to the surging crowd in the street below.

"A braver show, I fancy, *Pir Moorshid,* than your late patron the so-called Peishwa of the Mahrattas," Mirza Guffur suggested, with thinly concealed malice. "The much-vaunted Nana Sahib, who has suffered so many defeats at General Havelock's hands that he seems scarcely to merit the reward of 25,000 rupees which the British governor-general has placed on his head!"

"The Nana is a more trustworthy ally than the noble Man Singh," the Moulvi retorted. "He would betray us to the British if he thought it would be to his advantage."

Gomundi Singh, the long-serving *subedar* of native infantry whom the Hindu sepoys had elected as their commander, ventured a halfhearted protest at these insults to his fellow Brahmins, but the two Mohammedans affected not to have heard him, and he relapsed into his customary watchful silence. All his life he had been a simple soldier, content to serve the company with unquestioning loyalty, until he became entitled to a pension. Secure in the respect and affection with which his British officers regarded him, he had not wanted to join the mutiny but had been unable to resist the pressure the sepoys of his regiment had brought to bear on him, which in the end had overcome his scruples and compelled him to embrace their cause.

Now, admitted to the council of war by virtue of a rank he had never, in his wildest dreams, expected to attain, he frequently found himself ignored by the other members of the council, his opinion—even if it were sought—seldom if ever acted upon. He felt out of his depth in the company he had to keep, conscious that he was neither an aristocrat like Mirza Guffur nor an intellectual like the Moulvi. Since the death of *Rissaldar* Yakub Khan of Fisher's Horse—who had been elected to command of the cavalry and who had unhappily fallen victim to a lal-kote marksman a week or so ago—Gomundi Singh had become acutely aware of his own isolation. He and the more forceful Yakub Khan had been cast in the same mould. They were both professional soldiers, with more experience of war than any of the other council members, and although of different religions, on questions of military strategy they had been of like mind. He had made a point of supporting any proposal that the cavalry general put forward; in return, Yakub had always consulted him, and their alliance had precluded amateur interference in purely military matters.

Following Yakub Khan's unfortunate death, however, the Moulvi had begun to assert himself. Not content with his appointment as adviser to the Begum, he had assumed command of the cavalry on her authority alone, without a vote being taken. If his earlier threats were to be taken seriously, he might well be making a bid for command of the entire Oudh army. The Begum trusted him implicitly. He had her ear, and if the Moulvi could contrive to place the blame for yesterday's reverse on Mirza Guffur and himself, then Hazrat Mahal might give him the appointment he so clearly desired.

He wished that he could form a working alliance with Mirza Guffur, but the old artillery commander, whilst he disliked and mistrusted the Moulvi, was a good deal in awe of him. If there were to be a showdown, the old man would support his co-religionist. Of that there was little doubt, especially if a Hindu voice should be raised against him. It would therefore be wise to remain silent for as long as he could, Gomundi Singh knew . . . at all events until any damaging accusations were made. The situation would be vastly improved if only Man Singh would agree to join the council, but the wily Hindu leader had refused to do so and had told him privately only the previous evening that unless assured that the British cause was irretrievably lost he intended to hold aloof—and possibly even retire with his troops to his own stronghold at Shahgunge. Indeed, he had sheltered a number of British fugitives there and given them safe conduct to Lucknow.

The Moulvi turned away from the window. He said unpleasantly, as if he had read Gomundi Singh's thoughts, "I am told, General Singh, that you paid a visit to Man Singh yesterday evening, but failed to persuade him to attend our council meeting?"

"I . . . yes, that is so, Moulvi Sahib."

"But you did not see fit to inform me of what transpired

between you!" the Moulvi accused. "Had you done so, it would have spared me the unnecessary humiliation of receiving his refusal when I called upon him this morning."

Gomundi Singh was visibly disconcerted. "*You* called on the Lord Man Singh, Moulvi Sahib? I was not aware of your intention. Indeed, I—"

"Naturally I called on him. We require his aid. He has an army camped in our midst and must declare either for us or against us. Why did you not tell me what he said to you?"

Gomundi Singh flushed guiltily. Much of what Man Singh had said to him—had been confidential and he knew that he must guard his tongue, lest the Moulvi accuse him of treachery. "There was little opportunity," he defended plaintively. "Yesterday, you will recall, I was with my troops doing battle with Havelock Sahib. But I had, I assure you, intended to convey his views to the council, as he requested of me. The Lord Man Singh fears that—"

"And what does the Lord Man Singh fear, General Sahib?" The interruption came from the curtained archway at the entrance to the council chamber and Gomundi Singh turned, startled, to see that the Begum had entered, with her escort, and was regarding him with searching eyes. But her tone was neither angry nor accusing, and taking heart from this, he answered boldly, explaining Man Singh's uncertainty and the reasons underlying it.

Hazrat Mahal let him speak for a moment or two and then held up a small hand for silence, the gesture directed also at the Moulvi, who had hurried to her side to greet her with an obsequious *salaam*. "I have news for all of you," she announced and Gomundi Singh saw that she was smiling.

"News, Begum-ji?" old Mirza Guffur echoed. "Good news, I trust?"

"Very good news, General *Bahadur*," the Begum assured him triumphantly. She waited, savouring her triumph, and then, satisfied that she had their full attention, continued in ringing tones, "I myself called on Man Singh before coming here. He has given me his word that he will join us."

"*Here,* Begum Sahiba?" Gomundi Singh demanded, surprised out of his normal caution. "At the council meeting?"

"At the council meeting *and* with all his troops in the field!" Hazrat Mahal returned. She and Mammu Khan exchanged glances and the Moulvi-always the first to recover from any momentary surprise—asked suspiciously, "But at what price did you buy his allegiance, Begum Sahiba? There is a price to be paid, is there not?"

"Naturally there is a price," Mammu Khan put in harshly.

"And what is it?" the Moulvi persisted. His dark eyes were blazing in his pale thin face, the beetling brows drawn together in a wrathful scowl, as if he already knew the answer to his question and the knowledge displeased him mightily.

The Begum said, her voice now gentle and persuasive, "We are to put right yesterday's errors, Moulvi Sahib. Only a paltry handful of General Havelock's *lal-kote* soldiers have succeeded in entering the Residency—we are to make sure that no more do so, neither men nor guns. An attack must be launched on the Mod Munzil Palace and none must be permitted to escape."

"It was in any case our intention to attack the Moti Munzil," Mirza Guffur told her. "General Singh's troops have surrounded the palace and my guns opened fire at first light. The British have more wounded than fighting men to protect them and the *dhoolie*-bearers are afraid. They will take flight the instant they come under our fire."

"Havelock Sahib will have to send a force from the Residency to their aid, Begum Sahiba," Gomundi Singh added eagerly. "We are waiting only for word that they will do this and then we shall commence our attack. I do not believe that the Lord Man Singh's demand is unreasonable. We can meet it."

Contemptuously, the Moulvi cut him short. "That is not the full price, is it, Hazrat Mahal?" His tone was bitter. "Man Singh demands more . . . he seeks command of our whole army, does he not? Sepoys as well as Irregulars?"

Hazrat Mahal did not try to prevaricate. "He asks for such a command, *Pir Moorshid.*" She laid a slim, jewel-bedecked hand on his arm, entreating his understanding. "But only until the British are driven from Lucknow. Then he will relinquish it. He asks also that we send a *cossid,* in our joint names, to the Nana and to Tantia Topi—who, as you know, now commands the Gwalior troops on the Nana's behalf—urging them to launch an immediate attack on Cawnpore. A very weak force has been left there to defend the city. It will fall, since General Havelock will be unable to send aid now. With both Lucknow and Cawnpore in our hands, victory in Oudh will be assured." She smiled into his resentful eyes. "Have patience, Ahmad Ullah . . . you are *my* choice as commander. But it behooves us to go carefully. First we must defeat General Havelock and the formidable warrior who has accompanied him to the Residency . . . General Outram. These are brave, experienced soldiers, whom we must match and defeat decisively before we claim victory."

"True, Highness," the Moulvi conceded. "But we—" He was interrupted by the arrival of a *jemadar* of the 7th Cavalry who burst in to announce excitedly that a force was being assembled in the Residency, preparatory to a sally.

"They will assuredly try to save their wounded and the guns left behind in the Moti Munzil," he finished, breathing hard. "I observed that they have gun-cattle with them but no guns, and they are led by a Sahib with one arm, who is well known to me from Ajodhabad. Sheridan Sahib, of the Light Cavalry."

"Sheridan Sahib!" the Moulvi exclaimed in shocked dismay. Hazrat Mahal waved him to silence.

"The time has come," she stated, with emphasis. "We will adjourn this council meeting." Turning to the two old generals, she added urgently, "Do not delay. Go at once to your commands. Wipe out the *feringhis* to the last man! Victory will be ours if you do your work well."

Both men saluted and started towards the curtained archway, but the Moulvi, moving swiftly, was before them.

"I will give you victory, Hazrat Mahal!" he promised. "If you will give me the chief command until tomorrow's dawn. Do not fear that I shall fail. I have a score to settle with an old adversary."

"With Sheridan Sahib?" Hazrat Mahal suggested. "Well . . ." she hesitated for a moment and then inclined her head. "So be it, Ahmad Ullah. May Allah be with you and give you strength!"

HISTORICAL NOTES

➤➤➤ • ⋘⋘⋘

Events covered in *The Sepoy Mutiny* and
Massacre at Cawnpore

THE SO-CALLED Indian Mutiny was, in fact, not a rebellion
throughout the whole vast country but the revolt of one of the three
Presidency Armies—that of Bengal, which consisted of 150,000 hitherto loyal and well-disciplined native troops, commanded by British
officers in the employ of the Honourable East India Company.

The mutineers received encouragement and active aid from a
few Indian chiefs and princes, who were themselves driven to revolt
by a very real sense of grievance as a result of the Company's policy of annexing (annexation by right of lapse) native states and land
to which there was no direct heir. By means of this policy, imple-
mented by Lord Dalhousie-Governor-General from 1848 to 1856—
250,000 square miles were added to British Indian territory so that,
by 1857, the Company held sway over some 838,000 square miles.
Under Dalhousie, 21,000 plots of land, to which their owners could
not prove documentary right of tenure, were confiscated; the States
of Satara, Nagpur, and Jhansi were seized, and the Punjab and Scinde★
conquered by force of arms. Finally the ancient kingdom of Oudh—
from which the bulk of the sepoys of the Bengal Army were
recruited—was also annexed.

★ The Scinde campaign. 1843: War of the Sudej, 1845-46, and the
Second Sikh War, 1848–49

Added to the resentment, by both princes and peasants, of this arbitrary seizure of their land, the root cause of the Mutiny was the fear—which rapidly became a widespread conviction among the sepoys—that their British commanders, on instructions from the Company, had embarked on a deliberate campaign aimed at destroying their caste system, with the ultimate intention of compelling the entire army to embrace the Christian religion. The issue of supposedly tainted cartridges, and the sepoys' refusal to accept them, was the excuse for the outbreak which, by the time Lord Canning succeeded Lord Dalhousie as Governor-General, had become inevitable.

The time was well chosen. In 1857 Britain was still recovering from the ravages of the Crimean War, she was fighting in China, and had recently been fighting in Burma and Persia. As a result, India had been drained of white troops, the British numbering only 40,000, plus about 5,000 serving with native regiments, whilst the sepoys in the three Presidency Armies (Bengal, Madras, and Bombay) numbered 311,000, with the bulk of the artillery in their hands. The territory for which the Bengal Army was responsible included all northern India, from Calcutta to the Afghan frontier and the Punjab. The Punjab had only lately been subdued, and there was a constant threat of Border raids by the Afghan tribes, so that most of the available British regiments (also called Queen's regiments, to distinguish them from the Company's) were stationed at these danger points and on the Burmese frontier, with 10,000 British and Indian troops in the Punjab alone.

The 53rd Queen's Regiment of Foot was in Calcutta, the 10th at Dinapore, 400 miles up the Ganges river; the 32nd was at Lucknow (capital of Oudh) and a newly raised Company regiment, the 3rd Bengal European Fusiliers, at Agra. Thirty-eight miles northeast of Delhi—ancient capital of the Moguls—at Meerut, there was a strong European garrison, consisting of the 60th Rifles, 1,000 strong,

600 troopers of the 6th Dragoon Guards, a troop of horse artillery, and details of various other regiments, 2,200 men in all. Stationed with them were three native regiments—the 3rd Light Cavalry and the 11th and 20th Bengal Native Infantry, under the command of 75-year-old Major-General William Hewitt, whose division included Delhi, which had an entirely native garrison.

On the face of it, Meerut seemed the most unlikely station in all India to become the scene of a revolt by native troops, and the outbreak, when it came, took everyone—not least the Commanding General and his Brigadier, Archdale Wilson—so completely by surprise that they did virtually nothing to put it down, with the result that Delhi was lost.

There had, of course, been warnings, but for the most part these were ignored or treated with scorn and disbelief, and the officers of the Bengal native regiments continued, until the last, to place the most implicit trust in the loyalty of the sepoys they commanded. The first tangible warning came early in 1857, with the incident of the greased cartridges. The new Enfield rifle, which had proved its superiority in the Crimea, was ordered to be issued to the Army in place of the outdated Brown Bess musket. Both were muzzle-loaders, but the cartridge of the new weapon included a greased patch at the top which—like the earlier, ungreased type—had to be torn off with the teeth. The greased patch was used to assist in ramming home the bullet, which was a tight fit in the rifle barrel. It had apparently not occurred to the Ordnance Committee in England or, indeed, to anyone in India, that the composition of the greased patch might offend against the religious scruples of high-caste Hindu sepoys, of whom there were a great many in the Army of Bengal.

At the arsenal at Dum Dum, near Calcutta, a lascar of humble caste was abused by a Brahmin sepoy of the 34th Native Infantry. The man retaliated with the claim that the new Enfield cartridges were smeared with the fat of the cow (sacred to Hindus) and of the pig (considered unclean by Mohammedans). Biting it, the lascar jeered, would destroy the caste of the Hindu and the ceremonial purity of the Mohammedan, and this story spread like wildfire throughout the native regiments. The men were assured that they might grease the cartridges with their own ghee (native butter) or tear them by hand, but the sepoys still refused to accept them, and the leaders of both the Hindu and Mohammedan faiths—conscious that their own power was waning under British rule—fanned the flames of suspicion assiduously. Fakirs and holy men travelled from garrison to garrison and an ancient prophecy was revived and whispered among them—the Battle of Plassey had been fought in 1757 and John Company, the prediction ran, would last for exactly a hundred years, so that this year would see its fall.

Several native regiments were disbanded for refusal to accept the new cartridges and a sepoy named Mangal Pandy—who was to give his name to all mutineers a few months later—was executed at Berhampur, 100 miles from Calcutta, for firing on his British officers.

In Meerut, early on the morning of Saturday, 9th May, General Hewitt ordered a punishment parade of his garrison and, under the guns of the European artillery, he had eighty-five sowars of the 3rd Light Cavalry—men who had previously been condemned by court martial for refusal to accept the infamous cartridges—publicly stripped of their uniforms and put in irons. Next day, when the British troops were preparing for Church Parade, the Light Cavalry mutinied, released their condemned comrades from the jail, and then, joined by the two native infantry regiments, indulged in an orgy of arson and looting, slaughtered a number of Europeans, and finally set off for Delhi. General Hewitt's inept handling of the situation and his failure to pursue them sealed the fate of Delhi. The native troops there joined the mutineers from Meerut and, after an appalling massacre of Europeans and native Christians, the survivors were compelled to flee, and the eighty-year-old Shah Bahadur, last of the Moguls, was proclaimed Emperor of India. Delhi became the focal point of the Great Mutiny, and from all the outlying stations of northern India, during the ensuing weeks, more and more native troops rose in rebellion and, having in most cases killed their British officers or attempted to do so, they too made for Delhi.

The Governor-General, Lord Canning, and the Commander-in-Chief, General Anson, took what action they could to stem the tide of anarchy. Canning recalled British troops from Persia and Burma and sent for others then on their way to China; Anson, greatly hampered by lack of transport and difficulties in communication, nevertheless contrived to send a small and ill-equipped force to endeavour to recapture Delhi. Brigadier Archdale Wilson was ordered to march from Meerut to join him, with the 60th Rifles and the 6th Dragoon Guards, and the first successful action was fought against the mutineers at the Hindan River crossing outside Delhi on May 30th and 31st.

General Anson, weakened by his exertions, died of cholera in camp at Karnaul and was succeeded as Commander-in-Chief by a Crimean veteran, General Barnard. By June 8th, after fighting another successful action against the mutineers at Badli-ke-serai, six miles outside Delhi, the combined British force—numbering fewer than 3,000 men of all arms—established itself on the Ridge to await the arrival of reinforcements, guns, medical supplies, and ammunition, which would enable them to attack the city. Until these reached them, they could only wait—outnumbered by well over ten to one—whilst, in the Punjab, the Chief Commissioner, Sir John Lawrence, made strenuous efforts to send them succour. He formed a "Movable Column," lightly equipped and ready to move with speed against any area of disaffection, and disarmed a number of sepoy regiments, aware that before he dared denude the Punjab of British troops, he must make it and its frontiers secure. With the dynamic Nicholson succeeding to command of the Movable Column and a siege train in process of preparation, the recapture of Delhi became, at last, a less remote possibility than it had at first seemed.

But the preparations took time, and elsewhere in India the situation was critical as, in garrison after garrison, the pattern of Meerut was repeated—the native troops rose and the bazaar riffraff rose with them, eager to kill and plunder their white rulers. The districts were in a state of rebellion, communications were disrupted, the telegraph wires cut, and no traveller was safe, even on the Grand Trunk Road. The civil police threw in their lot with the mutineers, jails were broken into, and prisoners released to swell the growing ranks of lawless marauders. British officers and their families who managed to escape from their stations did so as fugitives, finding every man's hand against them. The Chief Commissioner of Oudh, Sir Henry Lawrence—elder brother of the ruler of the Punjab—with typical farsightedness, had made his own preparations to withstand a siege in his Residency at Lucknow, whilst doing everything in his power to prevent a general uprising. Such was the respect in which even his enemies held him that he almost succeeded; throughout May and June, whilst other stations suffered mutiny, Lawrence contrived to keep the peace in Lucknow, continuing secretly to fortify and provision the Residency. Reinforcements could only reach him from Calcutta; the recapture of Delhi was the first priority and all the resources of the Punjab had to be concentrated on this objective, since Delhi and the old Emperor were the key to the suppression of the revolt.

A source of grave anxiety was Cawnpore, 53 miles northeast of Lucknow, on the opposite bank of the River Ganges. The garrison was predominantly native, consisting of the 2nd Light Cavalry and the 1st, 53rd, and 56th Native Infantry. The station commander, Major-General Sir Hugh Wheeler, a veteran of the Sikh wars, had formed a close personal friendship with the adopted son of the last Peishwa of the Mahrattas, Dundoo Punth, a Hindu of Brahmin caste and the self-styled Maharajah of Bithur. Relying on the promises of this man—known best by his Mahratta title of Nana Sahib—Wheeler had agreed to call on the aid of his troops should his sepoys break out in mutiny. Even were they to do so, the Nana assured him, they would march immediately to join their comrades in Delhi, and all that Wheeler need fear would be attacks from the lawless elements of the native city. Accordingly, the old General decided against fortifying the stone-built Magazine, with its vast reserves of guns and ammunition, which had the disadvantage of lying six miles northwest of the city. Instead, after receiving the news of the outbreak in Meerut and the fall of Delhi, he constructed an earthwork entrenchment on the open plain to the south of the city and the Native Lines, close to the road from Allahabad, along which he expected his promised reinforcements to come.

Reinforcements were, indeed, being rushed north from Calcutta, over 600 miles away, but for all his frantic efforts the Governor-General, Lord Canning, had few European troops available. A wing of the Madras European Fusiliers, under the command of their Colonel, James Neill, reached Calcutta on 24th May from the Madras Presidency and Canning despatched them at once to Cawnpore. The small column reached Benares on 3rd June and Neill was compelled to delay his advance in order to put down a threatened insurrection there. It was the same story in Allahabad, where mutiny had already broken out prior to the arrival of the column on 11th June, after a forced march of 70 miles in three days.

Only a single company of Her Majesty's 84th and fifteen of the

Fusiliers actually reached Cawnpore at the end of May and, confident that Neill's column would follow in a matter of a week or so, General Wheeler sent half of the 84th and fifty men of the 32nd on to Lucknow to augment Sir Henry Lawrence's garrison. Aware, however, that his four native regiments were dangerously disaffected, he called on the Nana Sahib for the promised Bithur troops. When 300 were sent in response to his request, he placed both the Magazine and the Treasury under their protection and ordered all Europeans and Eurasian Christians to take refuge in the entrenchment.

Work on this had not been completed when he was compelled to occupy it but, trusting in his alliance with the Nana, Wheeler was not unduly worried. Conditions were unpleasantly crowded; he had two brick buildings—one a hospital for European troops, with a thatched roof—and a four-acre site, surrounded by a four-foot-high breastwork built of mud, already crumbling in the heat, and a single well, from which all drinking water had to be drawn. Into it came close to a thousand souls, of whom nearly 400 were women and children. To defend his position, he had nine light-calibre guns, 210 European soldiers—59 gunners and 70 invalids and convalescent men of the 32nd among them—about 200 officers and civilian males, 40 native Christian drummers, and 20 loyal native officers and sepoys, in addition to some 50 noncombatant Indian servants.

The native regiments mutinied during the night of 4th June. The Nana's troops yielded both Magazine and Treasury to them and the sepoys, without making any attempt to molest the garrison in the entrenchment, set off on the road to Delhi—as the Nana had predicted they would. He, however, in cynical betrayal of General Wheeler's trust, persuaded them to remain in Cawnpore under his own banner, and on the morning of 6th June, all four regiments launched an attack on the frail earthworks, swiftly followed by a bombardment by guns looted from the Magazine.

The garrison of Cawnpore held out heroically and against well-nigh impossible odds for three weeks.★ With the temperature standing at 130 degrees, lacking shade of any kind, their well under constant fire and their thatched-roofed hospital burnt to the ground, their defence is one of the epics of the Sepoy Mutiny. The ranks of the besiegers were swelled by mutineers from other stations, until they numbered in the region of eight or nine thousand; they had batteries of 24-pounder guns forming a ring of steel round the crumbling mud breastwork of the entrenchment and, at the height of the bombardment, as many as 300 missiles an hour were striking the battered buildings and raking the open compound. Two hundred and fifty of the defenders were killed—including almost all the trained artillerymen—but the guns continued to hold the enemy at bay, served by officers and civilians. Wounded infantry soldiers manned the shattered parapet, often without relief, beating off attacks by day and night, and on several occasions small parties of defenders made daring sallies to spike the insurgents' guns and blow up their ammunition.

The suffering endured by the women and children was appalling, with mental agony added to physical misery. Toward the end, when there were no medicines to treat the sick and rations had been reduced to a handful of uncooked grain and a few sips of water, only the conviction that Neill's column was on its way to their relief kept the hopes of the stricken garrison alive. Neill did not come, and all save two of their small 9-pounder guns were put out of action when the Nana sent a Eurasian woman, whom he had been holding captive, to offer the survivors a safe passage to Allahabad by river. He promised boats and swore a solemn oath that, if the garrison agreed

---

★See *The Sepoy Mutiny.*

to surrender their entrenchment and leave Cawnpore, they might do so under arms and without molestation.

Having little choice, these terms were accepted and, on the morning of the 27th June, their sick and wounded carried in palanquins and carts and on elephants provided by the Nana, the 437 survivors of the garrison made their way down to the Suttee Chowra *Ghat*, where boats were waiting for them. The embarkation had scarcely commenced when hidden guns opened up on them with grape and canister and, from the slope leading down to the landing place, sepoys poured a withering fire of musketry into those who were struggling, waist-deep in water, to board the boats. The straw-thatched awnings of the boats were set on fire, and a number of cavalry sowars spurred their horses into the shallows to sabre terrified women and children who had flung themselves overboard to escape the flames.

When the Nana at last ordered a halt to the ghastly massacre, 125 dazed and mud-spattered women and children were dragged ashore, many of them wounded. They were taken as hostages, but any men who had survived the treacherous attack were butchered out of hand. The same fate awaited those who had contrived to make their escape in a single leaking boat. Pursued by guns and cavalry on both banks, for three days and nights they held off their assailants, only to be taken by a *zamindar* on the Oudh side of the river when their boat drifted out of the main channel and ran aground. Only a handful, who were unwounded, reached the shore; they made a last gallant stand and four finally escaped after swimming for six miles downriver under a galling fire from sepoys on shore.

Conflicting rumours as to the fate of the Cawnpore garrison reached Allahabad some days later. By this time, Neill had quelled the mutineers, hanging many of them and blowing the ringleaders from the mouths of cannon, and a force was collecting there to relieve Cawnpore and reinforce Lucknow. Brigadier-General Henry Havelock, on his return from the campaign in Persia, had been appointed to command the relief force, and it was he who questioned the two native spies who had brought news of the fall of Sir Hugh Wheeler's garrison and the Nana Sahib's treachery. A number of his officers refused to believe the spies' report, but Havelock had no doubt that it was true; even when it was later contradicted, the Brigadier adhered to his belief and, learning that British women and children were being held hostage, he exerted every effort to get his force on the road to Cawnpore. Hampered, as always, by lack of transport, he gave the order to begin the march on Tuesday, 7th July. His force was small, consisting of the 64th Foot and the 78th Highlanders—like himself, fresh from Persia—two companies of the 84th and a detachment of Madras Fusiliers, 150 Sikhs of the Ferozepore Regiment, and a six-gun field battery, manned by a scratch force of gunners, under the command of Captain Maude. The cavalry were his weakest arm—apart from twenty "gentlemen volunteers" under Captain Lousada Barrow, he had only a troop of irregulars, of doubtful loyalty, and just under a thousand of his force were Europeans.

Ahead of him, a still smaller advance force had been despatched under the command of Captain Renaud of the Fusiliers—300 men of his own regiment, 400 Sikhs, 95 irregular cavalry sowars, and two guns—and, fearful lest the Nana launch an attack on Renaud before he could join forces with him, Havelock sent an urgent message, ordering the advance guard to wait and rendezvous with him outside Fatepur. After an exhausting march, in the worst season of the year, Havelock caught up with Renaud on 12th July, just in time to meet and defeat 3,500 of the Nana's rebel army, which was advancing, with a large force of cavalry and twelve guns, in the belief that only Renaud's handful were opposed to them. They were routed by

Havelock's superior tactical use of his artillery and Enfield riflemen: all twelve guns fell into his hands and his only losses were from heatstroke.

Still in appalling conditions, which alternated between blazing heat and torrential rain, the British column took Fatepur and continued its advance. The irregular cavalry refused to charge and had to be disarmed; the infantrymen were exhausted, plagued by thirst, and frequently unable to take time to cook and consume their rations. They were stricken by cholera and always heavily outnumbered but, spurred on by the knowledge that the lives of the Nana's hostages depended on them and inspired by the personal gallantry and splendid leadership displayed by Havelock himself, they routed the enemy at Aong, at the Panda Nudi bridge, and finally in a savage battle outside Cawnpore, where the 78th Highlanders in particular covered themselves with glory.

Between the 7th and the 16th July, they marched 126 miles and fought four actions, the last with barely 800 infantrymen in line and their only cavalry Barrow's twenty gentlemen volunteers, taking the Nana's well-sited 24-pounder guns at the point of the bayonet, in a series of charges which demanded the utmost in courage and steadiness of the weary, half-starved men. But it was to be in vain. They entered Cawnpore to find that the hapless women and children who had survived the siege and the massacre at the Suttee Chowra *Ghat,* together with other fugitives from upriver stations, 210 in all, had been mercilessly butchered by the Nana' orders on 15th July, following his defeat at the Panda Nudi crossing.

Near the burnt-out Assembly Rooms, in a small, yellow-painted brick building known as the Bibigarh—the House of Women—the ghastly evidence of the slaughter was still plainly to be seen. The place was a charnel house, inches deep in blood, with here and there a woman's bonnet, the frilled muslin frock of a child, books, a torn Bible, and, still hanging from the door, the flimsy rags with which a vain attempt had been made by those who had perished there to bar it to their murderers. With grim irony, the pages from a book entitled *Preparation for Death* lay scattered about the blood-stained floor and the walls were scarred with sabre-slashes and the marks of bullets. Some of the sword-cuts were low down, as if some poor, cowering woman or terrified child had tried to ward off the blows aimed at them by their brutal assassins.

In the courtyard outside, the bodies of the victims were found in a 50-foot-deep well, which was crammed to within six feet of the top with dismembered limbs and torsos stripped naked by savage hands. The battle-hardened men of the advance party, who were the first to find and uncover the well, turned from it, sickened and appalled, thirsting for the blood of the man who had perpetrated such an outrage. But the Nana had fled, after blowing up the Magazine, taking his treasure with him but abandoning Cawnpore to the victors. Havelock's bitter, vengeful soldiers marched to his palace at Bithur in search of him, but this, too, they found abandoned. The Nana was reported to have withdrawn, with 3,000 regular troops and a number of newly raised levies, to wait an opportunity to launch an attack on Havelock's rear, should he cross the Ganges into Oudh in an attempt to relieve Lucknow. After taking possession of the thirteen guns he had left behind, with their transport elephants, the British force set his palace on fire and returned to Cawnpore.

From Lucknow, borne by the courageous spy Ungud, came the melancholy news that Sir Henry Lawrence was dead. On the morning of 2nd July a round-shot had entered through the window of his upper room in the Residency, which had shattered his pelvis. Two days after receiving this terrible wound, he had handed over command to Colonel Inglis, of H.M.'s 32nd, and Major Banks, the Civil Commissioner, and lapsed finally into unconsciousness.

Lawrence had suffered a disastrous reverse on 30th June, when—yielding to the demands for action from the Financial Commissioner, Martin Gubbins—he had, against his better judgement, led a force of 700 men against the mutineers at Chinhat. Betrayed by his native gunners, who had deserted to the enemy, he had lost 300 men and five guns, including a 24-pounder howitzer, and the position was now desperate. With news of Lawrence's death, Inglis sent an urgent plea to Havelock for aid; Lucknow was completely invested; the besiegers numbered many thousands—without aid, it would be impossible to hold out for more than a few days.

Although his losses from cholera were now acute and only 227 men of H.M.'s 84th Foot, led by Colonel Neill from Allahabad, had reached him as reinforcements, Havelock decided that he had no choice but to endeavour to fight his way through to Lucknow. He adhered to his decision, even when a regretful message reached him by telegraph from Sir Patrick Grant, the Bengal Army's acting Commander-in-Chief, from Calcutta, with the warning that two European regiments he had been promised could not now be sent to him for at least two months. The sepoy regiments at Dinapore had mutinied; the 5th Fusiliers and the 90th Foot were required to deal with the outbreak. Havelock must rely on his own resources if he made any attempt to relieve Lucknow.

"If the worst comes to the worst," the General told his son Harry, recently appointed Deputy-Assistant adjutant-general in place of Major Stuart Beatson, who had died of cholera, "we can but die with our swords in our hands."

BOOKS CONSULTED

Government of India State Papers: edited G. W. Forrest, Calcutta Military Department Press, 1902. 2 vols.

The Sepoy War in India: J. W. Kaye, FRS., 3 vols., W. H. Allen, 1870.

History of the Indian Mutiny: Col. G. B. Malleson, CSI., 3 vols., Longmans, 1896.

History of the Indian Mutiny: T. Rice Holmes, Macmillan, 1898.

The Tale of the Great Mutiny: W. H. Fitchett, Smith, Elder, 1904.

The History of the Indian Mutiny: Charles Ball, 6 vols. London Printing & Publishing Co., circa 1860.

Addiscombe: Its Heroes and Men of Note: Col. H. M. Vibart, Constable, 1894.

Way to Glory: J. C. Pollock, John Murray, 1957 (Life of Havelock).

1857: S. N. Sen, Government of India Press (reprinted 1958).

The Sound of Fury: Richard Collier, Collins, 1963.

The History of India: James Grant, Cassell, circa 1888.

The Bengal Horse Artillery: Maj. Gen. B. P. Hughes, Arms & Armour Press, 1971.

Lucknow and the Oude Mutiny: Lt. Gen. Mcleod Innes, V. C., R. E. A. D. Innes & Co. 1896.

Journal of the Siege of Lucknow: Maria Germon, edited Michael Edwardes, Constable (orig. pubn. 1870).

The Orchid House: Michael Edwardes, Cassell, 1960.

Accounts of the Siege and Massacre at Cawnpore by Lt. Mowbray Thomson, 53rd. N. I., and G. W. Shepherd (Survivors).

The Illustrated London News, 1856-7-8.

My thanks to Mr. Victor Sutcliffe of Stroud, Gloucs. for his help in obtaining copies of a number of the above.

GLOSSARY OF INDIAN TERMS
➵➵➵ • ⬅⬅⬅

Achkan: knee-length tunic (also Chup Kan)

Ayah: nurse or maid servant

Babu: clerk, loosely applied to those able to write

Bazaar: market

Bearer: personal, usually head, servant

Bhang: hashish

Bhisti: water carrier

Brahmin: high-caste

Hindu Cantonments: European quarters, residences, civil or military, usually military

Chapatti: unleavened cake of wheat flour

Charpoy: string bed

Daffadar: sergeant, cavalry

Dhal: flour

Din: faith, Moslem war cry "For the Faith!"

Dhoolie: stretcher or covered litter

Eurasian: half-caste, usually children of British fathers and Indian mothers

Fakir/Sadhu: itinerant holy man, Hindu

Feringhi: foreigner, term of disrespect

Ghat: landing place, river bank, quay

Godown: storeroom, warehouse

Golandaz: gunner, native

Gram: coarse grain, usually fed to horses

Hanuman: Hindu monkey god

Havildar: sergeant, infantry

Jemadar: native officer, all arms, lieutenant

Khitmatgar: table servant

Lal-kote: British soldier

Lines: long rows of huts for accommodation of native troops

Moulvi: teacher of religion, Moslem

Nana: lit. grandfather, popular title bestowed on Mahratta chief

Oudh: kingdom of, recently annexed by Hon. East India Company

Paltan: regiment

Pandy: name for mutineers, taken from the first to revolt, Sepoy Mangal Pandy, 34th Native Infantry

Peishwa: ruler or king of the Mahratta race

Poorbeah: from the East, an inhabitant of Oudh

Puggree: turban

Raj: rule

Rissala: cavalry

Rissaldar/Rissaldar-Major: native officer, cavalry:

RSM Ryot: peasant small holder

Sepoy: infantry soldier

Sowar: cavalry trooper

Subadar/Subedar-Major: native officer, infantry

Sweeper: low-caste servant

Tulwar: sword or sabre

Vakeel: agent

Zamindar: landowner

Zenana: Harem quarters. Seraglio